MELODY CARABALLO

THE UNKINDNESS SAGA
BOOK #1

UNHINGED WITCH

Portal World

Unhinged Witch

Copyright © 2021 by Melody Caraballo

For information contact :
http://www.melodycaraballo.com

Cover design by : Designer K. J. Harrowick
Editors : Carly Hayward and Jess Lawrence
ISBN: 978-1-955532-02-0

First Edition: October 2021

10 9 8 7 6 5 4 3 2 1

To John Schubert, chasing dreams alone is nothing compared to having someone beside you.

MELODY CARABALLO

THE UNKINDNESS SAGA
BOOK #1

UNHINGED WITCH

Jen,
   Thanks for all the
help when I was
new in the jail.
Always stay Unhinged.

Melody
♡

Teri,
Thanks for all the help when I was new in the jail. Always Stay Unhinged.
Melody ♡

Chapter 1

OUR FEET HIT the pavement in unison. Running was the one thing I was good at... I think, my memory isn't the greatest. I could be really good at puzzles or Pictionary, but sometimes it's like there's a hole in my memory and I forget the small things. Tonight, like most nights, running was when that didn't bother me much.

The wind picked up, blowing my blonde-with-a-touch-of-orange hair in my face. I attempted to bleach it myself and it came out a little wonky. At my age, I should be able to dye my own hair, but my upbringing wasn't nurturing to beauty techniques, or anything at all. I wiped the stray strands out of the way and caught Caden glancing at me. Even after almost a year together, he would steal quick looks. My stomach fluttered. He'd started running with me about a month ago. I was positive he didn't enjoy it, but did it to spend more time with me.

"Ready to talk about it, Harmony?" Caden stayed in-beat with me as we ran. His long stride could have easily outran me.

Or maybe he ran with me because it was when I was most talkative. "I don't like waitressing." That many people make me nervous.

An older woman with silver-blue hair styled in a short bob wearing a scowl on her face charged down the sidewalk towards us. As she got closer, I jumped to the left to avoid her. She moved with me and her elbow caught my... my... side. At times, I forget little words too, but I'm working on it. The woman's eyes caught mine and grew wide; a tad too wide.

"Um. Sorry," I stammered.

"Do I know you?" The woman reached out her hand toward my unruly hair.

I stepped back and tucked the strands behind my ear. My gut yelled at me to turn and run. Would she follow me? Probably not. To her I was a random familiar face, or her waitress for the past month at The Rusty Palace. There was no way she actually knew me.

"What's your name, sweetie?" The words stumbled off her tongue, like being nice caused her pain. She stayed blocking my path. At first, I had assumed she was in a rush, but she was standing there chatting it up with me.

Caden had stopped too, crossed his arms and glared at the woman. I looked over at him. Seldom did he look mean, but for a brief second, he had. He swayed on his feet and the fabric of his shorts swished.

"Harmony." People always made me uneasy, but being rude to them never seemed right.

"I'm Vera, nice to meet you." She stuck out her bony

hand. Am I supposed to shake it? Or is it acceptable to wave? How long do I have to stand here?

"You too, ma'am."

Caden took my hand and led me away from the woman. He's good at sensing when someone makes me uncomfortable. When he isn't around I try to be nice but that doesn't always work and I turn and walk away mid-sentence. I guess that could be considered rude.

Once again, we were back in unison running. It was late, so there weren't many people around. A lot of the little shops were starting to close for the day. It's part of why I ran at night, to avoid large crowds. The other reason was I'm not a morning person. Nothing against people that can get up that early, but I would rather wait till mid-day.

The sun had set, leaving way for the full moon. Even if the streets weren't lined with bright lights, the city would have been illuminated. In many ways, the moon is full of magic. It steals power from the sun and shines in its own way.

"So, the job." Caden went right back to the convo we were having before the woman bumped into me. Did he not find it strange? Did his skin not crawl as she glanced him over? Maybe I was overthinking it. She probably did think I looked familiar. I was making a way bigger deal about it than it was.

"Some guy was yelling at me for... for..." What was the word? I tried breathing heavier to cover up my brain malfunction. Extra saliva pooled in my throat. I coughed hard, attempting to expel it. Caden immediately slammed his large hand on my back. Ouch. "I'm okay. I just choked on my spit."

"Sounds like a partial lie to me, but I'll let it go. As long as you're okay." Caden's hand caressed my back sending chills up my spine. His hazel-green eyes twinkled at me. This man is so caring and sweet.

"Anyway, the guy yelled at me for screwing up his order." I took off at a run again.

The man had ordered a hamburger with the cheese on the side. Who does that anyway? I had placed his food in front of him, smiled and turned to get to the next table. He'd called me back, rather loudly. I'd plastered on another smile and asked if he needed anything else.

He'd rolled his tongue across his lips, then asked if I knew what 'on the side' meant. Had my brain glitched? Did I really not know? My heart sank. He'd stared at me until I answered that it meant on the side. The man had nodded and then yelled at me for messing it up.

Had I been built with a backbone, I may have stood my ground. Instead I was built with running shoes. I turned and left. I didn't even tell anyone I quit. Since it's the fifteenth job I've given up on, I know they don't call you to find out why you disappeared mid-shift.

"Why didn't you tell the manager? People can't act like that. Quitting isn't always the answer, Harmony." Caden's voice lowered as he spoke. I know he meant well and was always trying to look out for me, but sometimes it annoyed me that he was always giving advice on how I should have done something. He should complain with me and then let it go.

"I'll find another job."

"You don't have to work at all. Stay home. Work on your journals. Go back to school."

I was a high school drop-out, sorta. I went back and got my Good Enough Diploma. He brought up me going to college every time I quit another job. School wasn't for me, forgetting the little things makes you look real bad. And I couldn't imagine what it would be like to take a test while dealing with that issue.

An issue that I was going to fix. About six months ago, I started journaling. Every day around noon I write for about twenty minutes or so. It's all about my past. There are so many holes. Granted, it could be easily explained. I went through trauma so I don't remember. Easy explanation. But there are full years missing.

Once I started writing it all down, I noticed how bad it was. And at times, some things I would remember one day, the next I would forget. Not to mention the word thing I have going on. Who forgets simple words while speaking? Alright, maybe that part is normal. But add it into the missing years of my life and I had convinced myself something was wrong. Probably not brain tumor wrong, but could be.

Caden knew about the journals, but not what I wrote in them. He was already overly worried about me. I didn't need him knowing I might be going insane. He would insist I go to a doctor and I don't have money or insurance for that. I will figure it out on my own.

"Wanna race home?" Caden winked at me. "I have a surprise for you."

"No," I breathed, but it was too late. Caden was already running at full speed.

Chapter 2

CADEN WAS SITTING on the steps to our apartment when I finally caught up to him. His elbows were on his knees and his phone was in his hand. He wasn't the type of guy to spend much time on his phone. In fact he was usually losing the damn thing because he barely used it. For a tech guy at a nerd store, he wasn't really into tech.

I panted heavily, stopping in front of him. Those long legs of his really give him the advantage. I grabbed the railing and bent over to catch my breath. Caden stood up and stroked my arm. He placed his hand on my back and guided me to stand tall. I was the runner and yet he constantly reminded me how to get air into your lungs. You need to 'open up the rib cage.' I wouldn't need so much air if he didn't turn everything into a competition. Almost every run became, 'who could get home faster.'

The stairs to our apartment were crumbling. The building had lost a few of its bricks over the years. Kinda like my missing memories. The grout in between them had been worn down in so many places I wasn't sure how the thing was still standing. The entire outside was a large contrast from the beauty inside.

Every apartment looked brand new. The crown molding and granite counter tops seemed a tad too ritzy for the neighborhood. Which could be why it was the most expensive complex in the area.

When Caden and I had moved in together I had lived in a small studio apartment on the other side of the city. It was sorta run down and may have had some rats, but it worked for me. Now he and I live in this amazing apartment.

He insisted on paying most of the bills. I may have trouble keeping jobs but that didn't mean I couldn't pay my share, usually. Every once in a while I miss a payment, but I'm working on it.

Our apartment was also nicely decorated. That had nothing to do with me. I never understood spending the time to put things on the walls and waste money on furnishings. Caden did all the sprucing up. He asked my opinion on everything, but I thought it was a little much. When he was hanging the pictures of us all over the living room, I helped. Well, I held the tools for him. So, technically we did it together.

Caden and I were standing outside the door to the apartment and he stared at me. I knew that look. He wanted to talk.

I placed my hand in the pocket of my gray sweatpants. Could this be about the woman on the street? She had bumped into me for no reason. Then she tried to converse with me. Had she done that on purpose? No. Obviously she didn't. I, again, was overthinking. I picked at the skin on the side of my thumb. I couldn't get it. So I pulled my hand out of my pocket and started chewing on my nail.

"Harmony, I am in love with you. I truly believe you and I can have a wonderful life together. I know everything you have been through and it's not fair. I want to make sure you never feel pain or that no one ever treats you badly again. I know we already live together, but I need reassurance. You love me right?" Caden swayed on his legs.

"Why wouldn't I?" I said through chewing my hangnail. I almost had it removed.

"I'm only making sure. There is a lot about me I haven't told you. We don't even have to live here. We can leave, go anywhere." Caden grabbed my hand, and placed it between his. Little moments like this had me so in love with him. He never hid his feelings for me. He always told me what he thought of us, and our relationship. Usually we weren't standing outside our apartment door, but I loved his romantic side.

"Wait, why are we... um... doing this in the hallway?" Unlike him, I had trouble sharing my feelings.

"There is a surprise inside. So I wanted to discuss us before you saw it."

Oh no. A sharp ache pierced my chest. The speech, the sparkle in his eyes. The way his lips are turned up at the corner. I love him so much, but I wasn't ready for this. I may never be, it's not something I wanted. Marriage means children, and they end up in foster care. The discomfort in my chest grew. I grabbed my hand from Caden's and placed it over my heart, begging the pain to leave.

He was really about to propose. I wanted to turn and run. It was what I was good at. But he and I lived together, so that wouldn't work. My feet turned toward the doors to the building. I could have taken off, even if only to escape this moment.

The door to our apartment opened before I could decide. Had Caden left the TV on? A small squeak filled the air. My heart went from a sharp strain to a warm thudding. I took a step forward. Did he have something else planned?

Another small peep, followed by a purr. I went into our apartment. The living room was empty. Well, not completely, it had the sofa and TV along with the wooden coffee table that Caden had built for us last month. But what I was looking for wasn't in there.

Across from the living room was our kitchen. Next to the shorter side of the.. um... island were two small dishes. The sounds continued. It had to be true, why else would there be two dishes? I walked past the bathroom and opened the door, nothing. The small noise returned, louder. I was getting close.

I reached our bedroom and my stomach erupted into tiny flutters. There are times when butterflies aren't a good sign, but right now they had to be. I hoped they were. My gut was telling me this was good news. Caden's side of the bed was closest to the door, so I had to walk around to my side.

Had I ever owned a pet before? I scanned my memories. Nothing. I didn't even remember being around an animal. Was I allergic? That would stink so bad if I was. But it didn't matter, this was one of the best things that had ever happened to me. The purr grew louder.

On the other side of the bed, my side, was a beautiful

dark cat. She looked up at me. All of her was black except a white patch around her right eye. She went back to her toy and played with it again, the squeaks filling the air.

Caden got me a cat.

"She's on loan. But we're probably going to keep her. If you want." Caden knelt next to me and held his hand out to pet her.

"On loan?" I wanted her forever. She came up to me and rubbed her body across my arm. A spark of warmth ran through me. Ginger, her name was Ginger. I didn't know how I knew, but I did.

"It's Penny's roommate's cat. Apparently her roommate took off and she asked if I could watch her, maybe even keep her."

Penny was Caden's co-worker at Tech-fix. I had never met her, but he had mentioned her before.

Even though Caden was saying Ginger was on loan, I felt like she was mine. Or more accurate, like I belonged to her. She brushed against my arm again, and I realized I was petting her head. She wanted me to scratch her belly.

"Let her know we can keep Ginger."

"How did you know her name?"

I didn't have an answer for him. It was like she had told me what her name was. Obviously, that was impossible. I couldn't tell him she looked like a Ginger. Her fur was the opposite of a redhead. Maybe it was like one of those big guys that everyone calls Tiny. Instead of answering him I shrugged and scooped Ginger up into my arms. She...um... I lost the word... She purred in response.

Ginger and I went back into the living room. I nestled my face against her, really hoping I wasn't allergic. She pressed her face back and I plopped us both on the sofa. As I was loving on her, my mind trailed back to the conversation with Caden.

It seemed a little off that he was talking about his feelings when he only wanted to cat-sit. Was I missing something? I closed my eyes, I had to be wrong about him proposing. That would not be okay. The cat was enough for us. Hopefully I could keep her. Penny's roommate was wrong for leaving her behind. She didn't deserve Ginger.

"What did you want to say in the hallway?" I asked him as he sat next to me on the sofa. The smell of amber and wood drifted into my nose; he always smelled good. He leaned in and pressed his lips against my cheek. A shiver ran through me. I love this man.

"When Penny asked me to take Ginger for a bit, it got me thinking." He stared at me for a few moments before he continued. For someone who never had trouble talking, he seemed to be short on words.

I blinked. If he ended up talking marriage, Ginger and I were gonna run.

"I don't think we should go see my parents next month," he said.

"Oh," I replied. The hole in my memories was messing with me. I couldn't think of any words I wanted to say. I was relieved, but why didn't he want me to meet his parents?

Last month, Caden had asked me to go with him. He said they lived in a huge place in Florida. We had planned on spending a week with them. My mom and dad died when I was young, so a huge part of me was looking forward to this.

But now he was taking it away, and I was actually

relieved. As much as I wanted parents and to be even closer to Caden, I also knew how it would have gone. I would have forgotten words, or been too quiet, or they would have thought my orange-ish hair was ugly. There were so many ways it would have gone wrong. Now I didn't have to worry about that.

"I want you to meet them. Someday. But for now, I love what we have. I love our life and I worry they will complicate things. And, maybe we could move?"

"Where would you want to go? You have a good job, and I'll get another one. As for Florida, it's fine. Parents don't ever like me, so I'm fine skipping that." I felt the warmth from Ginger against my neck. She was saying she was there for me.

"I can tell you aren't fine. I will make it up to you. But for now, it's best not to visit. We could go, just leave. I know you aren't used to staying in one place, because of the foster care. And work is scarce here. We could go somewhere else. I mean, if you want."

He was asking me to run. To pick up and leave would mean abandoning Philly. I quit another job, and yet despite how much I loved to run away from things, this time was different. I wanted to make a change. I have never had a home, and with Caden I had one. This time I would stay, this time I would, um… shit. I couldn't think of the word. But no matter, I wasn't taking off.

"I think we should stay. It's sweet you're worried about my career choices, but I will find something else." It was odd that he was asking me to move. It had to be his way of fixing my work situation.

He wrapped his arms around me and pulled me into him. His skin was electricity against mine. Ginger jumped out of my lap. She didn't want to be squished between us.

Caden kissed the top of my head. His hazel-green eyes shone bright and he pulled away to stare at me.

"It was just a suggestion," he whispered. I leaned into him and pressed my lips against his.

Chapter 3

A BELL ABOVE the door chimed as Caden held it open for me. The smell of wet dog tickled my nose. A large shaggy brown collie lay in the corner of the veterinary clinic. His fur had a damp appearance to it. The teenager holding his leash had water marks on the bottom of his jeans. I giggled and entered.

Ginger wore a sparkly pink collar and leash. I wasn't too keen on the color, but when I took her to the store, she had picked it out. Obviously, she couldn't have picked it out herself. Caden thought we should have gotten a cage to bring her here.

Really, we didn't even need to go to the vet. I tried to tell him she was fine. Penny's roommate had made her an appointment because she wasn't eating her food. My guess was she should have switched to soft food. But I've never owned a cat so maybe her roommate knew better. I ground my teeth.

"No, she didn't know better, or the woman wouldn't have left her cat," I thought I said to myself, but Caden turned in his chair and frowned.

"I'm sure she had a good reason." That was Caden, always looking for the bright side.

A short woman in Hello Kitty scrubs came into the waiting area. For me to call someone short is a big deal, since I'm only 5'3". She burst through the door and the room instantly became happier. She smiled and shook her head at the teenager with the wet dog. He shrugged back and stood. The collie shook and water flung across the room.

I wiped a few droplets off my face as the woman strode past me to the kid. Thankfully, I hadn't bothered with make-up. Girls that apply it every day are amazing. I could never figure out how to take the time to do it, unless it was a special occasion.

"You took him in the creek again. Boy, you're lucky your father is the vet." She then turned to me. "Our receptionist quit so I'll check you in when I come back."

With roughly fifteen jobs in my background, I never imagined being a receptionist. Having to talk to that many people made me, um... nervous. But if I was at a veterinary clinic, with animals maybe it wouldn't be so bad. There had to be something I was good at. I... um... Darn. Words are hard, but at times, whole thoughts disappear.

I grabbed my blue skull journal out of my purse. Ginger meowed as she jumped from my lap; she didn't appreciate me disturbing her. The journal was part of my plan. If there was a pattern to the words and phrases I would stutter on, I would find it. And if there wasn't one, it was nice to keep track of my day to day.

I wrote down: At vet clinic. I might try and get a job

here. Lost thoughts on why it would be a good place to work.

Caden wrapped his arm around my shoulders. When I had first started journaling he would ask a million questions. He was so interested in my memory holes and missing years. He still is, but lets me fill him in when I'm ready.

He squeezed me with his arm and placed a kiss on my head as the Hello Kitty woman walked back into the waiting room. She went behind the counter and clicked away at the computer. Caden scooped up Ginger and approached her. I put my things away and followed. By the time I got there, Ginger was checked in.

The nurse stepped out from behind the counter and grazed her hand along Ginger's fur. The black crystal she wore around her neck dangled in my cat's face. Well, maybe not mine yet. But I had high hopes.

"I'm Dara. You must be Savannah Joy. Funny naming a black cat Ginger." Nurse Dara put out her hand for me.

"No. I'm Harmony Laverack. We're cat-sitting." I took her hand and a tickle crawled down my arm. The charm caught the light and twinkled. I stepped back and stared at the woman.

"Black onyx. It's for protection." She grabbed it and didn't even mention the tickle. Not a word about it. I must have imagined it. Yup.

In the back room there were shelves filled with ripped up chew toys, treats and other distractions for the animals. Another one contained glass doors with veterinary equipment. The walls were covered with pictures of happy owners and their furry companions. Standing next to the tall metal exam table was an endearing older man wearing a floppy toupee. This man gave off good vibes, which most men didn't. Caden excluded. He smiled at me then waved for Caden to put Ginger on the table.

"Hi, there. You are precious, aren't you?" He ruffled her fur. "I'm Doctor Barker, nice to meet you, Ginger."

"He forgets his manners around humans. But I assure you, he is the best with animals." Nurse Dara twinkled her eyes at Dr. Barker. That look means love.

Dr. Barker ignored the comment and worked on his examination of my cat. I was already convinced she would be mine. She, um... wanted to live with me. Wanted! That word I forgot. I clenched my fists. People can't live like this. It's not normal. My brain freezes and I can't think. Ginger purred as if to tell me to relax.

After a few questions directed at Ginger, that Caden answered, Dr. Barker nodded and walked over to his computer. He typed away at a speed a slug would have been impressed by. Twenty minutes later he printed a sheet of paper and handed it to Caden. At the top, big bold letters told us soft food should help her eat. He could have said that, but I don't blame him for not talking to people.

I went to scoop up Ginger and she leapt from the table. All four of us scrambled to grab her but she was out of the room. I chased her down the hall and her fuzzy tail turned the corner.

"Grab her," Dr. Barker yelled. For someone that doesn't talk to people he sure can yell at them. Not that I blamed him, she could get hurt.

Caden's long legs easily strode past me. He was around the corner before I even reached it. Dr. Barker and Nurse Dara's feet slammed behind me. My heart pounded in my chest. Why would Ginger take off like that?

Around the corner there was a door wide open. A bright glow came from the room. I entered and shielded my eyes from the brightness. The entire room took me off guard.

The only normal thing in there was a tiny desk with a bright pink laptop. Every other inch of the room was covered in candles, crystals, and tiny bottles. There were even dream catchers and pendants hanging from the walls. I couldn't count how many trinkets if I tried. The curtains on the window were tied back allowing for the sun to reflect against every stone in the room.

I walked inside and saw Caden on his knees beside a table. Ginger was under it refusing to come out. The table above her was covered in green stones. Some were bigger than my hand. Others smaller than my pinky nail. If it fell they were both in trouble.

Caden clicked his tongue at her. She turned her tail up at him. She was chewing on something and had no intention of allowing him to take it from her. I knelt beside Caden and clicked my tongue as well. No luck.

"Shoot. Be careful. Don't knock anything over," Nurse Dara panted.

"Come here, Ginger," I whispered.

Ginger turned and sauntered over to me, her tail high and something clearly in her mouth. I shook my head at her and placed my hand out, palm upright. She dropped a wet plant or root of some kind into my hand and went over to Caden. Apparently she didn't want to be bothered with me at the moment.

"What is this?" I showed Nurse Dara.

"Ginger root. Great for spel... I mean stews." Nurse Dara took it and placed it in her pocket.

She'd been about to say spells. The rocks and spices and dream catchers. All the things in this room looked like a witch lived here. Obviously a real practicing witch that connects with Mother Nature and not one of the ones on TV that has a wand. I glanced at Nurse Dara, trying not to make it obvious. I could picture her meditating under the full moon with flowers in her hair. A Wiccan, that's what they were called.

"You're Wiccan. Very cool." I nodded.

"Yes. Does that interest you?" She played with the black onyx.

"No." I slapped my hand against my mouth. Why do I always blurt things out? Heat rose to my cheeks as I walked out.

"Funny Ginger was eating ginger. Weren't you?" Caden cooed to her as he carried her.

Wicca had fascinated me, so why did I say no? Why does my brain blab things out before I can stop it? I had once thought Chakra stones could heal me. I'd tried to focus, but I couldn't get into a meditative state.

Maybe Nurse Dara could help me, if I apologized for saying no. Why would a stranger even do that? If I worked here, that would make it less weird asking. Ugh, I had to get up the courage to get an application. I like places that had them online. I could fill it out from my phone without having to speak to anyone until the interview.

Unfortunately Barker's Veterinary Clinic didn't seem like a techy place. It was more a family-run business. Which had its appeal because it gave me good vibes. I could last here more than a few weeks.

"Ready?" Caden asked as he handed over his debit card to Nurse Dara.

"Are you hiring?" I asked the nurse. When she stared at me I added, "You said you were down a receptionist."

"How old are you, dear?" She handed Caden's card back to him.

"Twenty-two. I will work hard. And I'm good with animals." I pushed my shoulders back and stood as tall as I could muster.

"Doctor Barker doesn't like to be bothered. I like this place clean, and you have to be good with a computer. You don't talk a lot do you? Cause we need a worker, not someone that is gonna chat it up with everyone that walks in the door. Last girl would pop gum and ramble on. Nice kid, but she never took a breath."

I nodded. I didn't want to talk too much and ruin my chances of working here.

"Okay, you start tomorrow. Eight o'clock. And don't be late."

Yikes, that was early and fast. She must be desperate for a secretary.

Chapter 4

NO, NO, NO. I slammed my phone on the nightstand. With the sleep still in my eyes, I jumped out of bed. As I rubbed them, I went to the closet. I hadn't even decided what I was going to wear. Shit, I have twenty minutes to get to work.

The plan was to get up early and take my time with my outfit and hair. I sniffed my armpits; gonna need extra deodorant. Caden and I stayed up late celebrating my new job and there was a lot of sweat. Heat rose in my cheeks thinking about it. Caden still managed to get up early and head to the gym. He hadn't missed a day since we moved in together.

I tossed on a purple button-up blouse and black slacks. No time to even check to make sure it looks okay. Before heading out the door I grabbed a scrunchie and saw myself in the mirror. Yup, I looked like I was up late having sex. My hair was a knotted mess of craziness, so I wrapped it into a bun to hide the knots, then slipped my feet into sneakers and left.

As I jogged to work, I realized I left my purse at home. And to make matters more awesome, my phone was on the, um… the table by the bed. Ugh. The start to my day was not going well. How do morning people do this?

Barker's Veterinary Clinic was dark. No lights, nothing. It was locked. I went for my phone. Fuck. I left it, and already forgot that piece of information. There wasn't a single clock on the street. Was Nurse Dara late? There was no way I was early.

The last time I had done that I walked in on a conversation that shouldn't have been for my ears. Mrs. Watson and her husband were having a heated debate about me when I was nine. It was my third foster home, sort of. Luckily, I wasn't there long enough to count it. Mrs. Watson had told me to be at breakfast at seven. As an excited little girl to have a new family, I came downstairs to find Mrs. Watson whispering to her husband.

Even though it was a whisper, she was shouting at him. He had picked me out at the orphanage-type place. Mrs. Watson was furious about it. She said foster kids are homely and ugly, not attractive little girls. I stood in the doorway shaking. She spotted me and rounded on me. As she was explaining that I can't stay there, Mr. Watson was licking his lips at me. My stomach turned. I hated him so much. That image still haunts me.

I turned and vomited on the sidewalk.

"Oh dear, don't be nervous. First day can give people jitters." Nurse Dara patted my back.

Every part of my body wanted to turn and run. This

was beyond embarrassing. Thinking today was going to be a bad day, and vomiting in front of my new boss were two totally different things. I had expected to mess up at work. But this, oh this was terrible. Not to mention, Mr. Watson's face still swam in my vision.

"You need a drink. Come on." Nurse Dara placed her arm around me and guided me.

When we got inside, she had me sit behind the counter. The lights were still off. Bile still stung my throat. This first day was worse than being a dishwasher at a restaurant. I had left mid-shift, wet from the dish sprayer and smelling of old food. I didn't go back.

The lights flickered on and Dr. Barker waddled into the office. He glared at me. I opened my mouth to say something, then shut it. He didn't look happy with me being here.

"Miss Garcia, why is Ginger's owner sitting in the office looking paler than she did yesterday?" Dr. Barker shouted.

"Oh, Ven. I told you I hired her. And she looks pale cause she lost her cookies outside. Poor thing was so nervous. You scare people. If you would only show them how sweet you are," Nurse Dara yelled from the back.

Dr. Barker stared at me for a few moments, then walked out of the room. I really didn't blame him for not talking to me. People can be scary. And I didn't look like someone that was approachable. Normally, I didn't look so awful, but today I did. This is what I get for trying to wake up early.

Nurse Dara walked in with a large Mad Hatter teacup. It matched the Alice outfit she was wearing. For being in her mid-forties, she loved her kiddish scrubs.

Not that I was judging her. I found it charming.

The tea smelled of lavender and ginger, not the best combination. I tried not to drink it, but Nurse Dara insisted.

"Why did Doctor Barker seem offended by me being here?" I squeezed my eyes shut. Can't I ever think before I talk?

"Don't pay him no attention. He really is kind and sweet. That man has been through so much. He finds it easier to talk to animals. Humans can be evil sometimes. When his son Van was a baby, his wife was murdered." Nurse Dara skimmed her hand through her short, mousy-brown hair.

"Murdered?" I took a sip, it smelled gross but tasted of magic.

"Yea. Never found the killer. He hasn't been the same since. Had to raise Van all by himself. I help where I can but it's hard. You want to get on his good side, make him a sandwich for lunch. All men love them." Nurse Dara took a deep breath and walked away.

The bile in my throat was washed away by the tea. And it took away the nausea. Before I finished drinking it, Nurse Dara returned with a spray bottle and rag. She put me to work. I had to use Thieves Cleaner because it was organic and non-toxic to the animals.

For the next few hours, I cleaned everything. That office sparkled. I even went outside and cleaned up my vomit. Which was my fault, so I didn't mind. When clients arrived, Nurse Dara handled checking them in. She said she didn't want to overwhelm me.

Close to lunch, my stomach started to growl. I hadn't brought anything and there was no way to get food with my wallet at home. I had a few more hours left of work,

I could get through it. Be strong, Harmony. Gurgle. Shh. My belly was not happy with me. Nurse Dara walked by and jumped when she heard my stomach. She claimed I was going to waste away if I didn't eat something soon. I insisted I was fine, and she said I wasn't. Within seconds she had a plate of cheese and crackers in front of me. I could love this woman.

The bell above the door chimed. Caden held it open for a tall, angry woman that looked like she had recently gotten into a fight. Her jet black hair didn't move as she walked inside. Danger emanated from her. Despite the outer appearance, I felt calm around her. She must be one of those friends that hate everyone, but if you're in her circle she'll burn down cities for you.

"Hey, Cutie Pie, this is Penny Wren. I figured we could all go to lunch." Caden twinkled his eye at me.

"Oh. You are a tech person? I mean. Cool. I, um... wish I had known, but I'm eating already." I popped another cracker in my mouth. Of course I wanted to go and get to know this girl and why she appears so badass. But not right now. It's already been such a bad day. And I forgot to brush my teeth.

"Thanks. I know I don't look very techy. Can't judge a book. Or however that goes. Nice to meet you, Music." Penny held out her hand.

"Music?" I stared at the hand.

"She nicknames everyone. Calls me Ice Cream half the time. I tried calling you. Then when I got home from the gym I saw your keys and phone." He pulled both out of his pocket and handed them to me.

It took one more smile from him to convince me to go.

Penny stood at the entrance, arms folded, hip cocked to the side. A tall, skinny man with long, dirty hair approached her. I couldn't tell what he said to her, but within seconds he walked away, shoulders hunched. The man wore defeat poorly.

"What did he want?" Caden asked as we approached Penny.

"A date." Penny scrunched up her face. "I told him he was a loser if he thought picking up some random stranger was a good idea."

I shrugged, I didn't blame her. I got lucky with Caden, but not all men are like him.

The bell above the door chimed as we stepped into Joe's Diner. The red booths were striped with duct tape, masking the tears. Grime ran along the floors in place of baseboards. Shadows cast on the walls from flickering bulbs that hadn't burnt out yet.

A short woman in jean shorts popped a gum bubble as she asked, "Table for three?"

"Yea. And a bathroom, please?" I scanned the restaurant. The waitress pointed to the back.

A french fry crunched under my foot as I walked in the direction she had pointed. The mirror was not my friend. I had bumps in my hair and I had missed a button on my shirt. Not one person had pointed that out, not even Dara who had mentioned how much of a mess I looked. Using my fingers I combed through my mane and attempted to make myself look decent.

I found Caden and Penny in the back of the, um... restaurant, laughing at each other. Penny tossed sugar packets at Caden. He dodged one but got smacked in the face with the next. They were so familiar with each other, more like life-long friends than just co-workers.

I sat down next to Penny. Big mistake. She got me in the side of the face with a sugar packet. I teamed up with her and pelted Caden with a fresh volley.

Outnumbered, he ducked below the table. Not that I ever had any type of family, but had I this is what I would have wanted. A sister that could defend me and yet joke around with me. My face hurt from smiling.

"Coffee, also?" the waitress asked between snaps of gum. "Or are you guys gonna toss all the sugar at this hunky guy over here?"

"Um. Water please." I shifted in my seat dropping the remaining ammunition.

"Thanks, these girls are vicious." Caden sat up, grinning. His eyes twinkled.

The server blushed as she walked away. Penny chuckled and launched one last packet at Caden. It slapped him in the corner of his mouth. Penny snickered and grabbed a menu. Caden didn't retaliate, but picked up his and glanced it over.

I wanted to ask Penny about her roommate. If she returned, would she take her cat back? Hopefully I could keep Ginger. Someone who would leave their cat behind didn't... didn't. Ugh, my brain wasn't working. Again.

"So, did you find your roommate?" Caden asked. He had no problem with tough questions. I would have blurted it out.

"No, I still have time before I can worry. Rule... two... give it five days before we go searching." Penny sipped her coffee.

"Why five days? That's a dumb rule." I immediately regretted my word choice.

"It's a rule between us. Savvy will be fine."

She clearly didn't want to talk anymore so I shut my mouth and waited for my food. A bus boy came by with a large plate of fries for me. Caden got a BLT and Penny got bacon and eggs with extra bacon. I doused my fries in ketchup and ate them to keep myself from asking more questions. If my roommate was missing I wouldn't wait days to report it. I would be out looking for them.

As the last fry crossed my lips a gust of wind blew my hair in my face. I should have left it in a bun. There was now a glob of ketchup in it. I grabbed a napkin and attempted to clean it when I noticed her.

The tall woman with silver-blue hair and black eyes was across the restaurant staring at me. Caden could be right, I could have seen her at work before. Or he could have been mistaken. Fucking Vera. This could be a coincidence. Either way my food didn't want to stay down. I did what I do best; got up and ran out of the restaurant.

Chapter 5

I HEARD THE TIRES screech seconds before a woman shouted. A loud, shrill cry demanding attention echoed off the windows of the veterinary office. My veins turned cold. Something in that scream made my entire body icy.

"Help!"

I dropped the cleaning rag, stood up from my chair, and walked towards the entrance. What was that? I tossed open the door, headlights shone bright in my eyes, blocking my view.

I squinted, trying to see what was there. Part of me wanted to rush out into the night, the other part yelled at me to stay put. Whatever was out there was coming in.

A shadow approached holding something bulky. It seemed to shrink with every footstep. As it got closer, I heard whimpering. The soft, low mewl of an animal made my heart cringe, threatening to break it in half. The sound caused the hairs on my skin to prick up, one by one. Bile rose in my throat, threatening to escape.

"It's her leg." The voice was familiar.

"Come in," I said. If it wasn't for the injured animal I would have, um… slammed the door in her face.

Instead, I rushed them inside. This wasn't a coincidence, it couldn't be. I pushed aside my worry and did what I could to help.

Vera cradled the wounded animal like a newborn child. It was wrapped in a pale blue blanket. The cries bounced throughout the empty waiting room. I ushered her past the empty chairs and a saltwater fish tank, careful not to touch her.

"Doctor Barker!" I hollered and pushed on the heavy door separating the waiting room from the back offices. It swayed open allowing us both to enter.

I guided them to the treatment room. Dr. Barker was sitting at the computer with his headphones over his dark brown toupee. He had a sandwich in his hand and was watching yet another video about the history of cats. His large frame hung over the sides of the chair.

"Barker!" I yelled.

He jumped in his seat.

I didn't want to startle him, but we needed to help this animal and get this woman out of here. She had to go. When he turned, his face dropped. His perfectly made—by me—ham, turkey, and extra mustard sandwich fell to the floor, already forgotten. He yanked his headphones off as he stood.

"What happened?" he asked as he grabbed the bundle. He placed the swaddled dog on the metal table in the middle of the room. Unwrapping part of the pale blue blanket, he revealed a brown boxer dog who whimpered in pain. "Tell me!" he demanded, looking up at the lady. I couldn't believe how demanding and angry Dr. Barker appeared.

"She was playing in the backyard. I tossed the ball, but I didn't mean…" The owner's voice broke on every word. It had to be an act.

"This is Dr. Barker. He's the best," I said, my hand jetting out to comfort her. I immediately yanked it back. The raven tattoo on her arm seemed to pulsate as I got close.

"I'm Vera, this is Mrs. Who."

"Her hind leg appears to be broken. I'm going to have to sedate her. Harmony, come here and help hold her down while I muzzle her," Dr. Barker said as he examined the boxer.

No. I was frozen, too afraid to move. I was the secretary at the vet clinic—bookkeeping, scheduling appointments, answering phone calls—that was my job.

I had been here a few days, that's not long enough to do nurse work. Why did Nurse Dara have to leave early today? She didn't need to go to a sale of crystals at some weird witchy shop.

The thought of having to restrain the dog made my heart pound and palms sweat.

"Get over here and hold her down. Now," he growled, low and demanding.

Fuck. My heart beat faster as I took two steps forward. My sneakers slid across the tiled floor. The screech from my shoe made way too much noise in the tiny room. An apology caught in my throat. Vera spoke, but the words didn't reach my ears. The beating of my heart drowned out all other sound.

The dog looked up, her tongue flopping out of her

slightly opened mouth. Her eyes were sad, watery pools. Dr. Barker tugged on a portion of the blanket, and the wounded animal snapped at him. Teeth clashed down, but her head barely moved. Dr. Barker flinched and stepped back.

"Harmony." Anger laced his voice this time.

"Sorry," I mumbled as I approached the table. I was being so dramatic about this. Vera being here made me so uneasy and scared. Pull yourself together.

Mrs. Who squirmed as I tried to place my hands on her. Stop being a baby. I sucked in a breath and gently placed my palms on her backside. The fur was warm against my fingers.

Argh, no, not warm. Pinpricks of cold licked at my fingertips, moving their way through each one. Tingles of frostbite were left in the wake of the sensation. I looked down at my hands expecting to see black, blue, fire, frost—something. But there was nothing.

They looked as they always did—perfectly chipped nails and a freckle on my right one. There was no ice-fire, no frostbite.

"Okay, hold her very still," Dr. Barker demanded. He was across the table, adjusting the straps on the muzzle.

I fought the pain so I could hold her down even though I was losing control. A wave rippled through her skin. She struggled to move. I held her down, despite the boxer straining against my ice-burning hands. Mrs. Who barked, all trace of whimpering gone.

The boxer pushed up forcefully on all four legs. The momentum threw me back and I slammed against the wall. It was more shock that flung me than force. The pale blue blanket fell away and revealed a dog showing no sign of injury. As Mrs. Who leapt from the table, the covering tumbled to the floor. What? How?

"Harmony!" Dr. Barker yelled. "Grab her! She's going to hurt herself."

"I… didn't…" I tried to speak, my hands in the air as if I were a doctor about to perform surgery.

Vera knelt on one knee and opened her arms wide. Mrs. Who jumped directly into her embrace. She scratched behind the dog's ears as the boxer licked her face. "Who's a good girl?"

Dr. Barker set the muzzle on the metal table and knelt in front of Vera to inspect the boxer. At first, he appeared to be gentle with the hind leg. He poked again and she responded with a sloppy lick across the doctor's face.

Argh. The pain was still in my hands. I couldn't take it. I left the treatment room. The cold burning continued as I stumbled into the bathroom. Turning on the water, I placed my hands underneath.

Lukewarm water flowed over my fingers, the sensation draining away with it. Every second under the water was sunshine and happiness as it relieved the burn. Tears stung my eyes.

What was that? The animal's fur must have been warm from the blanket. Or static electricity. Yes. It must have been static electricity. I turned off the water, decided I was right and returned to the waiting room.

"She must have just been scared," Dr. Barker said.

"I really thought she broke something," Vera replied. Mrs. Who was on the ground between them chewing on her tail.

"It's late. Go home, get some rest. Come back in the morning, and we can do some x-rays as a precaution." He bent and ruffled the boxer's head.

"Thank you. Again. How much do I owe you?"

"We can worry about that tomorrow. Get some rest."

Vera bent and scooped up Mrs. Who. The boxer gave her tail one more nibble as she was lifted into the air. Vera cradled her pet in her arms; the pale blue covering was gone. I let go of the swinging door and rushed into the treatment room.

The blanket was still puddled on the floor. I bent to pick it up and my hand grazed a wet spot. As I unwrapped layers, I inspected it and saw streaks of crimson. Had that been there before?

It was still wet. Yet Mrs. Who hadn't been bleeding when she'd jumped off the table. I shook the inexplicable reasons for the blood from my mind. I was overthinking.

I placed the blanket in a plastic bag from one of the cabinets above the computer, blood already crusty on my hand when I went back into the waiting room. I would have stopped for a towel to wipe, but Vera was already leaving.

"Vera!" I snapped as she headed toward the exit.

The woman turned around, holding the door open with her backside. The dog was still in her arms, trying to get at her tail again. She opened her fingers to grasp at the bag.

Vera nodded at me and walked away. Did she grin? She couldn't have, I was overthinking this entire thing. Her car had been left on, and the headlights tossed a glow across her as she left. Either way, I did not trust that person. She probably drinks the blood of her enemies.

I turned on my heel toward the bathroom to wash my hands. I slowly walked past Dr. Barker, still standing in front of the fish tank.

As I passed him, he grabbed my wrist and pulled me

to face him. He had about two seconds to get his hands off of me. Foster care taught me to never let a man touch you without your permission.

"Sorry," he whispered and let go.

"It's okay." He wasn't good with people.

"Why are you here?" Dr. Barker asked.

"Oh, you mean me and not Nurse Dara? She had to go home early. I'm sorry about having trouble holding her down."

"You healed her," he said it like it was a fact. Obviously he was very wrong.

"Excuse me?"

"Do you not know you are a witch?" Dr. Barker scratched his head and his toupee moved.

The man was obviously losing his mind. He had to be messing with me. Or maybe he meant Wiccan like Nurse Dara. Yes. That had to be it. That makes sense. Because a witch with powers. That's not real. They don't exist. The blood on my hand flaked as I rubbed them together.

"You don't know. Oh you poor girl. Let me call Miss Garcia. She is better at talking to people. Don't be frightened." Dr. Barker turned toward the counter.

I did what I'm good at. I ran.

Chapter 6

IT'S NOT POSSIBLE. There was no way. Dr. Barker was messing with me. Or he had gone off the deep end. Walking home, I crossed my arms over my chest. The wind licked my skin and sent shivers down my body. For May it was rather chilly in Philly. It should be called the windy city. My jacket was still at the clinic, hanging on the coat rack. Fuck that; I wasn't going back to that quack's office. A witch. Ha.

Magic wasn't real. That stuff is in books and movies. My head pounded against my temples. I needed to wake up from this dream. No, this nightmare.

As I stumbled on, the night became darker, the clouds grew larger and covered the moon.

Streetlights illuminated the sidewalk, yet it still seemed too dark outside. The green, earthy scent of rain crept into my nose. My shoulders hung low as the thought of a storm dampened my already sour mood. I had a ten-minute walk ahead of me, and I didn't think I would make it home in time. I could run, but my brain was in, um… overdrive.

Something moved out of the corner of my eye—the flicker of a shadow across the street. I squinted. It scurried across the lane. There wasn't a single car on the road to threaten the safety of whatever was coming. As the thing scampered closer, I blinked and a black cat headed straight for me. Its body was the color of tar and looked just as sticky. The white patch over her right eye gave it away. Ginger.

I bent and Ginger ran at me, only a few feet away. I pursed my lips and flicked my tongue against the roof of my mouth. A clicking sound echoed through the night. As if in understanding, she leapt into the air.

Ginger landed directly in front of me—not near enough to touch, since there was a thick syrup matted on her. What did she get into? How did she even get out? Poor girl. She needed a bath, and I wasn't so sure she was gonna be willing. I can add 'bathe a cat' to the list of bizarre things happening this week. Right under being stalked by Vera and above vomiting. But far below burning in my hands. Magic can't be real. I was freaking out.

"Ginger, can you believe Doctor Barker told me I was a witch?" I scooped her up; her fur was slimy against my arm.

I can't believe you didn't know you are, Ginger spoke, but the words were in my mind.

No way did I hear that. She did not speak in my mind, because cats don't talk and I don't understand what they are saying. I wanted to drop her and run. But I was obviously imagining it. This is how I go crazy. The holes in my memory and years missing were bad enough.

But this stuff with the animals. It was too much. Too much.

A cold, wet drop slapped the top of my head. I can't be a witch, they don't exist. Another drop slapped my head. Why wouldn't it start to rain now? That makes sense. It might as well hurricane and storm cows. Ginger meowed and rubbed her little face against mine. The sticky syrup slimed up my cheek. Gee, thanks.

"Why are you meowing? I'm the one going crazy."

Are you gonna keep us in the rain or go home? You can cry later, Ginger snapped at me. She was a bitchy cat. The rain fell harder. Okay, Ginger did have a point. I can deal with all of this later. Wow. I agreed with a cat. A cat. I shook my head and trudged on.

When I reached my apartment, I stood there and looked at it. My keys and phone were in my coat back at the clinic. Of course. The taste of salt grazed my tongue. Confused, I tried to figure out where it came from. My eyes stung. I blinked the burn away and realized I was, um... crying. Soft tears rolled down my face. I sniffed a few times to prevent the snot from escaping my nose. Then big, ugly tears came. The more I tried to stop, the more I cried. I was being split in two.

None of it was real. It couldn't be. This shit happens to people in movies, not in real life. Witches, magic, healing, talking to animals. It wasn't. It wasn't. I wanted to go inside and crawl in my bed, but I had no way in.

Would you stop crying and let us in? Ginger hissed.

"I can't. I forgot my keys at the clinic," I cried.

When did you get so dumb? Your boy left a key under the mat. You must forget things a lot.

I took a deep, shaky breath in an attempt to get

myself under control. It took a while, but the slow, shallow breaths began to help. I pushed all thoughts of the day from my mind and lifted the mat. Part of me wished it wasn't there. Because if it wasn't, that would have meant Ginger wasn't talking to me. But it was right where she said it was. Fuck, I'm going crazy.

My clothes sloshed as I unlocked the door and stepped into the dark living room. Ginger jumped from my arms and scattered off. Mean cat. The heat had been off, since it's May, and a horrible chill ran through me. Big droplets of water fell to the floor from my clothes and hair. Grabbing the bottom of my shirt, I pulled it over my head.

Thwop.

The blouse slapped the floor. Pulling my slacks down caused a ripping suction sound to vibrate through the living room. Had I not been so drained, I might have remembered to take off my sneakers, but my brain was in overdrive today and not working properly. My pants were caught around my ankles. I clumsily sat down to remove my shoes and untangle them. I left my wet clothes on the floor and went for a much-needed hot shower. Today needed to end.

By the time the water ran cold, I was rejuvenated. My mind had been playing tricks on me. For the first time ever, I was working hard at a job. I had finally decided to stay in one place. I would still have to journal all of this, but it wasn't real. Yup, I was putting my brain to work, and it was messing with me. That's all.

With the towel still wrapped around my head, I got dressed. The clock shone bright; Caden wouldn't be here for another hour. I tossed on sweatpants and a tank top. Drying my hair, I went to the living room.

Something moved out of the corner of my eye. Bam.

The front door slammed. Caden couldn't be home yet. Oh no. I never took the key out of the door, anyone could be here. Vera could be in my apartment.

Footsteps.

I searched for a weapon, anything I could use to protect myself. Instead of standing there defenseless, I darted into the bathroom. Footsteps grew closer. I tossed open the cabinet. There was a toilet bowl brush and some cleanser. I grabbed the brush and aimed it high like a bat.

I walked out, prepared for battle. I looked left and right down the hall, but still didn't see Vera. She was being a little too quiet. I crept down the hall. If I had to, I would beat her with the brush and then run. Where was Ginger? She was being conveniently absent.

"Hello," Caden called out. "You shouldn't leave the key in the door. Anyone could come in."

I let out a long, slow breath. His eyes bulged out of his head when he saw me. Towel on my head, brush in hand, and ready to kill. I must have looked so cool. He laughed. At first, it was a small chuckle, but it quickly became a howl. He bent over and pointed at me.

"What?" Caden said through fits.

"I got scared." I joined him in laughing. How ridiculous. My nerves were so far on edge. Obviously Vera wasn't going to break into my apartment. I was being dramatic.

He was an hour early and had scared me. But he had an amazing, sexy bag in his hand from Faster Fast Food. They have the best french fries and cheeseburgers in Philly. Caden always had this way of knowing when I was craving something and would randomly come home with it.

I bounced on my heels and jumped on him. He wrapped his arm around me and kissed the top of my head as he apologized. I didn't even blame him, I laughed too. I wanted to explain to him everything that had happened.

He deserved to know. Maybe he would have some answers for me. He knew about my memory slip ups. He knew four years of my life were missing. And he was supportive and wonderful about it. How would he handle this?

"You okay?" He set me down. The dimple on his left cheek was barely there.

"Yes." I glanced down.

The light in his eyes grew stronger, slowly transforming him. Of course, there was no actual light, yet there was—something. A change took over him. It was as if the fog that had been surrounding him was being lifted. "Tell me the truth," he replied.

His muscles rippled through his shirt as he tensed. The logo of the tech shop he worked at looked oddly distorted under his bulging chest. The intensity in his eyes made him look like a fierce warrior. He stood there silently staring at me, as if he knew I was lying.

"I'm fine." I wanted him to let it go. And I wanted him. He was so attractive. He made sense to me. Caden was my solid ground. The one thing I could always count on. And for a little while longer I didn't want him to know. I didn't want to risk him thinking I was crazy. Right now, I needed him.

A heat rose inside me. Desire coursed through my body, a magnetic current pulling me towards him. I took a step forward, having to be close to him. Caden pulled me into him. Yes—this was what I wanted. All of him. The food hit the ground with a small thud. We can eat that later.

Flashes of his body against mine invaded my mind. Yes, this is what I need. Him. On impulse my hips flexed forward. He took one hand and placed it on my waist. My fingers trailed up his chest and traveled to the back of his neck, lingering in his hair. I pulled Caden's lips to mine. My mouth grazed his, and a shiver ran through him. His hand trembled against my hips.

I loved teasing him.

He yanked me into him, forcefully grinding. Warmth pooled between my legs and a moan escaped me as I rubbed against him. Caden opened his mouth to allow my tongue entrance. I kissed him harder as all other thoughts faded away.

Chapter 7

NORMALCY. THAT'S ALL I wanted. This crap with holes in my memory, magic, talking cats, and Vera was driving me crazy. The more I tried to get a grip, the more I was becoming unhinged. And the desire to run away grew stronger.

Two days ago, Dr. Barker claimed I was a witch. I made the mistake of forgetting my things at his clinic when I ran out. I had debated leaving them as a loss but I couldn't afford a new phone. Not that anyone aside from Caden calls me, but I still needed one to do my Sudoku puzzles. I wasn't good at them, but apparently they are good brain exercises and I needed that.

Nurse Dara had stopped by, asking me to come back to the office. I hid on the other side of the door pretending I wasn't home. Not that I fooled her, she knew I was there and told me when I was ready my job would be there. She also said if I wanted to talk, she would listen.

I wanted answers, but it was too hard. Could she even help me? Dr. Barker seemed to think she could. I would decide what to do later.

My dish is empty, Witch! Ginger hissed.

"Nope. You can't talk," I replied. "Besides, I fed you like five minutes ago."

I can only talk to you and other witches with your talent. And they would give me more food. Ginger rubbed her body against my leg.

I stood in the kitchen staring at a pot of water that wasn't boiling.

Ginger continued to complain that she was starving. I walked over to her bowl on the other side of the fridge and it was, in fact, not empty. Instead of arguing with her, I grabbed another can and refilled her dish.

Back at the stove, the water was boiling. I tossed in a box of angel hair pasta and a few dabs of olive oil. The meatballs were in the sauce and the bread was already buttered. It wasn't fancy, but it was the best I could do. Caden would be home soon and I wanted to have a nice date with him.

There would come a day where I had to tell him what was going on and he may leave. Not that I would, um… blame him.

But for now I wanted a normal night with him. The, um… darn it, I can't remember what I was thinking of. Whatever, I refused to focus on that. The food should be done soon and Caden will be home.

I want a meatball, Ginger demanded.

"No, you don't get human food. And stop talking to me. I want one day of nothing bizarre." I pulled the strainer out of the cupboard.

One ball and I will. If not, I won't shut up. Your choice, Witch.

Making deals with a cat was never on my agenda. Neither was anything that has happened lately. I set two meatballs in her very full dish and grabbed my journal. I wanted to write down as much as I could before the food was done.

I was sitting at the kitchen table, pen in hand, when the door opened. Caden was home. He entered with a bouquet of sunflowers. Once every week or every other week, depending on the life of them, he brought me fresh ones. I love him.

The timer for the noodles went off. Caden kissed me on the head and replaced the flowers in the vase on the table. I finished dinner and had it set out for us to devour. There was way too much pasta, I shouldn't have cooked the entire box.

Caden thanked me and dove right in. He didn't mention how unusual it was that I cooked. Or that I was still in my sweatpants and tank top. He had been the one to teach me and spaghetti was the only thing I learned. Aside from the heaping amount on each of our plates, it turned out edible.

"Our run tonight is gonna be tough with all these carbs in our bellies." Caden shoved another forkful into his mouth.

"I was thinking we could skip it. Stay inside and watch a movie." I wanted normal today and I was worried that I could bump into Vera or Dr. Barker. I refused to take a chance.

"Sounds good to me. I hate running. It'll be nice to hang out with you." He grinned, bits of basil stuck in his slightly crooked pearly whites.

"Why do you run if you hate it?"

"It's more time with you."

He said it so calmly, like that was enough of an answer. I wouldn't go lift weights with him every morning just to spend time with him. Mostly because I hate mornings. Caden is so wonderful. I couldn't imagine my life without him. But there was a chance I would have to. If I lost him. Ugh, It was a hard thought that crept into my head over and over.

After the meal, Caden and I prepared to cuddle on the sofa. He grabbed two sodas for us and I popped a bag of popcorn. I didn't even want it, but movie time deserved it. I set it down on the coffee table and placed the movie in the DVD player. He went into the bedroom to grab a blanket for us. This was perfect.

Knock. Knock.

You thought I was gonna disturb your stupid normal night. Ginger sauntered by.

Ding. Dong.

There was no way I was going to answer that door. It could be anybody and I had no desire to deal with them. If I didn't answer they would go away.

The banging and doorbell continued.

Ugh. I walked over and opened it, wishing I had one of those peep holes.

"Hey, Music. I tried calling you but your phone is going right to voicemail," Penny said.

"Hi, Princess. I, uh... left it at work. Want me to grab Caden?" My attempt at coming up with a nickname for her fell flat. She did remind me of royalty, but more of one of their guards than a girl running around in a dress eating figs. She stood in my doorway wearing all leather and had two sticks peeking from the top of her back. Wait... not sticks.

"Princess? Little odd. Anyway, no don't grab him, I

need you. I may have found a lead on my roommate, Savvy, so I'll be gone a while. I was making sure you are cool with keeping Ginger." She shifted and I got a full view of the things strapped to her back.

"Are those swords?" I had been having a hard time lately, so I was positive it was part of my imagination.

"Uh. Uh. Cosplay. I'm into dressing up. Music, you cool with Ginger?" She took a step back and I noticed a knife stuck in her boot. She did look like a Ninja Princess, but she didn't appear to be into cosplay.

I agreed to keep Ginger, I had planned on it anyway. Even though she was bitchy and not nice to me, I had grown attached to her. If I could stop her from talking to me she would be close to perfect.

Penny left and I decided tomorrow I would go to the clinic and get my phone and keys.

As long as Dr. Barker wasn't weird to me, I would consider Nurse Dara's offer to keep my job. It was a good place to work... and if he was right, then I would need them. But there was no way he could be right.

Caden came back into the living room complaining he couldn't find the extra soft blanket he loves.

I had planned on washing it and tossed it in the hamper a week ago. I needed to add laundry to my to-do list. Once we were settled on the sofa, I filled him in on Penny dropping by.

"Yea, she's into cosplay. She works at Tech-fix with me, she has a nerdy side," he said.

Caden put his arm around me and tilted my head to his. My lips found his, sending butterflies to erupt in my stomach. I deepened the kiss. He moaned into my mouth and slipped his free hand into my sweatpants. His finger found my clit. I was wet instantly. As he rubbed against me I grabbed his hair in an attempt to be closer. I needed him.

Tonight things would be normal. Tomorrow I would deal with whatever was happening to me.

Chapter 8

THE LIGHTS WERE already on and I had arrived ten minutes early. Through the glass door, Nurse Dara was wiping down the counter. Dr. Barker stood next to her, chatting away. She paused and laughed at what must have been a joke. His cheeks reddened. They were in love and I doubted either realized it.

I walked in and grabbed my coat off the rack. My phone was dead but I had brought a charger. Dr. Barker stopped talking, causing silence to fall over the clinic. The only sound was the bubbling of the filter in the fish tank. Shit. I should have ran. Turned around and jetted out of there.

Instead I walked over to the two people that might know what was happening to me. I still wasn't buying that I was a witch; they don't exist. No matter how much the evidence keeps piling up. I'm a foster child from Ohio. And there was nothing magical about that.

"I have some danishes in the back that I made. The cherry ones are a little overcooked. Once you eat, start cleaning. We don't have any patients for about an hour." Dara walked over and hugged me.

"Um, uh, okay," I stammered. She didn't mention anything else. Not me being gone for days, not the witchy thing, not ignoring her when she stopped by. Nurse Dara was offering me food.

I tossed my coat on the counter, defeated. She had me at danishes. As much as I wanted to run from this problem, I had to face it. If I was going crazy then I would sign myself into the looney bin. If this was real and I was a witch then... I still might sign myself in.

The cherry pastry was baked perfectly. The edges were a tad crispy but added to the flavor. I was on my third one when I noticed Nurse Dara's office was open. She was on the floor with her legs crossed. Her eyes were closed and she looked like she was asleep. The stones in the room seemed to glow.

A green and blue bird flew out of the room, directly at me. Its right wing flapped harder than its other. I stepped back and it landed on the table. It was a beautiful pirate animal, um... a parrot.

"Hello, pretty," I cooed.

D-d-don't call me pretty. I-I handsome, he spoke in my head.

"You're a parrot. Can't you speak? Get out of my head," I snapped.

I repeat wh-when I t-talk o-out loud, he stuttered. *You must be powerful to t-talk to me. I'm Sparky. M-my o-owner meditates too m-much.*

Great. Now a bird is talking to me. A twitchy one that could speak but chooses to communicate in my mind. I never gave much thought to what it would be like to be a witch. But I didn't think it would be talking animals. As far as powers go, it seemed a little weak. Although Sparky thinks I'm powerful. The healing part is cool. But I thought witches made spells, carried wands, and rode brooms. Shit, I was starting to convince myself this was real.

Sparky squawked at me. He didn't seem impressed with me. I wasn't either. He pecked at a danish on the table. I thought about stopping him, but it was Nurse Dara's pet. She probably fed him constantly. She feeds everyone.

I finished my food and said goodbye to him. He ignored me and continued to eat. Would Nurse Dara be upset with me that I fed her pet? Well, technically it was her food that he ate. I did neglect to stop him, but I was putting the blame on her.

She was still sitting on the floor of her crystal room when I passed. I had considered meditation to help search my brain for my missing memories, but it had been a big fail. Maybe if someone showed me what to do. There was only so much I could learn from videos on the internet. Asking her to help me did sound like a good idea. Unless she tried to talk to me about the incident with Mrs. Who.

Coming back to work after having left was hard enough. The fact that they acted as though nothing had happened made it easier. I was not ready to discuss anything. I pulled my journal out of my purse and jotted down a quick entry about Sparky. Yes, I had to clean, but I didn't want to forget what he had said to me.

After scrubbing the toilets, I started setting up the folders for the day. Each patient needed to have their file out so Nurse Dara could easily grab it. The first one of the day was a ferret named Sunset and his owner named Arlo. He didn't need to walk into the office for me to know what he was going to look like.

Ten minutes later, Arlo and Sunset did not disappoint. Arlo had long hair, yoga pants and a star pendant around his neck. He was a total hippy and I was beyond fascinated by him. His ferret peeked out of the pocket of his jacket. He nodded at me and explained his little dude wasn't doing so gnarly.

Nurse Dara came out from the back and embraced the man. He teared up a little into her shoulder. Sunset crawled out of the pocket and up Nurse Dara's arm. She didn't seem even slightly bothered by it. I love animals, but that would have startled me.

She tried to calm him down, but it wasn't working. For a brief moment I wondered if I could heal his pet. My hands burned at the memory of having done it before. Never mind, I could never handle that pain again. It was too much. The ferret crawled back into Arlo's pocket and disappeared.

"Are you meditating? You seem so stressed," Nurse Dara said.

"I can't. My little dude. He needs me," Arlo cried.

"You are no good to her in this state. Go into my room. Meditate. First, grab a danish from the back room. I will take care of Sunset."

Hours after Arlo and his little dude left, I was still working up the nerve to ask Nurse Dara for help. I swear she knew what I was up to. She would give me side looks and ask what was on my mind. I lied. As much as I wanted her help I was afraid to ask. Plus, I didn't want her to talk about the incident. So far she hadn't, but she might still.

As we were closing up, she came up to me and leaned on the desk. Nurse Dara handed me a brownie that I was sure she had baked. My mouth watered. How was this woman not married with multiple kids? I wanted to bang my head against the wall. Her baking and cooking skills should not correlate with marriage and kids. Ugh. That was awful of me to think.

I took a bite. Caramel oozed into my mouth. Wow. It was fantastic. I wished Nurse Dara was my mom. My heart crunched in on itself for a moment. I never had a mother, but I would have wanted her to be this woman. I had spent days ignoring her when she could have helped me.

"I need help," I blurted.

"Oh, child, I know. I am here for you. Do you want more brownies?" A plate was placed in front of me.

"Yes. I know Doctor Barker said to talk to you about, um... the thing. But I'm not ready. I was hoping you could teach me how to meditate." I took a massive bite of the brownie. I would have kept talking had my mouth been empty. I was nervous and I didn't want her to know about my memories.

Nurse Dara nodded and pulled me in for a hug. She was shorter but still managed to pull me into her boob area. It was a tad too close to her, but the comfort level overtook me. I never had parents. This must be what it's like to have one. I bet moms would do this. Pull you in as close as possible. Be there for you in hard times. Love you no matter what.

Tears trickled in the corner of my eye. I was afraid if she squeezed any tighter the tears would pop out. I hate crying because when I start it's so hard to stop. And with everything going on, I may end up a puddle on the floor.

Nurse Dara kept me in her arms as she guided me to her office. It was an awkward walk that tripped up my feet a few times. Dr. Barker walked by us and chirped about women. Had I seen us, I probably would have laughed. But it was a parent comfort level I had never had before.

We reached the room and she let me go. The crystals in the room seemed dull. They must have been glowing when she was meditating, I couldn't have imagined that. Or maybe I did and it was the light from the sun shining through and bouncing off of the trinkets. I would have to remember to ask her about that.

She dimmed the lights and lit a few of the candles. I wanted to ask what I was supposed to do, but I didn't want to sound dumb. As I stood there, she pulled out two mats from a closet I hadn't noticed. After she was set up she instructed me to sit cross-legged.

I counted breaths in and out with her until I stopped feeling silly. Nurse Dara kept instructing me to steady my thoughts. I couldn't. My mind was racing with everything that had happened recently. Witches, magic, healing, talking animals, it scared me so much. Yet a part of me, a small part, was curious about what it all meant.

"I hear your thoughts over here, girl. Relax. Think beaches or the color pink. Pick one thing, one small thing and focus on that," Nurse Dara whispered.

Hazel Green, Caden's eyes. Hazel Green. Hazel Green. All other thoughts drifted away. Which left room for a memory I was trying to suppress.

The day I was adopted by Benny Deter. I got to sit up front on the ride to his house. The big yellow door looked happy against the pale white. There were six bedrooms and two living rooms in total. The house was huge and piled with junk. I walked into boxes upon boxes on both sides. A small pathway led to the sofa. Dirty dishes were stacked on one of the cushions and the television lay on its side. The smell of mold stung my nose.

Mr. Deter pushed me forward. The house was filled to the brim. I got two feet in before I had to turn around. The staircase was hidden underneath mounds of paper. The bedroom that was given to me had heaps of clothing, most brand new with the tags still on. I stared at Mr. Deter.

"You said you like to clean. I have to straighten up this house in thirty days or I get evicted. Which means you get evicted." He walked away, leaving me in the pile of junk.

Not wanting to lose this chance at a home, I began clearing trash. A dumpster was dropped off in the driveway, and I filled it—twice. He refused to let me attend school until the house was finished. I had wanted to join the track team, so my heart was broken. I worked as fast as possible so I could get back into school.

As I tossed things away, Mr. Deter drank. The first week it was only a few beers. He was a funny drunk. He'd even helped me remove some of his belongings, calling me his little lifesaver. The six pack easily turned into a twelve pack. By week three of this routine, he was up to a case of beer each night. The entire first floor of the house was cleared. Grime and scum had once filled the cracks in the tiles. I scrubbed them with a bristle brush, proud of how they shined. Mr. Deter came home from work, and I expected his praise. There was no way the town would take away his place now. He had even mentioned adopting me.

On day twenty-two, he walked in with a bottle of

vodka. He flopped on the sofa and turned on the television. Now that it was upright, it worked. I greeted him with a smile and a ham and cheese sandwich. His eyes were drooping, and it appeared he had started drinking early.

"Do you think I want this?" he slurred.

"Um. I'm sorry. The upstairs is almost complete. We should be able to keep the house," I smiled.

"I want my stuff. Not this house. Stupid child." He stood and ripped the plate from my hands. His palm struck me across the face. Then, with the back of his hand, he struck me again. That was the first time he hit me. It wasn't the last. The state of Ohio allowed him to adopt me a year later. Even with the records of broken bones, missing school, and police calls. I was stuck living the constant nightmare. My only escape was the days I had track practice.

On my eighteenth birthday, I packed up everything I owned. It wasn't much since Mr. Deter ruined most of my stuff with his drunken rampages. As I was packing, he stumbled into my room.

He grabbed my bags and tossed them in the basement. I knew he would break another bone. Tears swelled in my eyes. He grabbed me and flung me on the bed. The clinking of handcuffs made me wet myself as he cuffed me to the bed. I should have left while he slept. Now it was too late.

For weeks he left me like that. He never touched me except to feed me. A bucket was left by my bed so I would stop pissing myself. After a month, he came home sober and released me. He apologized and begged me to stay. I grabbed what I could and left for Philadelphia.

Water filled my eyes. I opened them and realized I

was at the clinic. I was safe. But it didn't matter. The tears fell. I was sobbing when Nurse Dara wrapped her arms around me. The memory was always below the surface, ready to erupt. I had wanted the missing years, not this nightmare to replay.

Nurse Dara grabbed a smooth black crystal off the table. She placed it between my hands and pulled me back into her. The surface was slick and warm against my skin. My heart stopped racing and the sobbing became a dribble. She kept instructing me to take deep breaths, which I was trying.

"This is obsidian. It will help calm emotions. Put it in your pocket and always have it with you. With everything you have gone through and will go through... well, child, you may need this daily," Nurse Dara whispered in my ear.

Chapter 9

CADEN SLOWED HIS PACE as we ran. I gasped for air, wishing I had water to help with the burn in my throat. He reached out his hand, interlacing his fingers with mine, and squeezed. I sucked in a huge breath and slammed my feet against the pavement.

We were usually out for about half an hour, unless I was having a particularly bad day. Somehow, Caden could sense when I needed a longer run. After what happened yesterday during meditation, I needed this. It had been two hours and he still hadn't asked what was wrong.

At some point he was going to. I wanted to tell him the truth. To confide in him. To have him wrap his arms around me and tell me he will never leave me. Those things weren't going to happen. I slipped my hand into my pocket, my finger sliding over the smooth surface of the crystal. I exhaled slowly.

"I can help you with whatever's on your mind," Caden said.

The first time he had said he could help me was when we met. Last year, I had the latest and coolest phone on the market. Well, to me it was. The Cleaning Bugs, a maid service, had recently fired me for being late so I couldn't afford much. It was used, but the ad claimed it was refurbished.

When the phone came in the mail, it wouldn't go past the home screen. After a day of trying to fix it myself, I finally called the seller. There was no record of him and no return address. Frustrated, I contacted my service provider. I was redirected to Tech-fix. I thought it was a mistake till a man on the other end told me to come into the store and he could reset it.

Caden had smelled like, um… oak and electricity. A weird combination, but his attraction was immediate. He stood in the middle of the store at a booth. Next to him was a tall girl with jet black hair—Penny. She was helping a woman with fiery red hair.

I looked over to Caden and he told me he could help me. A few minutes later my phone was fixed and had his number programmed into it. Days later I got up the guts to text him. He asked me out on a date and we have been inseparable since.

"Careful!" a man shouted at me.

I jumped to the side and Caden followed suit. I had almost crashed into someone else while running. Wow. My luck hadn't been good. What were the chances?

Since the day Vera bumped into me my life was turned inside out. I always had the memory issues, but the rest. All of that happened after she showed up. I had been running and she was walking. A normal person would have stepped to the side. She didn't. I had to see Nurse Dara. She would know if a person could cause someone else to have magic. It sounded crazy, but so were talking cats.

I still didn't believe what was going on, but the evidence kept piling up. For some reason Nurse Dara believed I was a witch. It was time I talked to her and got to the bottom of this.

"Ready to call it a night?" I asked Caden.

"I was hoping we could talk," Caden replied.

"Actually, I was gonna go, um, see Nurse Dara. She doesn't live far, um, from here. I will meet you back at home," I stammered.

Caden pulled me in for a hug. His sweat smelled electric; I wanted to lick it off his skin. I closed my eyes. As much as I craved him, I had to focus. If Vera did cause magic inside me, then I needed answers. None of this made sense. Nurse Dara may have answers.

"Hey, you okay?" I asked. His face was scrunched up. I wasn't the only one dealing with something.

"Penny needs my help with her roommate. She thinks she knows where she is. I don't want to leave you, but she needs me. I love you. I'll be back in a few days," Caden replied.

"I love you too, babe. Be safe. Tell Ninja Princess I said hi." I didn't want him to leave, but it would be better if he wasn't around while I was dealing with my witchy issue.

"I'm not leaving till the morning. I'll see you at home when you're done at Dara's."

I kissed Caden goodbye and headed to Nurse Dara's house. She didn't live far from the clinic, but was about twenty minutes away from where I was currently.

A sad thought popped into my head. My heart

tightened and I hoped it wasn't true. If Vera did do this to me, if she was messing with me, I was in big trouble. She may have injured Mrs. Who to test me that day. If she was capable of doing that to an innocent animal, what would she do to me?

When I reached Nurse Dara's building complex I attempted to compose myself. I didn't want to appear as though I was losing my mind, although I was. The building was crumbling, with bright lights surrounding the entire perimeter illuminating the cracks. A camera hung above the entrance pointing at the list of tenants.

I pushed the one for Garcia that had a heart-dotted eye. She always had to make stuff extra. I stood waiting for her to come over the speaker. The door buzzed open. She didn't ask who it was. Should I have waited? I shrugged and entered.

Her apartment was on the third floor. I looked around for an elevator, but didn't see one. While searching I had walked past two staircases. I gritted my teeth and took them. I don't mind stairs, but my legs were wobbly from the long run.

Nurse Dara was in the hallway of her place with Sparky on her shoulder. Ugh. I didn't want to deal with a stammering, twitchy bird. I liked him, but talking animals were driving me mad.

The smell of rice and beans tickled my nose as I entered her apartment. It was one of my favorite Puerto Rican meals. The little black beans were so full of flavor and the yellow rice warms the belly. I wouldn't ask, but I hoped she had enough for me.

"Child, you smell. Were you running from someone?" Nurse Dara asked.

St-stinky but pretty w-witch, Sparky spoke in my mind.

"No. I run cause I enjoy it. Can we talk?"

Everything here was the opposite of what I had expected. She had a gray L-shaped sofa with an enormous TV across from it. Her dining room table was marble. The kitchen was off to the side and looked small for someone who was always cooking.

I had expected trinkets and candles everywhere. Aside from two black crystals on the glass coffee table and a few regular candles, there was nothing else that appeared wiccan.

"I have a room in the back for all that stuff," she said, reading my mind.

My stomach grumbled. The smell of her cooking was even stronger in here. Saliva pooled in my mouth.

Nurse Dara tsked at my growling belly. "Eat more, girl, or you're gonna waste away. After yoga I'll feed you."

"Yoga?" I had to have heard her wrong.

"Meditation brought up terrible memories, so instead let's try something new. It may help you open up, child."

She directed me to move the coffee table out of the way. Then she clicked on the TV and a yogi was already giving instructions. It was as though she had known I was coming and had everything ready. Nurse Dara placed two mats on the ground and told me to focus.

In high school, my track coach had us do this once a week. He said it was good to stretch out sore muscles and learn balance. I hadn't done it since, and was surprised at how quickly I fell back into the poses.

When the yogi did the warrior pose I started talking. By the time we said namaste, Nurse Dara was filled in with every weird witchy moment I had dealt with over the last couple weeks. She didn't interrupt me once, or act like I was crazy.

"I am from Arlynn. Everyone is a witch there. Except for me, I'm what they call a Dud. No magic. I left there and came to Philly thirty years ago. The crystals, herbs, and candles are as close as I'll ever get. No, child, don't look sad. I love my life. I only mean to say, I can't help you with your powers. But I am curious how you went so long without knowing. Normally your affinity would come through around puberty. You are twenty-two. Where are your parents?"

"Dead. They were in a fire. I don't have any other family. Is Arlynn in Texas? Do you think Vera is doing this to me?" My skin vibrated. This was all so much. But the fact that she believed me comforted me.

"I don't know how to unbind someone, but it can be done. It is possible Vera wants something from you, child. I would stay away from her." Nurse Dara stood and walked into the kitchen.

There was nothing I had that Vera could want. Nothing. I'm a former foster child that runs and quits every job I have. What would she want? My ability to not do anything? She does seem rather motivated. Maybe she did want to learn how to be a slacker. I couldn't fathom why this woman was turning up every time I turned around.

Nurse Dara was great to talk to, but I had expected more help and information. Instead I was left with more questions. Where was Arlynn? What was unbinding? What does Vera want?

The poor woman had become wiccan because she was a Dud. And she left her home by choice, I didn't understand that. Even if I was different from my family I would have stayed with them.

Sh-she d-d-didn't leave by ch-choice. They f-forced

her out, Sparky spoke in my head.

Wow. That was really sad. But how did Sparky read my thoughts?

Tho-thoughts on y-your f-face, p-p-pretty girl.

"This is labradorite,' Nurse Dara said, handing me a blue-green iridescent crystal. My hand tingled. The power of the stone, undeniable. "It helps with mind and stability. It should strengthen you. I will put a protection around the clinic in case Vera shows up again. I don't know her, but from what you said, she sounds evil. I packed you some rice and beans. You should get home, it's getting late."

I tossed my arms around Nurse Dara. She pulled me in for a hug and I melted into her warmth. Once again, I wished she was my mom.

Chapter 10

EVERY LIGHT IN the clinic was on. Ginger sat on the chair behind the counter, complaining that she was hungry. I tried to explain to her that she wasn't. On the counter was a steak knife I had taken from home. Hidden under a few plastic chairs was a baseball bat Nurse Dara had brought. We had a stopper in the big metal door that led to the back, so Ginger could slip out there. We weren't taking any chances.

"You remember the plan?" I asked.

Yes. If the evil woman kicks your ass I go get Nurse Dara. Ginger yawned.

The bell above the door chimed and, um... moths erupted in my belly. This was a bad idea.

Last night, on the walk home from Nurse Dara's, I had bumped into Vera, again. When she had come around the corner, I didn't even flinch. The woman seemed to be able to find me anywhere. She had tried to talk to me, but instead I asked her to meet me at the clinic. She gave me what looked like a bow and agreed. Weird woman.

Vera stepped through the door. Wind whipped my hair in my face; I needed to fix the color. Goosebumps trickled up my arm. With her in the room it was ten degrees colder. She smiled.

I should attack. She scared me. I didn't want to talk to her, but if I was ever going to get her to leave me alone, I had to. If this meeting didn't satisfy her, I'd be fucked. I would spend the rest of my life hiding from this woman.

"What did you do to me?" I asked, my voice shaking.

"I fixed you. They would have you without your magic. I simply unbound it," Vera said.

"Unbound? How was my magic bound? I would remember that." That wasn't true, my memory was screwed up.

"Would you? Do you remember everything? Do you have any memory issues? Anything you feel you should know, but don't?" Vera stepped closer.

She knew. Somehow she knew about my messed up mind. Could she have done this to me? Vera had the power to unbind my magic; did she have the ability to bind it? My heart was racing. How was this possible? She had to be lying. But she could be telling the truth. There was no way to tell. Didn't matter. I didn't trust her.

"They messed with you. Had they not, you would know who I am. We are friends. Practically best friends. To see you this way breaks my heart, the light and life inside you extinguished. Listen, you and I have the same goal. We are trying to help Arlynn. I need you. Come back home with me." Vera held out her scaly hand. Like I was gonna take it. Ha.

"Who messed with my memories? Why do you need me? Who are you?" I stepped back. Nurse Dara had mentioned Arlynn before. I would have to ask her about it.

"I am the leader of The Unkindness. We are a group of people trying to help Arlynn. Your magic is one of a kind. We need it if we have any chance of saving our people. I need you to use it to unlock someone that will help defeat the dictator of a king we have. Come with me." Her last words were demanding.

"I'm not going anywhere with you." I wrapped my fingers around the knife. The moths in my belly went haywire.

Wind swirled around the room. Ginger jumped from the chair and ran in the back. I held the blade in front of me. She may not have said she would take me by force, but she didn't need to. I could tell by her eyes that was her plan. I swished the weapon toward her and she howled with laughter.

It flew out of my hand, twirling inches from my face. Whatever magic Vera possessed she was using it to taunt me. Could wind be a magic talent? The knife flew through the air and landed in a picture of a dinosaur. I squeaked.

Vera yelled about me going with her, anger lacing every word. I dove and slid across the waiting room, grabbing the handle of the bat. I should have had it closer. I stood, attempting to conceal it behind my back.

A flick of the wrist from Vera and the bat was out of my hand. It skimmed across the room, taking the same path I had moments before. She was showing me her power. She wanted me to know at any moment she could snap her finger and make me go with her. Didn't matter.

Nothing could get me to leave. She was evil. I didn't know where Arlynn was, or who her people were, but I knew there was no way I was helping her. Whatever she had planned had to be world domination level stuff.

Even if there was a tiny chance she wasn't evil, I wouldn't leave Caden. But when he found out what I was, he would leave me. Um… my thought floated away as easily as the knife had. I needed to fix my brain.

Especially with this woman after me. As much as I wanted to believe this was all a dream, that I wasn't a witch, that magic didn't exist, it was becoming harder to deny. I had to accept it, to be able to stay away from Vera. I got up and inched back toward the counter.

A shadow of a man shone through the vet window. She had brought back up. From the looks of him, I may not be able to run fast enough. Every, um… bone in my body wanted to hightail out of there. But that would leave Nurse Dara and Ginger exposed. I got them into this mess, I had to protect them. Somehow.

The man yanked on the door. It wouldn't budge. I let out a sigh of relief; Nurse Dara wasn't sure if it was going to work. She had been in the back room, chanting a protection spell in case Vera had a partner.

Nurse Dara appeared with Ginger at her side. I had told that cat to stay in the back if things got bad. I didn't want her to get hurt. Obviously she didn't listen, I shouldn't have been surprised. She never listens. The crystal around Nurse Dara's neck glowed a bright white.

Vera laughed. Wind blew, pushing my clothes against my skin. My hair twirled above my head. Nurse Dara and Ginger stayed where they were. The water in the fish tank sloshed. I was in deep shit.

This will not be the last time I see you. If I can't get you to use your magic, I will find a way to take it. When you have your memories back, you will understand I am not the bad guy. The wind carried Vera's words to my ear.

Vera turned and flicked her hand at the exit. Glass shattered. The man on the other side jumped back, but it was too late. He was in the way of the shards flying. I winced, because he must have gotten sliced up. Vera stepped through the door and walked into the night.

Chapter 11

CANDLES LITTERED the entire area. Nurse Dara had turned her place into a ritual room, at least that's what she called it. She had crystals of varying colors of the rainbow scattered all over. Tiny jars were situated into an oval. In the center of it, where her coffee table was, was a bright blue mat.

Dr. Barker was in a metal chair off to the side. He insisted that he was present, but didn't want to actually partake. He claimed to believe in the mysteries of wicca but said that, as a Dud, he was useless. Part of me believed he was here to spend time with Nurse Dara. His eyes sparkled the same way Caden's did when he looked at me.

I wished he was here. Not that he would understand. But maybe he would be okay with it. I was in denial at first, but I was starting to believe I was a witch. What if he could too? Then I wouldn't have to lose the love of my life.

Nurse Dara directed me to lay on the mat and clear my mind. I tried, but I hadn't stopped thinking about Vera and what she could possibly want from me. Last night was a disaster. After Vera walked out, I almost crumpled to the ground. Nurse Dara was on me and had her arms around me. She refused to let me fall. Told me to keep my head up and stay strong. I didn't want to. I wanted all this to go away. But it wasn't going to.

She had brought me over to the counter and allowed me to sit down. With a cup of tea in hand, she let me ramble about everything I had been through. Everything Vera had done to me. I was pissed.

Vera had taken my choice away. I didn't want to be a witch, I didn't want powers. That woman forced it upon me. I was losing control. The hocus-pocus was clawing its way to the surface. I didn't want to be the freak that talks to animals or heals them. Yes, it's cool, but it hurts me.

Then Vera dropped the news about my memories. I had been trying to fix that problem on my own. I knew something was wrong with me. But the fact that someone had gone into my brain and messed it, that I was having trouble understanding, why would anyone do that?

Four years of my life gone. Those four years probably contained all my magic years. Could I have been running around casting during that time?

Nurse Dara tried to comfort me. She brought me a slice of cake she had baked during her lunch break. She had to have known I was gonna need it. As I ate she asked about one of the things she had overheard. Vera claimed her and I were on the same side.

There was no way that was true. Evil people are friends with someone like her, the kind that torture others for fun. Not someone like me. I'm not the type of person that would associate with Vera. That woman was darkness and horror. No matter what I had been through in my past, that wasn't me. I told Nurse Dara I didn't believe Vera.

She told me of a way she may be able to help and asked me to meet at her place the next day. As soon as I arrived at her house she had a glorious plate of nachos and cheese in front of me. I dived in as she set up what she called a ritual. She believed she could access my memories. That if magic hid them then magic could unhide them.

Dr. Barker helped her set up all the candles and, um... crystals. She would yell at him that he was being too rough and he would snap that he shouldn't be doing this. They bickered as though they had been married a long time. I wondered how long they had known each other. I wanted to ask but didn't think it was my business.

They should be, um... together. They made an adorable couple, and it was obvious they were in love. But Nurse Dara had said his wife was murdered; he probably didn't want to let her in his heart. The pain from that must be awful. I couldn't handle it if Caden was killed.

"Child, your mind is racing," Nurse Dara snapped.

I was laying on the mat surrounded by candles that I hadn't noticed were all lit. Nurse Dara had a sage thing that was burning in her hand. The smoke danced away from it. The white dress she wore was covered in smudges of soot. She stood above me, lips pursed.

"Sorry. I can't concentrate," I whispered.

"Sad excuse, Harmony Laverack. Dara Garcia is attempting to help you. If you don't want her help go elsewhere." Dr. Barker was his normal happy self.

L-listen t-t-to me. O-one, t-two, Sparky stammered.

He counted to ten and had to start back over at one. Nurse Dara hadn't taught him past that, which he was nice enough to explain in long, strained words. Poor Sparky had so much trouble speaking. I concentrated on every number. Other thoughts pushed at my brain and I ignored them. Sparky counted and I listened.

The smoke from the sage melted away. The sky opened up. It was bright orange with black iridescent clouds. A majestic castle painted the horizon. Mountains surrounded the other sides of where I was.

Three men stood above me. Fear ripped through me. I had never seen them before, but I knew who they were. Each one had on the same exact suit. Black pants, jacket, and a gray tie. They appeared to be part of a group, but aside from the secret service I didn't know anyone that ran around with their friends in matching suits.

One of the men was taller than the rest and appeared to be in charge. The second was a tiny man with a rat face and looked petrified. The last was a short, stocky man that had the same look as every bully I had ever come across. I was sure he spent his nights pulling the wings off of flies.

None of them looked at me, talking to each other as if I wasn't there. I was wearing a black bathing suit and sitting in a chair, ropes dangling from the arms. At one point I must have been strapped down.

There was no water around, but the smell of salt wafted my nose. I tried to remember how I got here. Why I was here.

Nothing. Anything before this moment was gone. They continued to talk, but their words didn't reach my ears. I opened my mouth to scream and no words left my lips. I stood up. Well, tried to. My body stiffened. I could sense every muscle, but they wouldn't obey. What was going on? Where was I?

In the distance, Nurse Dara's voice drifted. She was calling to me. A light hum of my name patted at my ears. I wanted to run to her. I wanted her to save me. A tear crawled out of the corner of my eye.

These assholes were the enemy. They were part of everything wrong with Arlynn. I hated them. I may not recognize them, but my soul knew what they were, pure evil. They were stripping witches of their memories. They were changing who they were. And they were about to change me.

"Donickey, are you sure she won't remember any of this?" the tall man asked.

"Sir, I have her memories here." The rat man held a small black bottle in his hand.

I bolted upright. Someone was screaming. I held my hands over my ears to stop the noise from piercing my brain. Tears flowed from my eyes. Arms flew around me. Sage burned my nose.

When I opened my eyes, Nurse Dara and Dr. Barker had their arms around me. The screaming continued. Aside from the light of the candles, the room was dark. I was back in Nurse Dara's apartment.

And I was the one screaming.

Chapter 12

"WHAT WAS THAT?" Dr. Barker asked when I stopped screaming.

How could I answer him? What I had seen was real. But I was in a different place with orange skies and magic buzzing in the air. There was nowhere like that in Philly. Or anywhere else.

I had walked into a memory, and the entire time I didn't forget a word or struggle to think. My mind had never been so clear before. I struggle daily to remember my past and those years that were gone. It took Nurse Dara one stroke of her sage.

"I think I was in Arlynn," I replied. It made sense; if it was magical then that's where I was.

"You went rigid and then sat up and screamed, child. Are you hungry? What did you see?" Nurse Dara stood up and headed to the kitchen. Food is always her solution.

She had a plate of cheese and crackers in front of me on the mat. I was gonna have trouble going to the bathroom later with all this dairy. I popped a little yellow square in my mouth, spicy. The cracker dulled the burn on my tongue. Nurse Dara handed me a glass of milk. Dr. Barker and Dara stared at me, waiting for me to tell them what happened. I didn't know how to describe it, and the way my skin still crawled.

After all the food was gone, even the spicy ones, I finally spoke. They asked me over and over to describe the three men. They had both lived in Arlynn and had no clue who they were. It was over thirty years ago for them, so I wasn't surprised they didn't know them. But the assholes did look the same age as them.

Dr. Barker sat back on his heels and scrunched up his face. He scratched his head, causing his toupee to move. I wanted to giggle, but my brain was in overdrive. He opened his mouth numerous times and then closed it again. I waited for him to speak, but he said nothing.

"They messed with me. I knew years of my life were missing, but those witches did it. They had a tiny bottle with what looked like black smoke." I ground my teeth.

Nurse Dara shook her head repeatedly. She stood up and paced between the candles and crystals. Dr. Barker stayed on his heels and chewed his inner lip. They weren't saying anything. I wanted to scream. I wanted them to do something. Say something. Anything. I got up and grabbed my purse.

"Where are you going?" Nurse Dara asked.

I didn't know. I wanted to run and keep going until my legs bled. I had always known there was something wrong with my mind, but I thought if I tried hard enough I could get my sanity back. Finding out I was a witch was terrible enough. I... I... ugh, I couldn't think.

"You have to go to Arlynn and get your memories back. I have a friend that could help you. My wife's brother lives in the forest there. He is a tad odd, but he knows everything. His name is Apples. Let me write down his information." Dr. Barker was rambling.

I wasn't sure where I was going, but Arlynn would not be it. I had no plans to go on some insane trip. For what reason? To locate a bottle? Nope. I had wanted to know who I was, but this wasn't right. Something about that bottle scared me. What would happen if I found it? Would it be just the missing years or my whole life?

Vera had said we were friends. She believed I could go save the people of Arlynn. That's not me. That's not what I do. Whatever memories were taken, they were better off where they were. I didn't want them.

Nurse Dara kept talking to me. I tightened my purse across my body and did what I do best; I ran.

The streets were bare. It was late at night and there wasn't anyone out. Usually around this time there were still a few people shopping. Tonight, there wasn't. The way my life had been going, I took that as a bad sign. Any minute Vera would appear from thin air.

The plan was to run until my head was clear. Instead I found myself at home.

My heart raced and my fingers tingled. I slammed my back against the wall and slouched down. How is this my life right now? This was becoming too much. I couldn't handle it.

Food. Witch, I am hungry, Ginger snapped.

I pulled myself up and grabbed a can of food out of the cupboard. I walked over to her dish and saw there was plenty of food in it. This cat was trying to annoy me. I stared her down.

I knew you would get up. You're welcome. Can't stay on the floor all night. Ginger showed me her tail and walked away.

Sneaky cat. She did force me off the floor. But I still wanted to fall apart. I wanted someone else to swoop in and save me. Caden. He would be able to do something, if he knew what was going on. Unless he committed me to a mental institution. I guess I would be safe in one of those.

With my journal in hand, I went to the bedroom. The light above was broken, so I clicked on the lamp on the nightstand. I had told Caden numerous times I would grab a new lightbulb, but I forgot. It had been burnt out for a few weeks and had fallen to the bottom of my to do list. At the top was: fix my mind.

Now that I knew what was wrong with me, I didn't want to be fixed. My memories could stay in Arlynn.

Maybe the journal could help me understand my powers. Writing it all down could show a pattern to what triggers it. Or learn what Vera wanted with me. As much as she said she wanted me to save the people of Arlynn, I didn't believe her. Aside from the fact that she doesn't seem the type to help anyone, ever, I'm useless.

My powers had healed a dog and allowed me to talk to a few animals. That doesn't equal save the world type of stuff. Animals are important and I love them, but they aren't people. She said people of Arlynn. I don't have whatever power she thinks I have.

I spent hours writing everything down. Even the way I felt when I was walking through my memory. I added small details about how Dr. Barker's toupee moved when he scrunched up his face. I had pages dedicated to Nurse Dara and her amazing food. I put everything into it.

My eyes grew heavy.

I hadn't taken off my sneakers yet, so I pushed each one off with my toes and flung them across the room. I snuggled under the blanket, wishing Caden was here. He always kept me so warm.

It was probably the fact that I had written down everything and finally gotten it off my chest, but when I fell asleep I slept the best I had in weeks.

"Babe. Babe. Harmony," Caden whispered, jarring me from sleep.

"Uh, hi. Did you find her?" I mumbled. Was I dreaming? I reached out to grab him. He pulled away from my touch.

"We need to talk." The light peeked through the curtains and fell on his face. He was covered in mud. Cuts rode along his arm and his shirt was ripped at the collar. Caden had been in a fight.

Chapter 13

I PACED BACK and forth picking at my nail beds. I touched his face and a tear fell from my cheek. What happened to him?

Caden wasn't a fighter. He had rippling muscles that were only used in the gym. To see him in this condition. It had to have been, um... Vera. She did this to him. She hurt him. I would make her pay.

I hadn't decided if I was going to tell him about my current dilemma. The choice was now taken from me. To protect him I would tell him what was going on. Ugh, I really hoped I didn't end up in a padded room.

"I should have told you sooner. I was scared. I need you to know, I am in love with you. We can run and never go back. We can go wherever you want. Harmony, I love you." Caden paced.

"I love you too. What happened to you?" I cupped his hand with mine.

He pulled away from me and walked into the other room. What the heck was that?

He looks worse than you. Ginger followed him out of the room.

My mind raced over what could have happened to him. It had to have been Vera. I refused to go with her and now she was getting back at me. It happens in movies all the time. Fuck. I had to tell him I was a witch. How do I even tell him that? 'Hi, Caden, I love you and I have magic powers.' Ha. That would go over well.

Caden walked back into the room with two cups of coffee. He handed me one and sat on the bed with the other. He took a sip and sighed heavily.

"I need you to know I really do love you. None of this was ever supposed to happen," he mumbled into his coffee.

"I love you too. Um, there is something I need to tell you." My heart pounded in my chest.

"I'm not from here," Caden blurted out.

Had he not heard me? I needed to talk. He needed to know what I was, not that I even really understood it.

"I'm from Arlynn." Caden set his cup down and knelt in front of me.

What? My head spun.

"It's... Shit, how do I explain this?" He placed his hands on my knees.

"You said Arlynn?" But that would mean... and he couldn't...

"It's a place hidden in the Bermuda Triangle. Arlynn isn't exactly a different dimension. It's more of an island that humans can't find. Our magic hides it. You won't find it on any map. There are actually a few islands there, but we live on the main one."

"But... but..." That would make him...

"I'm a witch." Caden stood.

Ha! Did you see that one coming? Ginger came back into the room and pounced on the bed.

"Well, we are both witches. I know this is a lot to take in. If you need a minute, I get it."

I got up and went into the bathroom. The water was lukewarm as I splashed it on my face. This wasn't happening. How could he be a witch too? What does this mean? I am going insane. That's the only explanation that adds up.

"Ahhh!" I screamed.

Caden charged into the bathroom as I sank to the floor. He wrapped his arms around me and sat with me.

My heart tried to jump out of my chest. My head wanted to roll off and hide under the sink. Every atom in my body shook. He couldn't have said that. There was no way he said that. How? He was my normal. But no. Caden Perry is a witch.

I clutched my head to prevent it from falling off. "How?"

"I was born in Arlynn, so were you. The Order sent me to Philly almost a year ago. I was to protect you while you were here. They altered your memories so you were safe. My mission would end when they called you back. Usually a year. That was why we were supposed to go to Florida, but as I said before we could not return. We could go anywhere," he rambled.

"Wait, what is The Order? Protect me? Altered memories?" My head was spinning. His words didn't make sense.

"The Order is like the police and military mixed. We protect the witches of Arlynn from all threats, like The Unkindness." He held me tight as he spoke which was good because I couldn't look at him. I was trying to process this massive info dump. "The Unkindness are an evil coven hellbent on destroying Arlynn. Their leader Ember Raven has been out for revenge on her father's death for the past six years. She won't stop until the royal family is dead."

The woman sounded like Vera. I was sifting through everything he said. I didn't understand it all.

"How do I fit into all of this?" I asked.

"The Order started The Witches Protection Program. They figured out who Ember Raven was targeting and then started sending them Earthside. I was only supposed to keep you safe, but I fell in love with you." Caden kissed the top of my head.

Ember Raven wanted me for the same reason Vera did, my magic. They needed it, but I wasn't sure why. Ember and Vera must be working together. That explains why Vera is after me.

"What did you mean by 'they altered my memories'? I remember being a foster kid, not a witch."

"It's for your protection. They implant a past, so you don't go looking for Arlynn or accidentally use your powers. I don't know why they gave you such terrible memories."

I stood up and clenched my fists. Terrible memories was a fucking understatement. They destroyed me. They had me believing it was all real; the foster homes, years of torture, feeling like no one would ever love me, dead parents.

Holy fuck! What kind of people do that! And Caden was in on it. He knew my past wasn't real, yet he let me cry to him for hours about it.

The Order sounded as awful as The Unkindness, maybe worse. What kind of person steals someone's memories and then gives them nightmares?

"Run with me. We don't have to go back. I'm sorry I lied to you." Caden stood. "I know this is all a shock."

"No." I was mad. He lied. This whole time I thought I was losing my mind he knew what was going on. "I don't believe you. I'm not a witch. You aren't a witch. None of this is real."

"You aren't surprised at all. Why aren't you?" He stared into my eyes.

Um... think, Harmony. Say something.

"My particular affinity can tell when someone is lying. I'm a truth detector."

I turned on my heels and ran. He didn't follow me out the door. He didn't follow me down the stairs. I stopped to see if he was behind me when I was a few blocks away and he wasn't. Yes, I was mad at him, but a part of me wanted him to follow.

I slowed down and started walking. Caden was a witch. Had he opened up to me sooner I wouldn't have had to spend the last few weeks alone. He could have helped me, but instead he took off with his friend and returned in tattered clothes. Where had he gone?

He was so busy filling me in on everything he had kept from me that he hadn't told me about that yet. He should have started with what happened and not his witch story.

I was someone he was protecting, not his girlfriend. I wanted to believe he loved me, but it was hard to trust him. Ha. A truth detector lied to me for the past year. The irony.

And my past! I was furious. They were monsters for what they did to me. Those memories made me who I was, but fuck, they could have added some good ones. Anything that resembled love would have been nice.

In front of me was a small restaurant with a few of

the light bulbs missing from the sign. I checked my jeans; ten dollars, cool I could grab a bite to eat. Growl, my stomach agreed. I could go for some french fries. I had never been to a restaurant that had bad ones. Especially fast food places.

The bell chimed and a young girl with a low ponytail approached me. She looked behind me as she asked how many were with me. Her face fell when I told her it was me.

I hated when people felt bad for someone eating alone. There was nothing wrong with it.

Granted, I was eating alone because my boyfriend had spent the last year lying to me. My blood tingled in my veins. Why hadn't he been honest with me from the beginning? Especially after he fell in love with me. Unless that was also a lie.

The waitress rushed over and grabbed my order. Water and french fries. She reminded me that it was still breakfast time, and I smiled at her. It could be because it was a dimly lit restaurant, but it wasn't busy.

A tall man with black hair and grass-green eyes sat across from me in the booth. He wore a dirty apron and hair net.

There was no reason for the cook to sit with me. If this man told me I was the key to the restaurant or I had more magical powers that I didn't know about, I was going to hit him. I had never hit someone before but he would be the first.

"Odd food choice in the morning. You must be having a bad day." He smiled at me.

"I'm having a bad day with my boyfriend." Why did I tell him that?

"My girlfriend has been sick for days. All I get is texts that she doesn't want to see me. You kind of look like her. But she has fiery red hair. You know how those gingers can be." He shrugged.

"So bring her soup. Aren't you a cook?"

"She would tell me if she wanted some. But I do make amazing soup. Apologize to your boyfriend. I'm sure you aren't perfect."

The man was a tool. The smugness rolled off of him. I was positive he didn't believe he was ever wrong.

His poor girlfriend was probably hiding from him. I laughed and he squinted his eyes at me. Sad part was he was right.

I'm far from perfect. I was so mad at Caden for not telling me he was a witch, but I also kept secrets. For weeks I kept everything from him, afraid of how he would react. He finally told me the truth and I ran away from him. Ugh. I really hated that this stranger was right. I rolled my eyes at him and slouched in the booth.

He got up and walked away from me. I had no idea why he felt the need to come talk to me. I didn't know him and he sure didn't know me. At least he didn't talk to me about anything magical. I wasn't going to apologize to Caden, but I would be taking his advice. Once I was done with my food I was going back home. I had to learn to stop running from my problems.

Chapter 14

MRS. WISNIEWSKI BLEW the whistle and let it drop. It dangled around her bony neck. Everyone ran forward from opposite sides of the gym. Caden was the first to reach the dodgeballs lined up at center court. He beat the fastest kid in class, Dereck Wittmeyer, to center court, grabbed the nearest projectile and fired. Splat! The ball smacked Dereck in the arm and he let out a sigh as he walked out of bounds.

Caden quickly grabbed another ball before anyone else could approach, taking two steps back to assess the competition. Most of the girls just sauntered forward, showing little interest in the game. The guys, though, were different. They all wanted to beat Caden at something and had told him on multiple occasions. He held the record for almost every sport that he competed in at East Arlynn High and even though dodgeball wasn't a real sporting competition, he *treated it like it was.*

Michael Broom, the school jock, grabbed a ball and ducked as Caden launched another at him. Three balls were simultaneously tossed at Caden—one from his own teammate! He easily dodged two of them. The third he caught. April Carmichael giggled as she walked out of bounds. A few more kids walked to the bleachers, expressions of boredom on their faces. They didn't want to bother with another game of 'Caden wins dodgeball.'

Shy, quiet, gangly Spencer Austin was hiding in the back when a ball rolled toward him. He picked it up and limply heaved it at Caden. The ball missed by about ten feet. A smile emerged on Caden's face as he countered and fired a ball at Spencer. He let out a yelp, sparks of energy erupting from his body.

The ball sizzled and exploded into a flock of paper cranes. They fluttered erratically toward the ceiling before bursting into flames, falling in glowing embers to the floor. Stella had her mouth half open, a twinkle in her eyes. She reached out towards the lone paper crane that had yet to detonate. Her boyfriend, Clark, nudged her with his elbow and whispered in her ear. The twinkle disappeared and her arm dropped.

Mrs. Wisniewski chirped the whistle. "What is the number one rule of gym class, kids?"

"No magic!" everyone shouted in unison.

"Spencer! Principal's office! Now!" She pointed a skeletal finger toward the door.

"But he didn't mean it. He was scared," Caden blurted out, trying to defend him. He didn't want the kid to get in trouble because of him. It wasn't fair.

The class erupted into laughter, all directed at Spencer. Some pointed; some shouted "scaredy-

witch." Others declared that he was scared of Caden and his big muscles. Redness seeped from Spencer's neck into his face as he ran out of the gym. Caden chased after him.

"Spencer, stop!" Caden bellowed down the long hallway.

"What!?" Spencer turned to face him, energy dripping from his clenched fists.

"I'm sorry. I didn't mean for that to happen." Caden took a step back.

Spencer huffed, his black hair flopped down on his face which deepened from embarrassed crimson to a hateful blood-red. "Of course you didn't! That's what's so annoying! You're so darned likeable." The drip of energy turning to a trickle.

"I'll make it up to you."

"How? They all think I'm afraid of you… and frankly, Caden? Sometimes I am. One day you will pay for this. One day I will hurt you."

"Is that a threat, Spencer?"

The scene faded. I sensed Caden's hands still holding on to either side of my face. When I came home from the restaurant he said he wanted to show me Arlynn. As a truth detector he could project his truth into my mind.

Caden adjusted his book bag. He searched the flow of students ushering out of the front doors. Every student that came out nodded at Caden, or waved. Some blew him kisses. He turned down the street.

Majestic merlot-colored trunks bowed gracefully, sprouting a leafy canopy the color of sunshine. The shady arch transformed the air into a buttery haze down the length of the street. A peacock-blue squirrel was jumping from one branch to another. An arbor sprite vaulted from a hollow in the tree to accost the squirrel. Caden could see its tiny fist in the air and a finger jabbed into the squirrel's snout.

A garden gnome in a red hat was at the trunk planting magenta-colored sunflowers. He tossed the tiny shovel into a wheelbarrow, a bogie leaning lazily against it. The bogie was roughly the same height as the gnome, but green and rather fat.

The crossing guard, Mr. Bill the Centaur, yelled at the gnome for throwing sharp objects too close to the road. Students stood waiting to cross the street. A rainbow of colors floated erratically into the air. Once off the school grounds, students were allowed to use magic—so most used it constantly and pervasively. Affinities developed around puberty, so high schoolers were always fighting to control the inevitable mishaps that came with the territory.

Sarah Johnson had recently discovered her affinity for air and hadn't stopped hovering above the ground since. She floated on the corner of the road waiting for Mr. Bill to give the signal to cross. A fairy fluttered by, bright blue wings flapping in Sarah's face. Those evil little fairies could be annoying buggers.

Caden chuckled and turned his eyes toward the vermillion sky. Ebony, iridescent clouds, brightly twinkling, hung low in the sky, evolving into a myriad of shapes—a house transforming into a grinning cat, two clouds metamorphosing into witches and waltzing on tiptoe with each other. He genuinely smiled. Clouds always cheered him up—even today, despite what had happened with Spencer.

"Why do you always look up?" a familiar voice called out.

"Why do you always look down?" Caden asked

Autumn. He tore his gaze away from the dancing clouds. "Someone like you should always have her head held high."

"You mean 'the help'?" Autumn asked.

"No, silly. Someone like you. On track to be valedictorian." Caden jammed his hands into his pockets.

Autumn Everette stood a few inches from him, her brown, frizzy hair framing her face. The clothes she wore hung loose around her shoulders. They used to belong to Caden's elder sister, Liz. Autumn couldn't afford new clothes, so Liz often gave her the clothes she no longer wore.

Liz had once offered to go shopping for Autumn, but she had politely refused. The only reason she would even take the hand-me-downs was because it was one less thing for her mother to buy.

"Are we waiting for Sandra?" Autumn asked, ignoring the previous question.

"We broke up. Let's go."

The two walked in silence, under the arch of trees that seemed a little too beautiful. The arbor sprite was still hollering at the squirrel, who refused to stop hopping from branch to branch, shaking the bright yellow leaves.

As they passed the tiny shops in the middle of town, Caden peered inside. Patrons were browsing through an array of miscellaneous antiques. Autumn kept her eyes on the road. Not once on their walks home did she ever bother to peek at what was inside the shops. Caden noticed that she showed little interest in what they sold.

The variety of items was wonderful. You could buy the latest gaming system, eye of snake, a cell phone, *flying bikes, or food for your pet pixie. One of the shops they passed was painted black with darker, tinted windows. He never knew what they sold, and his parents told him he couldn't go in there—no matter how old he was. Liz had said she'd gone in once and it wasn't worth it but wouldn't allude to what was in there.*

He still couldn't comprehend how he and Autumn had grown up under the same roof, yet lived two completely separate lives. She was part of what his mother referred to as 'the help,' a term that bothered Caden. He knew she was, technically, but why should she be treated as such? His mother told him to stop walking her home, that he shouldn't be seen with people below his station.

A man walked out of the shadow of a dark alleyway. He was adorned with a tattoo of a Raven down his right arm. The ink still pulsed as if brand-new. His hair was long, black and oily, and his breath smelled of liquor. He got a little too close to Autumn for Caden's comfort. Wrapping an arm around her waist, he shifted her to his left side in one swift motion, away from the sinister man. She was his responsibility. If anything happened to her, he would be to blame. They were both sixteen, but Autumn's mom always asked him to look out for her.

As the scene faded, I lifted my hands to Caden's. I had so many questions. He kept his hands on my face and another scene played in my head.

Five castle turrets stretched up to the black, iridescent clouds. Caden used to laze in the soft grass of the courtyard and watch the clouds chase each other around the turrets. His brother would lay with him, too, until he grew older and thought it childish.

"Aren't you coming?" Autumn pulled his attention

away.

"I was gonna train," he mumbled.

*"No, Caden. Your parents will be furious with you."
Autumn grabbed his hand and dragged him through
the entrance of the castle. "You know they don't want
you fighting. Stop defying them. You think they won't
find out that you spar with James every night?"*

*Although the outside of the castle was all gray stone
and looked like something you would find in Scotland,
the inside was not. The walls were painted in shades
of tan; the floors were hardwood. His mother had
imported the crown molding from different parts of
England, claiming the witches didn't make it properly
here. He knew his mom liked it just because it was
expensive.*

*As he walked in, Melon, his pet dragon, scuttled up
to him. He was still a baby and hadn't started breathing
fire yet. Melon was no bigger than a full-grown cat, but
still had difficulty shimmying up Caden's leg. After a
quick lick across his face, Melon flew off. Caden
laughed as Melon tried to stay in the air. He was very
chubby for a dragon and his baby wings had trouble
keeping up with him. Caden's mom told him to stop
feeding him table scraps, but he couldn't help it. Melon
loved witch food, and Caden loved spoiling him.*

*Autumn shook her head and smiled at the departing
dragon. She pushed up onto her tippy-toes and gave
Caden a peck on the cheek, as a sister would do.
"Happy birthday!"*

*Before he could reply, she ran off. Thanks, but I
could have gone all day without hearing that, he
thought. He trudged to the kitchen, stomach growling.
His bookbag was still slung over his shoulder. He would
have brought it to his room, but the grumble in his*

stomach overruled his desire to relieve himself of the heavy bag.

The kitchen was excessive, the size of a small house, and obnoxiously silver. His mother had even painted the cabinets gray. Well, paid someone to do it. She called it modern; Caden called it over the top. His mother was standing by the center island, wearing too-tight blue jeans, a skimpy tank top, and looking like an older woman trying to relive the golden days of her youth. The worst part was the pure gold crown resting atop her head. She wore it all the time. Caden couldn't understand it. Everyone knew she was the Queen of Arlynn. His father, the king, only wore his crown when attending court or in the course of his royal duties.

"Hi, Caden. How was school?" his mother, Donna asked.

Before he had a chance to respond, his brother, Liam, sauntered in sucking all the attention in his direction. His head was held high, back straight as an arrow, carrying a round tray. It took Caden a minute to register that he had a birthday cake in his hands. The blaze of the candles suddenly lighting nearly blinded him.

Liam's affinity was fire, and he used it every chance he got. The candles on Caden's cake were no exception. Every year Liam set the cake ablaze, burning it beyond recognition. It was one of many reasons Caden hated his birthday.

"Hey, kiddo, can you tone it down on the flames?" Their dad, Kane, sauntered in and smiled.

"You know Caden loves the flames," Liam replied, but in the same breath the flames diminished to a normal-sized flicker.

They sang Happy Birthday Witch to Caden, while he

stood there and sulked. Liz would have made it bearable, but she was on a sabbatical. Once they were finished, he blew out the candles and turned on his heel to hurry off to his room, book bag still slung over his shoulder. He refused to eat a half-melted cake.

Before he had the chance, three men in identical black suits, ties, and shiny black shoes breezed past him—The Order. Big butterflies erupted in Caden's stomach. This was what he wanted for his future. He hadn't made a wish on his candles, but now he did. I want to be in The Order. Caden knew these men well. He had been practicing daily to become one of them.

The man on the left was Joseph Wittmeyer. He was taller than the rest and the leader of The Order. A life-long position, the only way to ascend to Commander was to wait until the current one died. Rumor had it, poison sped up the process. Jonathon Donickey, the tiny man to the right, looked much like a rat. He was next in line for the lead position. Since he cherished the ground Wittmeyer walked upon, no one believed him capable of assassination. However, as a rule, Donickey never stood next to Wittmeyer. Braxton had that position, always between them, like an unspoken threat—death to those who made an attempt on the life of the Commander. Dylan Braxton's squat, stocky appearance didn't fool anyone. He was the enforcer. In high school he had used his affinity for electricity to torment kids he didn't like. He did still torment witches, but the current of electricity was stronger—more focused—now.

"Your Majesties," Wittmeyer said as they all simultaneously bowed. "A word please."

"Speak," King Kane demanded.

"The princes?" Wittmeyer adjusted his tie, averting

his eyes to avoid looking at the two young men.

"Liam will be king one day. As for Caden? He plans to join The Order... if he proves deserving of the role. Speak."

Caden didn't miss the truth in his words. His father did not believe him worthy of The Order.

"Highness, we were attacked. The Ravens have formed a coven, calling themselves The Unkindness. We had believed it was only the Raven family who were after you, but they have followers now. Over a hundred. They plan to overthrow you," Wittmeyer said. The other two stood silent.

"The attack?" King Kane asked, frown lines etching into his face.

"It was on Highland Beach. We didn't know their numbers had grown. They are branching out from Sapris. They killed Mitchell. We followed them back to The Raven's home and burned it to the ground." Braxton smiled.

"Did you kill them?" Queen Donna asked. "Them... and their children, I mean."

Caden stood frozen. He felt like this conversation wasn't meant for him. He knew The Order had been chasing The Raven family for years, but to kill their children. It made his stomach twist. He pushed down the taste of bile.

"We believe their children, Ember and Grace Raven, perished in the fire."

The King and Queen let out sighs of relief. Caden turned and ran from the kitchen.

Chapter 15

CADEN PULLED HIS hands away and squeezed them. He explained using magic cool-burned the hands. I rolled my eyes. Yeah, I knew that. Flashes of me healing the dog fluttered in my vision, the pain still haunted me.

"I told you I would explain about being a witch, now please explain how you know you are one." Caden blew on his hands.

When I came home from the restaurant, Caden was sitting on the sofa, freshly showered. I bombarded him with questions. Why hadn't he told me? Why did they take my memories? Why tell me now? What happened to him? What's Arlynn like? Had he lived there forever? What exactly did his power mean?

My brain had been, um... spinning with all the questions. Had I known he was a witch things would have been easier. He could have helped me with Vera.

At least I had thought he could until he told me where he had been.

Penny had heard rumors that her roommate Savvy was in South Carolina. She could have driven alone, but if Savvy had been taken Penny would need help. Rumor was The Unkindness had found Savvy and planned to take her back to Arlynn.

I wanted to interrupt his story; The Unkindness kept coming and Vera claimed to be their leader, but that woman was a liar. Caden said Ember Raven was their leader. Vera also stated I was her friend. Which wasn't possible. I planned on asking him more about it when he was done with his story.

Caden had gone with Penny to South Carolina and searched everywhere for Savvy. He said his particular affinity helps with asking if anyone had seen her, because he could tell if they were lying. A man on the beach spotted Savvy heading to a sleazy hotel with a woman and two men.

They found the hotel and Savvy, but the woman and men attacked them. While the fight was going on, Savvy got away. Penny continued to follow Savvy in hopes of getting her back. Caden was going to go with her, but the woman... When Caden realized it was Vera, he knew I was in trouble.

Once he was done with his story, he showed me Arlynn. Why he chose those particular visions I wasn't sure, but I did get to see the beauty of the place. There seemed to be no pain, trauma, or foster homes there. It appeared perfect. But it wasn't. They fuck with witches' memories and hunt them down.

"You said Ember Raven was leader of The Unkindness, but in the vision The Order killed her as a child." I took a sip of the cold coffee he had made earlier.

"We thought she was dead. Until she was sixteen when she emerged with an entire coven of evil witches at her back." He grabbed the cup from me and filled it.

"Sixteen? That's so young." Even after everything I went through I couldn't imagine being that hateful at such a young age. Mad enough to raise an army against the royal family seems crazy.

"She wanted revenge. The witches wanted someone to follow. It was a perfect match. Enough about her. How do you know you're a witch?" he asked.

I wasn't ready. I needed a distraction for a little while, I had to clear my head.

My hands grazed his. Electricity pulsated through my veins. I had been trying so hard to keep us normal that I pushed him away. He lied to me, but I didn't tell him the truth either. Had either one of us been smart enough to open up, we could have been helping each other. I love this man.

I brushed my fingers down his arm, lightly. A tease. My heart raced. He stood still. Heat rose between us. I needed him. I needed to run my tongue across his bare chest.

"I know what you're doing. This is important. We need to discuss this." Caden pulled my hand away.

I didn't want to talk right now. I needed time. I shifted on top of him. He kept his hand on my arm as I grabbed the bottom of his shirt and pulled it over his head.

He released his hands and grabbed my ass instead. I ground my body into his. He wanted this as much as I did. His throbbing member pushed against me. My pussy pulsated with the need for him.

"You know how to distract me," he said with a smile. He may have wanted to stop me, but he gave in, giving me the distraction I needed.

Caden dug his fingers into my ass and moaned. I licked my lips and ground into him. As his hands traced up my back, touching my skin, ripples of pleasure ran through me. This was love. No matter what happened between us, no matter who started keeping secrets first, we loved each other. We were two magnets constantly pulling each other close.

Our lips met, and I let out a moan. I wanted him, all of him. He picked me up and tossed me back against the sofa. Within moments my clothes were off and he was sliding inside me. This time we were making love as witches.

An hour later I was satisfied and drenched in sweat. His eyes flashed green every time I smiled at him. It must be some witchy thing.

"You are fantastic. I love you so much. But, Harmony, it's time. We need to talk." He sighed.

With a huff, I went into the bedroom to grab my journal. It would be easier to fill him in if I had my notes. My brain misfires and I wanted to make sure he knew everything. The journal wasn't on the bed where I had left it. After a few minutes, I found it shoved under the bed in between a few towels.

Witch, someone is here! Ginger screamed.

Fuck.

I ran into the living room. Caden wasn't on the sofa, but the space wasn't empty. A tall skinny hag of a woman was sitting on the sofa. Vera. She wore a black pencil skirt and shiny high heels. Her hair was in a perfect angle bob, like it always was. The woman was evil but she did have style.

I followed the gaze of her eyes. Caden was on the ceiling, his back flat against it and wind slapping at his hair. Vera held him up there with her affinity, damn wind. I wanted to scream. I wanted to pull Caden down.

"I will kill you!" Caden yelled.

Vera flicked her hand at him and wind choked his words.

A vision of scratching her eyes out crossed my mind. But I also wanted to run. I turned my head to the door.

"You run and I kill your boy toy," Vera growled.

"What do you want from me? I'm not the person you think I am!" I shouted.

"But you are. You're not the person you think you are. The Order fucked with your memories. You aren't some sad little foster kid from Ohio. You are a strong woman and my friend. Together we can free our people. The king is killing witches. He fucks with their memory, claiming to protect them. He wants anyone that can stand in his way dead. And you are included in that. The Order altered your mind, but who do you think was in charge? The king." Vera spoke each word with precision.

Had she thrown knives at my chest, it would have been better. Could she really be lying? Most of what she said was true. The Order stole my memories, I had made that connection from Caden's vision, and he had admitted to knowing I was never a foster child. The years of torture I went through weren't real. There never was a Mr. Deter who tied me to my bed for weeks.

I hated them for what they did to me. Vera and The Order were both evil and I wanted nothing to do with either of them.

Who was I? Was I really Vera's friend? Was the king of Arlynn really bad? If he was, Caden was his son— did that make him evil as well? I was getting more questions than answers lately.

"Come with me." Vera stood.

I should have told her to fuck off. I should have peeled Caden off the ceiling and ran with him. There were so many things I should have done at that moment. Scratching her eyes out crossed my vision again.

"I will, but not yet. Let Caden down and I will meet you tomorrow night at the vet clinic," I whispered.

"Why should I believe you, child?" Vera asked.

"You need my magic. If you could have taken it you would have. Maybe you need me to use it. Either way, you have made it clear you need me. Take me by force and I will never help you." Vera was much stronger than me, and could have easily made me go with her. For some reason she hadn't. It could be because she believes we are friends. More than likely I was right and she couldn't use my magic without me.

"Clever girl, maybe all of you is not lost." Vera flicked her hand.

Caden crashed down onto the table he built.

Chapter 16

"YOU LIED," CADEN SAID as he pulled himself off the broken table. Of course he knew; being a walking truth detector had to be a cool power. Way too many people had lied to me recently and it would be nice to know when they were. Caden rubbed his shoulder as he walked over to me. For such a hard fall he didn't seem to be in too much pain. I would have been crying if that were me.

"I did. I'm stalling," I said. I grabbed my journal off the floor and sat on the sofa. "I'm leaving, but before that I need to hold up my part of the deal."

He sat next to me, still nursing his shoulder. I kissed his hand and opened the journal. He didn't ask about me saying I was leaving. I was planning on asking him to go with me, but first I had a few things to do. Three things to be exact. The first was telling him my side. Him and I had been keeping secrets from each other for too long.

I told him everything. And I let him read some of the entries I had written.

"The missing memories are a part of The Order altering your mind. It's still new," he explained. "We can go get them. I know you've been trying to fix your mind. I don't know where they're hidden, but I can help you find them."

"It doesn't matter. I don't care about that anymore, or even why they did it. They altered memories of who I was before and I'm guessing if I found them, it would change who I am." I didn't need to know why they stole them or where they were. My plan had nothing to do with the person I was. It was all about who I am. I am a former foster kid, track star, job quitter who is in love with Caden. Whatever happened before that didn't define me. If I chose to find my memories, I would lose the person I am. Fuck that.

Caden listened to everything I told him. He hugged me and kissed my hands as I spoke. Every time he went to interject, I stopped him. I needed to get this all out. As I told him about the dog, a few tears fell. Why do I cry so much? He wiped away my tears and pulled me into him. When I was done I shut the journal, got up and put it in my purse.

"So where are we going?' he asked.

"I'm not sure, but if Savvy can run from The Unkindness so can I. If you come with me, I doubt The Order will still want you in their little club."

I went into the bedroom. My bookbag was in the back of the closet. I hadn't used it since I left Mr. Deter. I had fled with only a bookbag and did just fine. The Order may have given me the worst fucking past possible, but it was useful. Because of that I knew how to run.

Witch, where are you going? I'm hungry, Ginger snapped.

She had been gone for a few hours, I hadn't even noticed she came back. I assumed she was playing in whatever sap she had on her the day I found her in the alley. I had asked her where she goes, but she nicely informed me it was none of my business.

"I'm leaving and you're coming with me." No way was I leaving her here, no matter how mean she was to me.

Fine, but bring enough food for me. I would like some meatballs. Ginger turned and walked out of the room.

Caden came in as I tossed my, um... underwear in the bag. I stared at him ready to give my big speech on why I was running, but the words escaped me. I had been doing really well with my thoughts that for a moment I thought my brain was patching up. I, of course, was wrong. I couldn't think of what to say to him.

He went over to the closet and grabbed his gym bag. He tossed his dirty clothes on the floor and went over to the dresser. As he packed, I thought of what to say. He had already said he was going, but giving up his dream of joining The Order for me was a bit extreme. He could go back to Arlynn and be the person he was meant to be.

"I want to go with you. I love you, whoever you are. I don't care if your mind was fucked with. I don't care about The Order. Only you matter," Caden said as he packed. Leave it to him to know what was on my mind.

"I love you." I zipped up my bag and walked into the kitchen.

Ginger would be rotten if I didn't bring enough food for her. She was already rotten, but when she was hungry she was worse. Once Caden and I found a good place to stay, I would search for Savvy. She needed to know her cat was in good hands, even if she did leave her behind. I understood why she did it. Hiding from a pack of evil witches couldn't be easy.

A few minutes later we were all in the car. Ginger was in the back seat complaining about not having a pillow to sleep on. She was never happy. Caden's car was a red sporty-looking thing. I didn't even have a driver's license so I was playing navigator. Which worked because he didn't know where we were going.

The first stop wasn't far. It was my goodbye stop. There were few people I knew in Philly, or anywhere really, and this one was the only person I wanted to say goodbye to. In the little time I had known her she had made a huge impact on my life.

Caden came with me, and Ginger stayed in the car. She did demand we ask for a pillow. I went to hit the button for Garcia, but she had already buzzed us in. How did that woman always know when I was showing up? For a Dud she, um… was magical.

I had expected the smell of something amazing cooking but there wasn't any. Odd. Nurse Dara must not be feeling good. When I entered, she was standing in the kitchen making sandwiches. She had a mini cooler on the counter next to a few sodas and some ice pouches. Was she going somewhere too?

"I hope you like ham and cheese. I also made a few peanut butter and jelly sandwiches. Will Ginger be okay with a small Tupperware of meatballs?" Nurse Dara asked.

"How did you know I was leaving? And that Ginger wanted meatballs?" I asked.

O-owner k-k-knows all! Sparky squawked.

Nurse Dara shrugged and continued to pack the cooler. Sparky flew by. The candles were all lit and the crystals in the living room were shining bright. It looked like she had finished meditating and then went right to preparing food for us.

Dr. Barker walked out of the back of the apartment. His toupee was on backwards along with his t-shirt. I caught eyes with Nurse Dara and raised my eyebrows twice. Good for her. Her cheeks blushed and she went back to the food.

"Um… I just wanted to say thank you for everything. I'm going to miss you." I walked around the counter to hug her.

"This isn't goodbye. You will see me again, but I fear it won't be for a very long time." Tears dripped from the corners of her eyes. Fuck, this was awful.

"Thank you for being there for her," Caden said. His hands were in his pockets.

Nurse Dara pulled away from me and went over to Caden. She wrapped her arms around him before he had the chance to pull his hands from his pockets. He whispered another thank you to her. She nodded and went back to the cooler. She placed all the food and drinks in it and closed the lid.

My heart tore. I didn't care what was in my memories, and what was stolen from me. This woman was the closest I had ever had to a mother. Departing, even if she said we would see each other again, sucked. There could be a real mother out there somewhere in Arlynn. But she never came looking for me.

"Caden, can you grab the cooler? Harmony grab the small black pillow on the couch. It should be good enough for Ginger." Nurse Dara pointed. There was no way she was a Dud. She had some form of psychic powers.

We both did as we were told. Then I hugged her one more time. Tears spilled from my eyes. I didn't want to leave her. But if Vera was willing to go after Caden, then that put her at risk as well. Leaving was best for everyone. I waved to Dr. Barker and he nodded back. The man really didn't like to talk to people.

"Don't forget your crystals," Nurse Dara called down the hall as we were leaving.

Ginger was satisfied with the pillow. She claimed it wasn't the best one, but would do for now. I didn't tell her about the meatballs yet. The car didn't need grease all over it. With everything secure, Caden asked where to next.

"We have one more stop. There's a little restaurant not far from here."

"You want french fries, now?" His mouth fell open.

"It's not for fries. I spoke to the chef there earlier, but I didn't realize who he was until I saw your visions. Ready to face up to Spencer again?" He had aged, but I had no doubt it was him and I didn't believe in coincidences anymore.

Chapter 17

THE BELL ABOVE the door chimed as Caden and I walked in. A woman with a high ponytail was at the hostess booth. The other girl must have gone home for the day. Her eyes sparkled at Caden as she glanced him over. A tinge of jealousy washed over me.

She grabbed two menus and started rambling off the specials of the day. "Our specials are turkey club, salmon, oh and fries smothered in gravy."

My mouth watered. I shook my head. Focus. "Ma'am, we were looking for the cook that works here, um…" I couldn't remember his name.

"Spencer Austin. Is he here?" Caden interjected.

The hostess dropped the menus back down and rolled her eyes. Geez, we asked if someone worked here, not for her to do anything. She cocked her hand on her hip.

"Like I told the last people looking for him, he isn't

here." She turned and walked away.

Caden and I snapped our heads toward each other. Last people? Who else would be out looking for him? Vera popped into my head. I wasn't sure what she would want with him. I had met him for roughly five minutes before and I didn't like him. So, it wasn't a far stretch that he was on Vera's side.

I shrugged and went back to the car. Ginger snapped that I didn't come back with food. I popped open the cooler and gave her a few meatballs. I would have to get the grease out of the seats later. She purred and started nibbling fast. The poor thing was going to choke on them if she didn't slow down.

"I could interrogate the workers and find out where Spencer is," Caden said as he sat in his seat.

His suggestion wasn't a bad idea. I had considered breaking in at night and checking pay stubs. One of the foster homes I was in locked me in the basement and I learned how to pick the lock so I could get food out of the kitchen.

Ugh. That wasn't even real. The Order had messed with my memories and given me a terrible childhood. That made no sense. I would have been fine without all the trauma.

Witch! Ginger yelled between meatball bites.

"We could break in," I suggested.

Witch! Ginger snapped.

"We could wait till tomorrow and follow him home from work," Caden said.

Witch!

"What?" I snapped back. That cat had a knack for being bratty. It's gonna be a long trip with her. I love her, but ugh.

I know where Spencer lives. Don't look at me like

that. I was watching him. He's Owner's boyfriend. I thought he knew where she was. I even fell in a trash can watching him. Got all sticky. Ginger purred.

The night she was in the alley, she had been covered in sap. I couldn't believe she was spying on him. Wait! All the words she had said were being processed one by one. Owner's boyfriend.

"Spencer is Savvy's boyfriend. We need to get over there fast. Ginger knows the way," I said. There really are no coincidences.

Caden's mouth dropped as he put the car in drive. He looked as shocked as I was. Spencer was the kid from Caden's vision, and Savvy's boyfriend. He came and sat with me at the restaurant. That wasn't because I ordered french fries for breakfast. He knew me. There was no other explanation.

We pulled up to the apartment complex Ginger directed us to. It was a few blocks from my apartment, I had walked by it on the way home from the clinic a few times. He was so close, could he have been watching me? I didn't trust anyone and this man made my stomach turn.

I jumped out of the car as soon as Caden put it in park, yet he still beat me to the door. Them long legs of his really came in handy. I wiggled my tiny little legs. If I wasn't a track runner, I wouldn't make it anywhere fast.

Caden pounded on the door. There was no buzzer for the entrance into the building so we went right up to apartment two. I would have to buy Ginger extra meatballs. She really helped me with this one.

I giggled. A few weeks ago I would have freaked out about a cat helping me find someone. Now, it was becoming normal to talk to animals. Once my life calmed down I would have to work on honing my powers. I had healed a dog, how many more animals could I help? What else did my powers mean?

There was no answer at Spencer's door, but I heard footsteps. The woman at the restaurant had said people were looking for him. Could they have found him before we did?

I pulled out a tiny screwdriver and flathead from my purse. Since my time in that basement, I carried them with me everywhere. They normally stayed at the bottom of my purse and were only pulled out when someone needed their glasses tightened. It didn't happen often, but I always had them.

As I was fiddling with the lock, Caden gasped. I shrugged and went back to picking the lock. Not all of us were the king's kid. Even though my memories weren't real, they were to me. And right now they came in handy.

I unlocked the door and pushed it open. Way too many people forget to snap the deadbolt. After this, Spencer may not forget again. We walked in and saw an old man with balding hair sitting on the sofa. He had on a pair of dingy white boxers and nothing else.

Down the hallway was a duffle bag on the floor. Clothing spewed out of it. There was no sign of Spencer.

"Get out!" the balding man hollered. His voice was off and scratchy, like it didn't belong to him.

Caden jumped over the end table and grabbed the man by the throat. I screamed. He was on top of the man, choking him. What the hell was wrong with Caden? The stranger was turning blue.

I stood frozen. Caden was killing this man and I froze.

"Caden, chill," he coughed.

Caden removed his hands from the man, but stayed on top of him. A ripple went through the man's skin. It was like someone had a huge blow dryer on him. One second he was the old man, the next he was Spencer, dressed in sweatpants and a black hoodie. What the fuck?

"He's an illusionist. He changes what you see, but he could never fix his voice," Caden explained to me as he got off of Spencer.

"I see you're still a know-it-all dickhead." Spencer rubbed his throat.

"I will process that at another time. You knew who I was at the restaurant. Why didn't you say anything? And where are you going?" I pointed at the bag in the hallway.

"Yes. I know you. But don't ask any questions. I won't tell you." He got up and grabbed his bag from the hallway.

I couldn't stand this guy. He was such a tool. I understood why Caden didn't like him. He spewed cockiness and it annoyed the crap outta me. He knew me, yet tried to say not to ask him any questions. What was wrong with this guy? I didn't know Savvy, but I was starting to wonder about what kind of person she was. First leaving Ginger behind and then dating this guy.

"Where are you going?" Caden asked.

"To find Savvy. After your little girlfriend came by the restaurant I realized something was up. Does she know you've been lying to her for, what, a year now? She was pissed at you earlier. Not surprised." Spencer tossed the bag over his shoulder.

I wanted to hit him. This guy was a total douche bucket. Caden clenched his jaw; he must have had the same thought as me. We could both beat the crap out of him. It would be fun. I shook my head. Violence is never my thing.

"You're coming with us. We'll find Savvy," I said. Nothing is a coincidence and I needed to know what he knew about me.

"Fine. I'm not driving. Penny is in Georgia, which means Savvy might be close." Spencer held his head high and walked out the door. I really didn't like him.

Chapter 18

CADEN PULLED ONTO the dirt road, dust flying into the air. The neon sign read 'May's Motel, Vacancy.' The place looked as broken as the road. Bricks were missing; paint was peeling. A rat scuttled across the parking lot.

"Nope! Not happening!" Spencer shouted as he pushed the lock down on his side of the car in the back seat.

I agree with the idiot, Ginger chimed in. Oh great, they get along.

I stared out the window as Spencer and Caden argued. They had been like this the entire time. Six hours of them bickering about stuff that happened in high school. The hate between them was strong.

Another rat darted across the parking lot, stopped directly in front of the car, and stared at me. The thing glared its beady little eyes. Another approached, then another. Within seconds, ten little vermin were in front of me. It was as if they were trying to tell me something. I rolled down the window. The leader of them came to my side of the window. *Run.*

I pushed the palms of my hands against my temples. The leader repeated, *Run*, over and over. We already were. What did he expect us to do? Ginger hissed. She was not pleased with this many rats near her.

"I'm gonna park the car and go in. I'll get two rooms. Spencer, you will pay at the next stop," Caden said.

Caden's beloved red car spluttered. It rocked back and forth causing me to slam forward and get jerked back by the seatbelt. After a loud poof, the car went silent. The vermin scurried away. I turned to Caden, scared.

Three black jeeps sped into the parking lot. Dust flew into the air and caused a thick layer to settle on the windows. I sank into my seat as Caden turned to me, his eyes darker than before. I peered through the windshield unable to see who was there.

I turned back to check on Ginger. She was off her fluffy pillow and on the floor. Spencer looked petrified. I rolled my eyes; for a big tough guy he was such a baby. The dust settled outside and the windows cleared as if they were never covered in the first place.

My heart pounded. We should have left when the damn rat said so. The three jeeps were still circling us. They were dark with tinted windows. Even the front windshields were pitch black. Tires screeched to a stop simultaneously, as if on cue, one on each side of me and blocking us in front. Someone stepped out of the driver's side of the one closest.

A tall, frail woman got out and looked directly into Caden's car. Her angled bob cut swayed as she moved, and she was dressed in a black pant suit. I tried to calm the shaking in my hands, but this bitch wouldn't leave me alone. Vera.

Caden opened his mouth to speak and was cut off by the crunching of metal. His door was collapsing in on itself like a soda can. I looked around, confused. No one was touching it. He unlatched his seatbelt, gave me a wink, and lifted his leg, kicking out at it. There wasn't much left of it, and it went flying into the car next to them.

A gush of wind whooshed into the car. My hair twirled in on itself, spiraling like a cone above my head. My sweatpants whipped against my skin. Poor Ginger cried in the back seat. Spencer tried to speak but I couldn't hear his words over the noise.

The blast of wind lifted Caden up, and he hovered in the air just above his seat. His hands grabbed for the steering wheel. One final gush and he was pulled feet-first out of the car, the steering wheel clutched in his hands

Vera laughed as Caden flew toward her. She pulled back her arm and flung air at him. Neon blue lines emanated from her hands, like the brightest flashlight I had ever seen had been turned on. The light turned to vines and smacked Caden in his chest. He vibrated as the blue light crawled over his skin. Tendrils of blue wrapped around his chest and worked their way down his arms and legs to his fingertips and toes.

I was frozen. My eyes bulged out of my head as I watched the scene unfold. I didn't understand what was happening. My heart threatened to jump from my chest. Caden was elevated, convulsing as the tendrils engulfed him. Grabbing at the strands, he pulled them off, flinging them to the ground where they evaporated.

Then, Caden did the strangest thing; he flung his hand back at Vera. In thin waves, the air turned a dark green. Struck, Vera fell back to the ground. Since when did magic have weird lighting coming from people? I didn't have that.

Someone yanked on my door.

"Listen, I study magic. You are stronger than you think. You can mimic animals. Try to be a lion or something. Get us out of this!" Spencer yelled.

Another yank and my door was pulled off the hinges. A man, not much older than me, smiled through the gaping hole.

"Come on," he said as he held out his hand.

"Come on, what?" I asked. My head spun. What did Spencer mean by mimic a lion? I searched for Caden. He was still in the air, tossing dark green waves at Vera.

"It's time to go, Em... Harmony," he said, hand still extended.

"Fuck you!" I tried to think of a lion, but all I could think of was the Raven tattoo on the man's neck. A bird wouldn't help me.

He grabbed my arm. I was yanked out of the car in one fell swoop, the momentum causing me to fall to the ground. My knees scraped on the gravel. Tears stung. I lay face down, refusing to move. Dirt and rock rubbed into my palms. I breathed deeply and closed my eyes. Think. Lion. Lion. Birds. Bats. Ugh.

An arm hooked into each of mine and pulled me upright. My eyes shot open to see who was holding me. One was the man who knew my name; the other was a woman I'd never seen. I became a dead weight. My toes dangled just above the parking lot as I was dragged towards Vera, who still hadn't gotten up.

Caden had his fists clenched as purple tendrils wrapped around them, restraining him. Another person had taken Vera's place and was tossing a pulse of violet-colored air at Caden.

Vera smiled at me and pulled herself upright. I wriggled and thrashed as I tried to break free of them. I moved my face to the male attacker's arm. Lion. Sinking my teeth in hard, I tasted copper. He jerked his arm, and I bit down harder. Not exactly what I thought about with lions but it worked.

"Stop, Harmony," the man begged. "We're trying to help you."

I unclenched my jaw, and blood flowed from the male's arm, his blue t-shirt soaking in crimson. I spat onto the ground. He released me, and I fell hard onto my knees.

"Vera, I am not going with you. Leave me the fuck alone!" I wiped my sleeve across my mouth.

"You are one of us, Harmony. Come with me. We need you. We need to save the people of Arlynn. His kind lock people in prison for life, no matter the crime," Vera said as she wiped her clothes down.

"I am not one of you. You are The Unkindness. That ain't me!" I shouted

Caden's entire body tensed. Dark-green light spread over his body, completely engulfing him. I could no longer see the purple and blue tendrils that had been there a moment ago. Even his eyes had a light emanating from them.

People flooded out of the jeeps. I counted at least another eight others. Each one of them wore the same look of animosity. One woman had a large inky-black raven tattooed down the left side of her face. They stepped closer to the glowing green ball of fire that was

Caden. The same tendrils, but in a wide range of colors, emanated from their hands toward him. Red, orange, purple, even pink vines flowed through the air. I could barely breathe as they closed in on Caden.

"Stupid boy, you're dead!" Vera laughed as blue tendrils flew out of her hands.

Bats. Why did I keep thinking of bats? The crystal in my pocket shocked my leg. I placed my hand in my pocket. There were two crystals but one had electricity pouring from it. I clenched it. In school I learned some bats had a sound that could break glass. Fuck, I hoped this worked.

I screamed. The sound vibrated in my throat, welling up from the pit of my stomach. It was different. I closed my mouth and the scream was severed into immediate silence.

The power inside me tingled at the base of my throat. *Yell,* it demanded.

Every atom in my body vibrated. The tingles trickled down my body. It was familiar to me, this feeling of power. Spencer was right, I could mimic animals.

I screamed again.

The tingles became hot pinpricks. Vera clutched her hands to her ears as she fell. Caden dropped, the green light dissipating. The others hit the ground as well. All the beautiful colors permeating the air—gone.

I screamed louder.

The fire coursed through my body. The sound of breaking glass sliced through the air. Shards twinkled and clinked as they fell, embedding in my skin. Everyone lay on the ground covering their ears. Blood poured from between their fingers as they writhed on the ground. Crimson swirled in the dirt, mixing into a thick red mud. Tiny shards of glass from the motel windows covered everyone, reflecting the sunlight and blinding me. I lifted my hand to shield my eyes from the sun. Caden was on the ground, his hands flat to the earth and no longer covering his ears. His blood flowed.

I closed my mouth and silence spread like a blanket, covering the parking lot. No one moved. Everyone lay unconscious. I stood, stumbled, and fell. It took two more tries to get up and go forward on trembling legs. I was covered in tiny lacerations. I stumbled to Caden and fell next to him, my knees once again scraping the ground.

Tears dripped from my face, and mixed with the bloodstained mud.

"Get up!" I demanded.

A faint moan from one of the others permeated the air, reminding me I didn't have much time. I slapped him. It always worked in the movies. Fuck. What was I gonna do? I went to the nearest car, since Caden's was missing doors, and opened the back seat.

Pulling Caden to the car proved to be difficult given I barely weighed 130 pounds. He was much larger than me—and solid muscle. Spencer stumbled next to me. I scrunched up my face and he covered his ears with his hands, showing what he did while I screamed. A few drops of blood were in his ears, but he seemed to be handling it better that everyone else.

He helped me get Caden into the backseat of the car. I stumbled and ran over to Caden's car to grab our bags, my purse, and the cooler. Ginger jumped out of the car and ran over to the other. Spencer was behind me pulling his stuff out of the vehicle. He also grabbed Ginger's damn pillow.

As I got in the driver's seat, I took one last peek at

the parking lot. Vera rolled onto her back, the blood already drying in her ears. This woman really wasn't giving up. I hated her.

The car roared to life as I turned the keys. I pulled on the gear shift—nothing. I had never actually driven. Spencer yelled at me to push the break and put it into gear. He was in the back seat with Caden. Ginger sat in the passenger's seat.

The car swayed as I pushed on the gas pedal. I coughed as dirt flew into the car. But I didn't let go of the gas. The needle on the dashboard wobbled past eighty. I pushed harder. We had to get away.

I drove for hours without talking to Spencer. A few times Caden had moaned. Spencer said he was still breathing. He believed that when he fell from the air, he hit his head hard. It didn't take a genius to figure that out from the goose egg on his forehead.

My stomach growled, but I ignored it. It wasn't until the gas light came on that I decided to pull over. I slowed into the lot of a gas station, hopefully we were far enough away from Vera. That woman was pure evil.

Walking up to the station, I looked down. My sweatpants and tank top were full of tiny tears and spattered with mud. Luckily, there was no one around. I didn't want people to see me in this state. Not that I care what people think, but I was in rough shape. I hadn't even checked to see if my face was still bloody after biting that creep. The cashier rolled his eyes as I entered the store. The look remained on his face as I paid for the energy drinks, chips, and gas. My eyes stung, he looked at me the same way everyone did when they found out I was a foster kid. I didn't want people's pity.

The gas tank release was another struggle for me. I

had no idea where it was. The lever had to be around the dashboard area somewhere, but I couldn't find it. My hand felt around aimlessly searching for it. Spencer sat there in silence, refusing to help me.

"Music, it's right underneath," a woman's voice said.

I jumped out of my skin. "Oh!" I turned to see a tall slender woman leaning against the car. Her arms were crossed, her hip cocked at an angle. She wore a tight leather coat and tighter black pants. Danger emanated from her.

"I didn't think you were ever gonna stop." She laughed.

"Penny!" I charged forward and tossed my arms around her.

Chapter 19

SPENCER RUSHED TOWARD Penny. I still had my arms wrapped around her as she clenched her body. She raised her boot up to her hand and slipped a knife out. Nobody likes Spencer, not surprised. I'd known him for a day and wanted to hit him. Penny probably had a lot of hate for this man. How did Savvy, um… like him?

"You bitch!" Spencer yelled.

"Aw, mad Savvy ran away from you? I don't blame her." Penny twirled the knife in her hand.

Ginger got off her pillow, sauntered over to Penny and rubbed her body against her. Penny bent and scratched her head, telling her how much she missed her and that they would find Savvy.

"Wait, how did you find us?" I asked. I hadn't texted her since we left Philly. The plan was to meet up with her when we got to Georgia. We were still somewhere in Tennessee. It wasn't a direct route but we weren't trying to be followed by Vera. That wasn't going so well.

I doubted Spencer had called her, he didn't seem to like her at all. Caden was still passed out in the back seat. Ugh, Caden really needed to wake up soon. My heart sank.

"Caden and I have family locators on our phones. When no one was answering me I checked it and, bam, here I am. Why do you have Tool with you?" Penny pointed at Spencer.

"For the last time, stop calling me that!" Spencer whined. He waved his hand in the air.

Penny jerked. The palms of her hands went to her eyes. She pulled them away, growled and rubbed her eyes. Spencer had done something to her. He was an illusionist so he fucked with her somehow.

She clenched the knife in her hand and jumped at Spencer. His back slammed against the jeep as she pressed the blade against his throat. For someone of my height I would have had to stand on my tippy toes. But Penny was tall. That girl was danger. I loved it.

"Unblind me! Or I will kill you!" Penny ground her teeth as she spoke.

Oh fuck! Spencer blinded her. I was impressed and annoyed. He really is a dick. But Penny had attacked him without being able to see; that girl was seriously awesome. She must be a fierce person to deal with in Arlynn.

I bet Spencer just bullied people and pulled the wings off of fairies. Aside from his good looks, which I would never admit, he had nothing going for him. And Penny was about to slice his throat so his looks weren't getting him too far.

"Fuck you!" Spencer spat at Penny.

Their bickering reminded me of two little birds fighting over the same piece of food. I wasn't sure why, but my brain is messed up. The vision of two black birds grew stronger in my mind. Ravens. Wings flapping in the air. Swoosh.

Spencer pulled his head back and thrust it forward, slamming into Penny. She stumbled back, grabbing her nose. Blood flowed. Asshole. He broke her nose. Swoosh.

Hundreds of birds flapped their wings. The sky darkened, blocking out the sun as inky black ravens swam toward us. Spencer and Penny ducked. They swooped down and hovered above us. I held out my arms and a few landed on me. They were all talking at once and I couldn't understand a word they said. Wow. They were beautiful.

"Send them away!" Spencer yelled through the noise.

Had I done this? My magic had to do with healing, mimicking, and talking to animals. Could I also summon them? The vision of birds had become so clear in my mind. My power is the coolest. How do I get them to leave? Wait. I had an idea.

"Agree to get along or they stay!" I yelled at Penny and Spencer.

"Fine," Spencer screamed.

"Unblind me, asshole!" Penny shouted.

Spencer waved his hand at Penny's face. She blinked a few times then gave me a thumbs up. It was as close as she was going to get to agreeing.

I closed my eyes. How was I supposed to get them to leave? I had called them by thinking of them, maybe if I thought of them flying away. I started with one, envisioning him soaring away. He took off. Then I pictured another flying away, and another. The final one left and I opened my eyes.

The gas station was again empty except for us. Penny was now holding her nose, blood still pouring from between her fingers. Once I was done getting the info I could from Spencer, he was gone.

I walked toward the store to grab some napkins for Penny. The clerk stepped back when I entered. He didn't even respond when I asked him where the napkins were. Nor did he say goodbye when I left. Rude.

Outside, Spencer had moved his tool self to the passenger's seat. Ha, Penny called him Tool. She had a knack for nicknames. He really was one.

Penny sat in the back seat with Caden's head in her lap. One hand stroked his hair, the other held her nose. I moved her hand away and cleaned up as much blood as I could without water or moving her. She then got up and asked me what had happened.

I quickly filled her in on Vera and me mimicking the animal. Aside from a few nods she didn't respond. She unzipped her black fanny pack that had blended into her leather pants. Her hand went way past where it should have. The fanny pack swallowed half of her arm. How much room was in there?

A few things rattled inside the bag. Seriously, how big was it on the inside? It sounded like she was searching through an entire store. She pulled her hand out and held up a tiny bottle. A pair of goggles was stuck to her finger. She shook her hand and they fell back in.

She unscrewed the bottle and the strong scent of peppers touched my nose. Yikes. She waved it in front of Caden's face and he bolted upright. His hand flew to the goose egg on his head. He rubbed it furiously as he took a few gasps of air. Whatever Penny had was pretty strong.

"How long was I out? Harmony, are you and Ginger okay? Penny, when did you get here?"

"We have to go. I still can't find Savvy. I've called some witches in Georgia. They'll let me know if they spot her. If I don't find her soon I have to return to Arlynn and confront The Order." Penny's words fell on the last sentence.

"Then let's go. Caden I'll fill you in when we get to a hotel. We still have a long way to get to Georgia." I hugged Penny and hopped in the driver's seat.

Penny walked over to a badass white Kawasaki motorcycle. Strapped to the side of the bike was a long brown sheath holding what looked to be a genuine samurai sword. The handle was adorned with an emerald dragon, flames erupting from its mouth. I smiled. Having this ninja princess on my side was a good thing. And if Vera attacks again, I know she will help.

Chapter 20

THE WATER HAD BEEN beating against my skin
for an hour, but I stayed in the shower. I was numb;
nothing was right. I hated what my life had become. I
was now a girl that some evil woman chased down. I
knew I would have to leave the bathroom and face life.
On the drive here, I filled in Caden on what he had
missed. Spencer tried chiming in but we both cut him
off.

Once we made it to Georgia, we found a decent hotel
and got three rooms. Spencer and Penny refused to
share. They probably would have killed each other, so
I didn't blame them.

I was fine the entire drive. Even when we reached
the room. It wasn't until I was in the shower, alone, that
I broke down. The tears flowed, mixing with the dirt and
blood that was washed away by the water.

A knock on the door. I knew it was Caden, even

though I had told him I needed some time. The bathroom was the only place I was going to get some privacy and collect my thoughts. Another knock. It was time to face him. I turned off the water and grabbed a towel. Leaving a trail of puddled footsteps, I let Caden in.

"Hi," I whispered.

Caden stood frozen. I continued to cry and he wrapped his arms around me. I hadn't bothered to dry off from the shower. The air in the hotel room was cool and licked my skin, causing goosebumps to erupt over my body. He grabbed another towel off the rack and wiped me down.

When he reached between my legs, butterflies erupted in my stomach. The cool air contradicted the heat burning inside me. I was crying and horny. What was wrong with me? Caden kissed away my tears.

I wrapped my arms around his neck, our bodies pressed against each other. He stood still, his heart beating against my chest, his breath warm against my cheek. My face turned up to his, and I held his gaze. I couldn't help but taste his glistening lips. His arms flew around me grabbing my bottom, fingers digging into me. Caden pressed his lips against me, slowly at first, then with more ferocity. All thoughts of what happened drifted away.

He lifted me into the air, and I wrapped my legs around his waist. The towel fell away. His groin was swollen and ready for me. The only thing preventing him from entering me were his jeans. The rough material against my pussy sent a shiver through me. He turned and lay me on the bed, not breaking our kiss. I tightened my legs around his waist and ground against him. I needed him inside me. Needed to forget.

Witch! I am in the room! Knock it off! Ginger spat.

At least she wasn't complaining about food. I pulled away from Caden and he squinted at me. "Sorry, I have to let Ginger out. She's being an ass." I hurried and let her out so I could return to Caden.

I went back to bed and climbed on top of him, kneeling down and pressing my lips against his. He grabbed my ass and rolled me onto my back in one swift motion. I let out a soft moan as he kissed me. He nibbled a trail down my neck, licking at my collarbone. As he rubbed his cock against me, I let out a soft moan. He traced his tongue down my chest finding my swollen nipples. He pulled a tiny nub into his mouth, suckling hard. Mmmm. I begged him to continue, I was so close to the edge. He released my nipple, and stopped rubbing his cock against me.

Such a tease. A moment later, he found my other nipple. As he caressed it with his tongue, it puckered for him. I let out another moan and he went back to grinding his cock against my wet pussy. Maybe not a tease.

His tongue traced a path down my stomach. This time, the goosebumps exploding over my skin were not because of the chill air. The heat inside me grew stronger, and his touch drove me wild, the intensity almost too much. As he moved down my body, his erection was no longer pressed against me, and I ached for him. The emptiness inside me grew. I needed him.

"Is this okay?" he asked as his lips kissed just above where I wanted him.

"Please," I begged. I'm sure he asked because moments before I had been crying. I pushed those thoughts aside, again.

I grabbed at the sheets when his kisses reached my clit. My hips raised to meet his exploring tongue and he pushed me back down. Slowly, he ran his tongue along my slit. I tried to buck toward him, but his hands kept me firmly in place. A moan tore through the hotel room when he finally ran his tongue against my clit. This was what I wanted.

Caden licked my pussy and I was soaked. He flicked his tongue against me, until I was ready to explode. He slowed, lazily stroking me, denying me climax again. Then he took his hand from my hip and circled a finger around my entrance. His tongue pressed against me and I let out another moan.

His finger slid inside easily. In and out, slowly, as he sucked on my swollen nub. He moaned against me; the vibration sent ripples of heat through my skin. I dug my fingers into his hair. Caden made a come-hither motion with his finger and rubbed against my g-spot. I screamed in ecstasy. He rubbed and licked harder, faster. Fuck, my climax tipped over the edge, I moaned, enraptured, as it ran through my body in waves.

When it was over, I collapsed onto the bed. My heart raced. The orgasm was pure, sensual, and sexy as hell. Caden joined me on the bed and pulled me into his arms. I reached down and rubbed his jeans, his cock was still hard and ready. Good. I had big plans for it. I unzipped his pants. His dick was freed and I wrapped my mouth around it.

Once we finished, I flopped on the bed exhausted. He lay next to me, still breathing heavily. He pulled me into him and kissed the top of my forehead. I started to drift off to sleep, but I forced my eyes open and peered into his.

"What happens to Penny if she returns without

Savvy?"

"She'll be fired from The Order. But we will find Savvy." Caden kissed me again.

"Are you still okay with us leaving after we help Penny?" I hadn't changed my mind about that. I didn't want to go to Arlynn. Whoever I was wasn't who I am now.

"Yes. It was originally my idea to go somewhere else. I love you. I love our life together. We go back and that changes. It's against the rules to date your charge."

"I love you too. You're okay with leaving The Order? That has always been your dream."

"It was, till I met you."

I snuggled into him. There were more questions I wanted to ask, but it didn't matter. Only our love did. As soon as we located Savvy for Penny we were gone. I still wasn't sure where. Texas seemed like a good place to move to. They had beaches and everything was bigger there. And it seemed far enough from Philly, and Arlynn. Not that I was sure you could outrun someone like Vera, but I was gonna try.

Caden got up and put on his sweatpants. I let out a sigh. He giggled and crawled back into the bed. "I was going to go to the store and get us some food."

I wrapped my arms around him. I didn't want to be left alone right now. When I expressed that, he pulled out his phone and called Penny. I got out of bed and tossed on clothes. If she was gonna babysit me, I needed to be dressed.

Knock, Knock. Penny and Ginger were here.

Witch, tell him I want meatballs. Ginger sauntered into the room and pounced on the bed with me.

Chapter 21

THE DOOR RATTLING against the chain jarred me awake. My eyes shot open, forgetting where I was for a moment, the flapping of wings from my dream still fresh in my mind. A thousand ravens had swept down on me, calling out to me. I had thought it was a nightmare, but they weren't there to hurt me. They were sad and needed me.

I sat upright, the blanket sliding from my body and I heard the rattle again. Penny bolted up from the chair she had fallen asleep in, drool still glistening in the corner of her mouth. Ginger stretched out and fell back asleep. When Caden had left for the store, Penny and I had fallen asleep talking.

Klink. Boom. The door flew open and slammed against the wall. A picture shook. The lamp on the nightstand fell over.

Penny grabbed the samurai sword leaning on the

side of the chair. She unsheathed it, and sparks of magic erupted from the blade as she took a protective stance in front of the bed.

"Wake," Penny whispered to the sword.

The intruder stomped forward revealing himself—Caden. He panted heavily. From ear to jaw was a long, deep wound, weeping blood. His clothes were torn and covered in dirt.

"We have to go. They found me," he heaved in obvious pain.

"Caden! Your face!" I tossed the blanket aside as I got out of bed. Penny hurled her hand out to stop me, remaining in the protective stance. She was acting like something was wrong with Caden. Was she still dreaming?

"Hurry up," Caden demanded.

"Ice Cream?" Penny said to Caden. She threw over her shoulder, "Harmony, get Ginger."

I scooped Ginger up, who protested at having been woken. Caden remained in the doorway panting. He was in obvious pain and Penny wasn't running to him. Had she lost her mind?

"Ice Cream?" Penny repeated.

"Yeah, I got some. Come on, let's *go*! They'll be here any second. Vera followed me," Caden said. He wiped the sleeve of his shirt along the gash on his face.

Penny lifted her left leg to pull a knife out of her boot. My face scrunched up as I slid on my sneakers.

"Are you ready?" Penny asked without looking back.

"Yes, let's go." I grabbed my bag and started walking toward her.

The knife sighed through the air before I realized Penny had chucked it, hilt and blade somersaulting, directly at Caden. He pivoted but wasn't fast enough. It sliced into his arm.

"What the hell?" I gasped.

He pulled a knife from his jeans and hurled it at Penny. Hadn't he been wearing sweatpants? She sliced it with her sword. Sparks of magic sizzled into the air. Caden shot out his hand toward Penny, slithering brown tendrils of magic extending out to her.

She used her samuri to counterattack. They rebounded off the blade and sprang back at Caden, punching him dead center. He hunched over, cursing violently. Penny closed the gap between them and kicked him in the balls—hard. He keeled over, smacking his head against the desk.

He grabbed at Penny's leg, pulling her down so her weapon was stuck underneath her. Caden yanked Penny toward him and grabbed her throat, squeezing. Penny's beautiful porcelain skin quickly turned red.

I dropped Ginger back on the bed. I had to do something. He was killing her. There was a severe lack of animals in here to summon. I could mimic one. Which one? Fuck, think.

Penny gasped.

With my free hand I grabbed the lamp that had fallen and slammed it into Caden's head. Blood poured from the gash it opened up. He slumped onto Penny, releasing her throat.

I rolled him off of her and checked his pulse. Good, I thought I had killed him. Penny grabbed her sword and held it above his head.

"No, you can't kill him." I held my hand out.

"Why not?" Penny frowned.

"He may have information for us." It was the only valid excuse I could think of. I wanted to run. I wanted this whole mess gone. The problem was, this shit wasn't going away. So for now, I would have to gather as much information as possible. Maybe learn why this man wanted me dead.

I yanked the sheet from underneath Ginger. She pounced off the bed onto the chair Penny had been sleeping on. I directed Penny to help me sit the person up that had used his magic to look like Caden. It was the same power Spencer had used back at his apartment.

Spencer.

I stomped out of the room toward his. He better be in there. If he used his illusions to trick me, I would kill him. I pounded on the door. Nothing. Why would Spencer change his image to Caden and try to get Penny and I to leave with him? I knocked again. Nothing.

He was a dead man.

The door opened. Spencer stood there in his boxers rubbing at his eyes.

"You are so lucky. There is a man in my room with the same power as you. Get dressed and meet me there," I demanded. I turned and walked back to my room before I added 'please.'

Back in the room, Penny was ripping the sheet into long strips. The man groaned. He still wore Caden's face. I helped her tie his hands and feet.

Spencer walked in and cackled. "You two sure this isn't Caden? Cause that would be funny."

"His magic color is brown, he didn't know Penny's nickname for him, and he tried to kill her. Yes, I'm sure," I snapped.

And he didn't have my meatballs. Ginger chimed in.

I slapped the man's face. He didn't wake up. I tried that a few more times before Penny stopped me. If he was part of Vera's crew we probably shouldn't be standing in the hotel room with him. The rest of them could be here and we were allowing them to surround us.

Penny slipped her hand into her fanny pack. She pulled out the same bottle she had used to wake up Caden. The spicy smell itched my nose. That stuff was potent. She waved it in front of him and he coughed.

"What is wrong with you two?" the man asked.

"Who are you and why are you trying to kill us?" Penny held her sword to his throat.

At that moment, Caden, the real one, walked into the room. His jaw dropped. He had take-out in his hands and he set it on the table as he scratched his head. He knelt in front of the man and touched the gash along his face. He pulled it away and his hand was clean. No blood. That was also an illusion. But the cut on his head wasn't. I had given him that one.

The man rippled. His body morphed to a short, scrawny man with balding hair. He didn't look like the type of person that would be chasing a band of misfits for a crazy witch. He had a Raven tattoo on his forearm. Every one of Vera's goons had it, including her. It was their gang symbol. Yet I dreamt of ravens. Weird.

"Let's try this again. Why are you trying to kill us?" I asked.

"Not kill. I want the reward for you. The red-headed witch was captured, and brought back to Arlynn. She was worth a ton and you're worth more," he whimpered.

Red-head. Savvy! Shit. They had found her. Which meant Penny would be returning to Arlynn. She would either admit to The Order that Savvy was captured or try to retrieve her from The Unkindness. If I was her, I would run.

"Are you part of Vera's crew?" I wasn't sure how to ask if Vera was close without tipping him off.

"No. Yes. Sort of. I want to be. And if I return you to her, she'll grant me entry into her circle. I was a part of them when Ember Raven ran things. But Vera took over and is a lot stricter. To get in you have to prove yourself. I bring you back and I'll be in."

It didn't matter. Even if he wasn't in Vera's inner group we had to leave. At any moment she could be closing in on us. And sitting in a hotel room wasn't my smartest plan. Caden ran over and grabbed his bag. He must have read my mind.

I followed suit and grabbed my belongings. Penny had a choice to make. If she wanted to run with us, I would be cool with her coming. As for Spencer he could do whatever he wanted, but coming with us wasn't an option. I couldn't stand being around him much longer. He was a tool.

"I have to go to Arlynn," Penny said.

"You could run with us," I said.

"Run? No. Come with me, please. I could use your help. And what about Caden?"

"I'm not going to Arlynn. I'm taking off," I replied. I didn't know how to explain about my memories and how I didn't want them back.

"I'm going with Harmony." Caden grabbed his phone charger out of the outlet.

Spencer stood in the corner with a smirk on his face. I really hated him. The man sitting on the floor stayed silent. He shouldn't be part of this conversation. I pointed at him and walked out of the room. The rest of my misfit band followed me into the hallway.

Witch, carry me. Ginger huffed.

"We need to go to Arlynn," Penny demanded.

"Not happening. I'm going to Texas." I stomped my foot. Childish, but hey I was adamant.

"Texas? Your memories are in Arlynn. Nothing is in Texas." Penny placed her hand on her hip and looked at Caden.

"I go where she goes." Caden pointed at me.

I vote Italy. They must have good meatballs. Ginger purred.

"You must reclaim your memories," Penny pleaded.

"How about no." I practically stuck out my tongue.

"Does The Order mean nothing to you?" Penny asked Caden.

He shrugged. This man really does love me.

Spencer whispered under his breath.

"What?" I snapped at him.

"Nothing. I was just gonna say if I had a sister, I would want my memories of her." Spencer smirked. "But it's your life, Harmony, do what you want."

Chapter 22

UM... SISTER. WHAT? Um... how? Sister.

"Sister?" Penny and Caden asked simultaneously.

"Shit. I promised I wouldn't say anything." Spencer scratched his head.

Um... I... Fuck. The thought of parents crossed my mind, and I easily dismissed it. They didn't go searching for me so I didn't need them in my life. But aside from parents it hadn't crossed my mind that I had a family.

A sister. Was she older, younger, bratty? I wanted to know her. Did I have anyone else? Aunts, uncles, brothers, a kid?

I dismissed the thought of a child. The Order may suck, but I think if they started separating parents from kids there would be an uprising. Yet, they separated me from my sister.

A sister. My gut told me to run. I didn't know where,

or for how long. My legs wanted to stretch. I wanted the cool air to hit my lungs. To be free so I could clear my head. I turned on my heels. Run. All of me screamed.

I walked. One foot in front of the other. Slowly. I forced myself to walk down the hall and out of the hotel. I had so much to discuss with everyone, but not in the earshot of the man we tied up. Running wasn't an option today.

Penny and Caden wrapped their arms around Spencer's shoulders like they were buddies. It was a possessive move. They were showing their control over him. They wanted him dead. That was before he dropped the bomb. Then he claims he promised someone not to say anything.

Outside the hotel room my heart sank. Vera could be anywhere, she could be watching me right now. I had expected her to jump out at me. Or wind to blow me up into the air.

Something.

When nothing happened my heart didn't ease. There was no way to trust this woman.

Even though the man had claimed to not be part of her circle, there was no way to prove he was telling the truth.

We had to get moving. I had planned on running, but now I knew there was someone out there that was my family I needed a new plan.

"The red truck." Caden pulled out a key fob and hit it. "We couldn't drive around in the enemy's car forever."

I nodded and went to it, holding the door open for Ginger. She stared at me until I picked her up and set her on the passenger seat. I climbed up and sat next to her. Spencer and Penny climbed in the back while

Caden hopped in and started it up.

"Where to?" he asked.

"Get us out of here. Then we can discuss where we're going." I said. I still didn't know exactly what I was going to do. Caden and Penny's input were crucial. So was Spencer's, but that tool didn't seem to want to talk.

Penny jumped out of the truck and grabbed her Kawasaki. Caden followed her and helped her place it in the back. They both climbed back in and buckled up.

"My charge is in Arlynn. We must go there," Penny demanded as soon as we left the parking lot.

"I agree with Penny," Spencer nodded. They'd come a long way from attacking each other yesterday.

"What do you know about Harmony's sister?" Penny asked.

"I made promises to keep my mouth shut. Look, I'm agreeing with you that we should go to Arlynn. Stop pestering me." Spencer crossed his arms.

I could torture him, summon hundreds of birds to destroy him. I shook my head. I barely understood my power. It could easily backfire and there was still no guarantee he would tell me anything.

Thirty minutes later, Caden pulled over.

Shit.

This was my time to talk. I knew what I had to do. I knew my plan. But was this the right decision?

"Let's go to Arlynn," I blurted before I changed my mind. Running was so much easier.

"Are you sure?" Caden pulled my hand to his lips.

"No. But my sister is there. I have to find her. Plus Savvy is there, she could be with the same kind of people as Vera. I don't know her but she's important to Penny. We find my sister and Savvy and then we leave. We can do that right? Like leave? How does that all work?"

Home doesn't have good meatballs. Can we stay here? Ginger chimed in. *I don't want to go home.*

I would address Ginger's reservations later. I would have thought she would be happy to find Savvy. Yet she seemed upset to go home. Wait. Home? She was from Arlynn. I had assumed Savvy got her when she got to Philly, but Ginger was hers from there. It was kinda cool. Ginger was a magical cat. That would explain why she wasn't surprised I'm a witch.

Penny, Caden, and Spencer were all yapping at once. I honestly couldn't understand what they were saying. They kept cutting each other off. None of them were allowing anyone to get a word in. They were trying to devise a plan. Too many leaders trying to make a decision. I sat there until they finally stopped talking.

"Anyone gonna actually explain the ins and outs of Arlynn or are you guys going to keep arguing?" I crossed my arms.

They all started talking again. I opened my eyes wide and chewed the inside of my mouth. These three were killing me. After a few more minutes, I pointed at Caden.

"So Arlynn is located in the Bermuda Triangle. To get there we have to get to Florida. There is a boat that will take us there." Caden checked his watch. "It's Wednesday. The boat only shows up on Saturdays. You could request early pick up in emergencies, but I don't think we should draw attention to ourselves."

"Savvy could be killed if we wait till Saturday!" Penny yelled.

"It would be longer including travel time. We need emergency pick up. My poor Savvy must be so scared without me." Spencer sighed.

"Emergency transport would alert The Order and then we'd all be in trouble, and who would help Savvy?" Caden complained.

"Okay. We go to Florida. Wait till Saturday. If Vera wanted her dead she wouldn't have bothered taking her to Arlynn. Once there, we find both girls. Then Caden and I leave." I scratched at Ginger's fur. She purred in agreement. She didn't want to go to Arlynn at all.

They huffed, but agreed. I couldn't believe I sounded so authoritative. I was pretty impressed with myself. I was never a leader, only a runner. And yet here I was taking charge of my friends. Well, Spencer wasn't a friend. He was a complete tool.

Caden put the vehicle in drive and pulled back onto the road. Spencer and Penny complained that they were hungry and Ginger chimed in that she agreed. This was going to be a long trip.

I opened the bag Caden had brought. He had a few burgers and french fries. I passed out the burgers to the back.

Spencer complained it was cold. I expected Penny to pull a microwave from her fanny pack. Instead she unwrapped the cold burger and took a bite.

I started with the fries. They were cold and mushy. I love all fries, but this was a little much. My stomach rumbled. I tried the burger instead. Eh, it was edible. Ginger rubbed her nose against my arm.

Caden had bought meatballs, too. This cat was beyond spoiled.

I opened the Styrofoam container for her and she lapped up the pasta sauce that was poured over them. She ate all three within seconds.

"Your next meal will be cat food," I said.

Witch, you haven't even reached Arlynn and you're being a bitch. Ginger turned her tail to me.

"You can be such a hateful cat," I spat.

Chapter 23

PALM TREES LINED the roads, and mopeds weaved through traffic. Boats and cruise ships were afloat on the bright blue ocean. A dog on a skateboard cruised by on the sidewalk. Beachgoers shopped a variety of boutiques. The boardwalk was abuzz with people.

We had finally gotten to Florida. Well, we'd arrived a few hours ago, but apparently we still had to get to Rondo. All I wanted was to hang on the beach, soak up the sun, and go on the rides on the boardwalk. Running away would have been a better option, but I had to find my sister.

Penny pulled into the first hotel she saw; she had taken over driving about halfway here. It looked fancy and sat right on the beach. I planned on spending some time on the sand. It was a stupid idea, but I didn't care. So far Vera hadn't attacked in view of people. I doubted she would attack me on the beach.

I hopped out and scooped up Ginger who was still pissed at me. Everyone else got out of the truck and grabbed their things. We got our rooms, but this time Penny and Spencer had to share because they only had two left. They weren't happy but it would only be for one night. The other nights they had rooms available.

Caden dropped his stuff on the bed and flopped down.

"I'm gonna go check out the beach." I tossed my bag in a chair. I hadn't bothered to bring a bathing suit or shorts.

"You aren't worried about Vera?"

"No. I doubt she's gonna attack us in front of witnesses."

People pushed babies in strollers, others jogged by. Children dragged their unwilling parents into the arcade and pizza shops. A man rolled by in short-shorts, bare-chested, and on old-timey skates. The boardwalk was brimming with life.

Caden walked into the first shop. I told him I didn't care where we went on the shore as long as we soaked up some sun. Part of me wanted to go for a run to clear my head. But I didn't think he would be down.

The shop was all bathing suits—rows and rows of skimpy suits and swim trunks. A guy in flip-flops and dreadlocks greeted us as we walked through the entrance. Caden informed him we were looking for some suits and I grinned. He smiled at me and squeezed my hand. A bright pink bikini with fat white polka dots hung on the back wall. I released Caden's hand and went straight for it. Normally I wouldn't wear something so skimpy, but I almost died a few times recently.

When I came out of the changing room, Caden was waiting for me. He had found plain black swim trunks that hung low on his hip, displaying the perfect V-line. For a moment I thought of tracing that line with my tongue to discover what lay beneath. My eyes glazed over the rest of his rippling muscles all the way up to his grin. The dimple on his cheek materialized as he smiled at me.

I did a twirl to show off my suit. It was a tad too revealing, but it fit me really well. He smiled harder and nodded in approval. I turned to head back to the dressing room when he stopped me.

"Don't change. We're heading right to the beach. Leave it on," he said as he grabbed his belongings.

I nodded and collected my things. Next to the register was a display of flip-flops. I grabbed a pair for myself and Caden, asking him if they were okay to get. He nodded as he paid for everything.

During the short walk, I bounced on my heels. I was going on and on about the things I wanted to do. There were jet skis and surfboards and parasailing. Caden told me we could do whatever I desired.

A day at the beach was so needed. I had been so concerned with everything going on, I was becoming unhinged. Even with my fake memories I don't remember going to the ocean. Maybe in Arlynn I had, which sorta made sense since it's an island. But I didn't remember it, so it didn't count. Today may be one of the last normal days Caden and I had, and I was taking full advantage of it.

A grass-roofed tiki stand stood a few feet away, advertising jet-skis on a white sign. I skipped over to it, Caden not far behind. He told the man we wanted to rent two for an hour. I insisted on longer, but it was already noon and we only had so much time to do it all. After a crash course on safety and operating instructions, the Jet-Ski man fitted us with lifejackets. Butterflies erupted in my stomach as I gunned the throttle. It flew forward and I had to hold on tight to stay aboard. The guy told me I could go crazy as we got further out to sea. Caden navigated his effortlessly as he rode alongside me.

Once we got further out, I got a little reckless. I stood up and did doughnuts. The water sprayed high into the air soaking us both. Caden laughed and splashed me back with his. I cackled and did a few more circles. Then I stopped to stare at the beautiful waves. We were far enough away from the shore that it seemed to be only us in the vast ocean. Caden pulled up next to me and I closed my eyes.

"What are you doing?" he asked.

"Shh," I replied. The power inside me stirred. This was a great chance to practice. I concentrated, visualizing every detail. I had never seen one in real life. Well, not that I remembered anyway, but I had seen enough on television to know what they looked like. Water sprayed my face. The echoing clicks of the animal proved it had worked. I opened my eyes. Wow.

A dolphin was right beside me, clicking away. It sprayed water in my face again. I turned off my jet ski and Caden followed suit as I glided into the cool water. A shiver ran through me, the ocean was freezing. My hand went out to the dolphin and it rubbed its nose against me as it clicked again. Caden was right next to me and put his hand out as well.

What can I assist you with? the animal asked.

"Nothing. I was practicing my powers. And I always

wanted to see one of you up close," I replied.

Then I will leave you. Take care. With one final display of sprayed water, the dolphin swam away.

Caden grabbed my life jacket and pulled me into him. His lips tasted of salt as he kissed me. I loved him. And I know he loved me. I was lucky to have him. Everything was constantly happening. Nothing was normal anymore, even this. I didn't know what Arlynn held for me and that scared me. I planned on finding my sister, and then leaving. I wasn't gonna dwell on that. I swam back to my jet-ski drifting a few feet away from me.

Caden swam over to his. I revved the throttle as I headed back, and pushed aside thoughts of Arlynn because today was for Caden—the man I was in love with.

When we returned to the tiki hut, I was debating our next activity. Caden wanted to keep me on the ground and do something nice, like sunbathing. I wanted to parasail, but my stomach grumbled, deciding for me. We both tossed on our t-shirts and went on the hunt for food. I wanted fries, but the taste of cold mushy ones were still on my mind. I would have to eat something different.

The pizza place was sandwiched between the arcade and the rides. I ordered a cheese and bacon pizza. Caden and I always ordered the same kind. We could have gotten half pepperoni and half mushrooms with bacon all over. But sometime in the past year we decided to agree on what kind we got. We both loved bacon.

"Are you happy to go back to Arlynn?" I asked as I took a sip of water.

"No. I didn't leave much behind. My parents are only

concerned with my brother becoming king and finding my sister a husband. The only one I miss is Melon, my dragon. Are you nervous about getting your memories back?" Caden fiddled with his straw wrapper.

"I'm not getting my memories back. I want to find my sister, but I don't want my memories. I like who I am."

"You would still be you, but with more memories, I think. Huh. Yea, I don't know how that would work actually. Okay, so no putting them back in your brain. But we should still find them to protect them. Vera has it out for you, if she gets them, she could use them against you."

Fuck. He was right. I had no desire to even locate them. They could have rotted in someone's basement or lab for all I cared. I didn't want them. I didn't even want to touch them. But I couldn't let Vera have something she could use against me. That was another reason I had to find my sister. If she knew I had one, she could harm her. My list of things I had to do was growing and all I wanted was to enjoy today with Caden.

After devouring most of the pizza, my stomach was too full for parasailing. Probably for the best. Being up in the air did have a different meaning after Vera kept throwing Caden in the air. Instead of doing a death-defying act I asked Caden if he wanted to play in the arcade. He nodded and we headed next door.

No surprise, he kicked my butt in every game we played. No wonder Spencer had gotten pissy with him for beating him, he was great at everything. The good thing was we had a boatload of tickets. As we were heading to leave, Caden pointed to a black machine in the far corner.

Pictures weren't really my thing. Caden had a few

selfies on his phone of us, but that was about it. He was the one always pushing for pics of us. I tried to tell him I have a bunch of tiny cuts on my face from the attack in the motel parking lot. He didn't care. I let out a sigh and walked with him.

Caden pulled back the curtain and waved his hand for me to enter. I took a half bow at him, going in first. He sat down and inserted a five-dollar bill. I growled at him, baring my teeth, attempting to be silly for the pictures. The flash was too bright and we both blinked. He pulled me into him, kissing my cheek; that would be a cute one. The next few I grabbed his cheeks and squeezed. He laughed and stuck his tongue out at me.

He collected our film and exited. Caden wrapped his arm around my shoulders and drew me in close. He kissed the top of my head; I melted into him.

The arcade began to bore me shortly after. Caden was great at every game we played. He won twice at Skee-Ball. Air hockey was basically him playing with himself and the puck—all too easy for him. I asked if we could go, but Caden had a bag overflowing with tickets he had won.

"Let me turn these in real fast. Don't move." Caden gave me a peck and ran off.

I played Pinball while he turned in his winnings. I did better at games when I wasn't competing against him. I had lost the third ball when he returned with a rather large grin on his face.

"Close your eyes and turn around," he demanded.

I shrugged and obeyed. Something cold grazed my chest and ran up my collar bone. My eyes sprang open and I looked down to see what he had put around my neck—a thin silver chain with a dangling silver heart. I turned to see Caden sheepishly grinning at me. He was beyond adorable. This kind of jewelry I could handle. Hopefully he never tried to propose. Marriage wasn't for me.

Twirling the necklace, I interlaced my free hand with Caden's. I loved his sweet romantic side. Well, I loved all of him. He squeezed my fingers between his and we headed to the beach. It was getting late and we both wanted to soak up the sun before we had to head in for the night.

We had till Saturday to hang out in Florida. As long as no one tried to kill us, it was going to be like a mini vacation. Day one was already a huge success. I pulled my journal out of my purse and filled it in on what happened the last couple days, since I had been too busy to write in it.

Caden snored softly next to me on the sand. We hadn't been in our chair rentals for more than five minutes before he fell asleep. Our rental umbrella kept the sun from burning my skin, but made seeing in my journal a little hard. I adjusted the umbrella.

In the distance, four men in jean shorts and tank tops walked close to the boardwalk. I wouldn't have paid much attention to them but they wore combat boots. One was short with black hair. Another was skinny with a raven tattoo across the right side of his face. The man in the back had ravens tattooed on his hands. The last man looked like he hadn't eaten in weeks. A little odd for Florida.

The starving man on the left shifted. Behind him was a tall fragile woman with a short bob haircut. Fucking evil woman. Vera.

Chapter 24

VERA WAS AT the other end of the beach, walking behind her henchmen. A woman was laid out on a towel soaking up the sun and Vera kicked up sand into her face. She really enjoyed torturing people. The woman stood up and started waving her hands at Vera.

I closed my journal and placed it in my bag. Caden snored softly. I touched his arm to rouse him without having him jump. He rolled over and stretched. I covered his mouth. His eyes opened and he raised his eyebrows. I pointed in Vera's direction.

She was still arguing with the woman. I couldn't figure out why she hadn't thrown her into the air. It could have been because of the people still milling about. Not that there were too many, but I doubted Vera wanted to expose us all. Who knows, the woman is evil.

Caden grabbed his bag while staying low. The

umbrella was still blocking us from her view. We needed to find a way out of here without her seeing us. Although I had been getting better about running away, this was a time to run. I'd had enough of this woman hunting me down. She followed me all the way to Florida.

Why? I didn't see what she wanted with me. Even if I had some cool magic she liked, she was a bit much. There were plenty of other witches, and I was sure they had better powers than me. I had animal magic; it seemed Caden, Spencer, and Penny all had a better affinity than me. I didn't even know what magic Savvy had, but hers was probably stronger as well.

Storm clouds rolled in. Waves grew higher in the ocean, slapping against the shore. The remaining people around us were packing up their belongings. A little girl ran from the ocean towards her waiting mother. The weather was forcing people to find shelter. I guess one of Vera's henchmen can control the weather. Again, another stronger affinity than mine.

Caden pulled the umbrella from the sand. I peeked around to see the woman turning from Vera. As she was packing up her belongings, a gust of wind tossed more sand onto her things.

The henchmen and Vera continued toward us. They were a good distance away but we still had to get moving. Caden tilted the umbrella over his shoulder to block us from their view. He looked like all the other people bringing their umbrellas up to the rental hut. I left the chairs, which I shouldn't have. It sucked that the workers would have to go back and get them. But I was concerned about being captured by Vera.

Lightning struck a few feet away, lighting up the sky. Rain followed. Droplets fell in the sand in front of us.

We picked up our speed. Thunder boomed in the distance. The storm had come in fast; it had to be a witch.

The wind picked up. *Swoosh*. The umbrella smacked into me and then flew into the air. Shit. I turned around. Vera pointed in my direction and the henchmen took off running.

Fuck. I dug my heels in the sand and pushed off. Caden ran right beside me. We hit the ramp that led from the boardwalk to the beach. Once my feet hit solid ground the running became easier. I searched for a place to hide. Rain slammed into my face. Lightning struck a foot away.

My heart dropped into my stomach. Facing Vera was bad enough; her and her henchmen were too much. They were too powerful. I ran. Most of the people had taken off before the rain had started. A few remained, but they were also running.

I risked a glance behind me. The men were following so we turned into the arcade. We couldn't hide here but I had noticed a back exit when we were in the photo booth. A man yelled at us for running as we flew past him.

Caden slammed into the door in the back. Locked. How is that even possible? We were screwed. I crouched behind the ticket counter and Caden hunched behind me. I peeked over the top as the two men walked into the arcade. We were dead.

The glass ticket counter we hid behind held all the prizes. There was a hook with the necklaces that matched the one around my neck. Tons of stuffed animals lined the walls. The rows in the counter held many other prizes like finger traps and bouncy balls.

"What are we gonna do?" I asked.

"I distract them and you run. You have to get out of here and get back to Penny and Ginger." Caden clenched his jaw.

"That's not happening. I'm not leaving you."

"Summon something to distract them. My tendrils should be able to break the door lock. And then we both run. Is that better?" he whispered.

I nodded. But how was I going to summon an animal into the arcade? The only animals I could think of were ocean ones. And there was no way a shark was going to come munching through here. I slid open the case and Caden squinted at me.

There was a container of bouncy balls in there. It wasn't the best plan, but it was something. I grabbed the entire container and launched it at the two men. Hundreds of balls bounced off the walls.

Caden tossed a green tendril at the lock. Smoke erupted from the deadbolt as it melted and dribbled down the door. After I mastered my animal summoning thing, I would have to concentrate on my tendrils. I still didn't know what color they were or how to get them to come out.

Ping, ping, ping. The balls were slamming into everything. The man that yelled at us for running was trying to catch them. Vera's henchmen stood there as they flung into them. Had they been smarter, they would have walked right past them. Luckily for me they were stupid and appeared to be waiting for them to stop bouncing.

While staying hunched down I scuttled over to the back. With the lock melted it easily opened. Caden followed me out and we both took off. The hotel wasn't far, but I didn't want Vera to follow and put the others in danger.

I ran past the hotel and across the street. Then I backtracked to the hotel and went to the side entrance. Penny and Spencer were on the eighth floor. I entered the stairwell and took two steps at a time. I didn't trust the elevator.

When we reached their room, I had half expected the door to be off its hinges. Everything looked fine so I knocked. Penny answered, rubbing the sleep out of her eyes.

"Ice cream?" Penny asked Caden.

"Stupid nickname. Anyway we have to go." Caden pushed past her into the room.

Penny followed him and grabbed her stuff. Spencer was snoring on his bed. Caden pushed on his back, telling him to wake up and hurry. He mumbled that Penny kept him up with her mouth breathing. These two were never going to get along.

Witch, you left my food in your room. Go get it, then we leave. Ginger rubbed her side against my leg.

As much as I didn't want to obey the cat, she was right. Not only was her food there, but so was all my stuff and Caden's. We were on the third floor. It would be an easy snatch and grab before we left.

Ten minutes later, we were outside the hotel with all of our belongings. Ginger was still complaining that we didn't have enough food for her. She was such a pain, but also the coolest cat. We were on the side hidden from view behind a bunch of tall bushes.

I had thought we were going to jump right in the truck and leave. Wrong. All four men, and Vera, were leaning against it. I wondered if Vera knew it was ours. I didn't believe in coincidences anymore.

The stockier henchman pulled a knife from his boot. Was that an Arlynn thing? Penny carried hers in the same spot. I should get a knife and start wearing boots too. The man stabbed the tire. Caden swore under his breath.

Then, the man jumped into the bed of the truck. Penny stood, but I grabbed her and pulled her down. Caden covered her mouth with his hand. Penny's fists clenched. The man lifted his blade into the air and sliced downward. The tires were hidden, but it was obvious what the man had done. He sliced the tires on Penny's Kawasaki.

She squirmed and I held her down. She would have gotten herself killed if she tried to attack them. There were four of us, but they were stronger. And I barely counted; I had only been a witch for a few weeks.

We stayed hidden in the bushes until Vera and her men walked off. Then we stayed there for a while longer to make sure they were actually gone. I was still shaky when we stood. Penny charged forward. She grabbed the side of the truck bed and jumped inside the back in one swift movement. Such a Ninja Princess. Beautiful.

Her face scrunched up and she looked around. She scratched her head and bent back down. When she stood again her mouth was half open.

"Once I saw what they were doing, I put an illusion on the guy to make him think he sliced your tires." Spencer shrugged.

Caden opened the back and helped Penny lift the bike out. It was fully intact. Not a scratch on it. Spencer did a nice thing, weird. He could have put an illusion on all of them so we could get away, but I was happy he helped out Penny.

"Thanks, Tool. Now we have to find a place to hide till Saturday."

Chapter 25

WE WALKED AWAY from the hotel arguing. Not a big surprise there; agreeing was not our strong suit. Three-and-a-half days of hiding seemed almost impossible. It was going to be hard enough for us to all get along with Spencer.

"I could get a room at a hotel and be fine. Vera wants Harmony not me," Spencer argued.

"Leave her out to dry and I won't help you find Savvy," Penny snapped. It seemed like she was already over him saving her bike.

He shrugged and kept walking. The rain had let up, which meant the henchmen had either moved on or simply stopped making it rain. We were in Florida, one of the warmest, most beautiful places I had ever been and we were clueless on where to go.

"Since you guys can't figure this out, and refuse to sacrifice Harmony, let's stay in the woods," Spencer said. "We have a better chance somewhere we can hide and have an advantage if they do find us."

It took a few hours to find a suitable place. I hated that Spencer had come up with the idea, but it was a good one. Birds chirped as we finally found a good place to crash and stay for the next couple days. My feet were killing me.

A few times Caden had offered to give me a piggyback ride. As sweet as that was, there was no way I could allow it. I didn't want the others to see me as weak. Ginger had no issue with how she was viewed. We all took turns carrying her and not once had she put her feet on the ground.

When we reached a clearing in the trees I flopped down. My body ached. Caden sat beside me, asking if I was okay. Too tired to answer, I nodded.

Penny reached into her fanny pack and pulled out two sleeping bags and pillows. Spencer questioned where the rest was. Penny had enough for her and Savvy; she hadn't planned on traveling with anyone else.

Caden unzipped one of the sleeping bags for him and I. He placed a pillow on it and tried to get me to lay down. Spencer reluctantly agreed to share one with Penny. She agreed as long as they took shifts keeping watch on us.

Um... Shit. I had a thought that disappeared. It was important.

No one grabbed my pillow! I hate you witches! Ginger snuggled on the pillow that Caden and I were supposed to share.

What had I been thinking? Oh. Duh. "Can't we put up a protection spell so we can all sleep?"

"It takes a very powerful witch to do that. I could put

up an illusion but I would need an onyx crystal to make it strong enough." Spencer lay down on the sleeping bag.

Nurse Dara had claimed to be a Dud, but she had done a protection spell on the vet clinic. Vera's sidekick hadn't even been able to come in because of the spell. Why would she claim to be a Dud and move to Philly? I thought of the way she looked at Dr. Barker. Love. It's the reason most of us do stupid things.

I reached into my pocket and pulled out the black stone Nurse Dara had given me. She seemed to know everything that was going to happen. I had no doubt she knew I was going to need it at this very moment. Nurse Dara was a powerful witch and the closest thing I had to a mom. Ugh, I missed her.

"Will this do?" I held the crystal up.

"Yes." Spencer snatched it from my hand. "This will take a few minutes, but we'll be safe."

Caden pulled me into his arms and cuddled on the sleeping bag, without the pillow that Ginger had claimed for herself. Little brat. I drifted off to sleep.

For the next few days, we stayed within the confines of Spencer's illusion. Penny had all the food we could need, except meatballs. That fanny pack she had really held everything. Well there wasn't a microwave so the canned ravioli were cold, but I was thankful for the food.

I tried to get Spencer to open up. I wanted to know what he knew about my sister and me. He just kept claiming he'd made promises and wouldn't say anything. I was annoyed with him. It made no sense he would keep it such a secret.

Every time our conversation got heated, Caden would step in. He hated Spencer and wanted a reason to hit him. Which he reminded Spencer of every few minutes. The days dragged on.

For the past few weeks everything had been so fast paced and now that things had slowed down I didn't know how to handle it. So when everyone was quiet and dealing with their own thoughts I wrote in my journal. I had stopped using it as a plan to try and fix my mind, but I enjoyed writing all the craziness of my life in it.

When Saturday morning came we were all ready to go. Ginger was non-stop about how the boat had meatballs. They weren't the best, but she was happy with them. Savvy should have called her Meatball instead of Ginger.

We packed up to head to the docks. According to Caden it was a pretty long walk. I picked up the onyx crystal that Spencer had on the ground in the protective circle. He claimed there was no more magic in it but I didn't care. It was from Nurse Dara and I wasn't going to leave it behind.

Five hours later and we were back in the middle of another set of woods. For some reason I had thought Florida was all beaches and golf courses. But there were a lot of forests here. I had no clue where I was going so I had to wait for Caden to direct me.

A path led to a narrow opening. At the end was a shallow river. We stayed back, protected from view. A few people had walked down to sit by the river. Caden explained that many witches travel back and forth.

At exactly midnight, the yacht simply appeared. It was far too large for the depth of the river; the bottom should have been scraping the riverbed.

As I nuzzled into Caden, he put his arm around my waist and kissed the top of my forehead. "Watch," he whispered, pointing to the boat.

It was dark, but the river now glowed a dull, rosy pink. My eyes followed Caden's finger to find the cause for the odd coloring. A woman stood on the edge of the boat, only visible by the magical blue glow emanating from her hands. The river rippled against the magic. I stood in awe, waiting to see what would happen next. Thick roots surfaced from the riverbed, interweaving with bits of fallen trees and driftwood. A bridge began to form, crossing the distance from the yacht to the riverbank. Curling vines designed themselves into intricate handrails. Miscellaneous debris—a tire, fishing pole, and a boot—became entwined in the vines.

"How?" I asked, wonder lacing the question.

"Lucy, the captain of *The Ugly Duckling*, has an affinity for wood. She's been doing this run for over sixty years," Penny replied as she wheeled her bike over to us.

At last, the bridge was complete, finishing with a gentle splash at their feet. Penny pushed her Kawasaki onto it and walked to the yacht. Caden laced his fingers into mine and strolled across with me. Ginger had somehow convinced Spencer to carry her.

"Welcome back, Prince Caden. And Harmony, if I remember correctly." Lucy gave a curtsy as we boarded *The Ugly Duckling*. "We will have your quarters prepared for you. They should be ready before we hit the border. Amy is cooking meals for each of you."

"Thank you," Caden said.

Lucy couldn't have been older than forty, yet she had been doing this run for over sixty years. She was young, beautiful, and looked like she belonged on the cover of a magazine. Her eyeliner was shaped into perfect wingtips. I couldn't even dye my hair correctly.

"How did she know my name?" I asked, once they were out of earshot.

"You left Arylnn on this boat. Let's hit the kitchen. I'm starving. Amy cooks a mean meal," Caden said as he pulled me toward the stern.

"I'm gonna walk around, explore a bit," I said. Caden, Spencer, Ginger, and Penny all offered to go with me, but I told them no. I needed a moment to myself.

I walked to the back of the boat, and in the floor was a staircase, with odd, swirling designs, but absolutely beautiful in its intricacy. I took the stairs, holding onto the marble railing. As I descended, the steps spiraled. It was fancy. I reached the first landing, finding a long hallway with a lot of doors. The next floor was identical to the one above. I kept going. Five floors later and it seemed I had reached the end. It really was enormous. So many floors impossibly fit under the boat. Magic. It had to be a butt-ton of magic.

I stepped off the staircase to the bottommost floor. Unlike the others, the walls looked as though they were made of gold. Grazing the wall with a finger, I decided they probably were. The dingy, carpet looked wrong against the shining walls. A dark, brown streak ran down the center of the aisle. Why would they be carpeted so far below deck? It seemed rather silly. Not that I knew anything about design. I lived in an attic before.

I walked forward and grabbed a door handle. Locked. Ugh. The next four doors were locked as well. At the very end of the hall, two glass doors led into an expansive library. Shelves and shelves of books covered the walls from top to bottom. Crossing my fingers, I tried the door. It opened. The smell of musty, ancient paper hit my nose. It was intoxicating. This was the real magic. My hands grazed the spines of titles I had never heard of—for good reason.

1001 Recipes for Eye of Squirrel.
Ten Things to Know About Fairy Juice
A Dud's Guide to Living with a Witch
The Ugly Duckling Records

I grabbed the last and flipped through the pages. It was a roster of passengers dating back to 1959. I flipped through, trying to find my name. Near the final pages, I found Penny Wren. Next was Grace Raven. I had heard that name before, but I couldn't think of where. Further down was Prince Caden Perry. My boyfriend, a prince; it's still weird to me. Another Raven and many more names I didn't recognize.

Gurgle. My stomach didn't care about names. It wanted food. I put the book back on the shelf next to an atlas of Arlynn—one day I would like to take a peek at that.

Gurgle. I'm going, relax, tummy. I took the stairs two at a time to get back to the deck. My legs tired quickly. I had walked way too much for one day. Lucy had said something about our quarters being prepared and I couldn't wait to rest. When I reached the top of the stairs Caden was standing there.

"Your food is ready," he said, beaming.

I laughed. "Yes, Prince Caden."

Even though Caden had told me I'd been on this boat before, I had no recollection of it—of ever being on *any* boat. This one, though, was particularly beautiful and had lights that wrapped around the entire upper deck, woven in and out of the railings. The stern had a mini diner with a few tables screwed to the floor.

A stocky woman, who must be Amy, stood behind a

long counter. She was cooking steaks and a vegetable medley on the grill. I slumped into a stool at the counter, Caden and Penny on either side of me. I could have gone for french fries but the steak smelled amazing.

Amy walked away and returned with a handful of potatoes. She began peeling them. Oh my, she was making fresh french fries. My mouth opened wide. Wow, she was as cool as Nurse Dara.

Witch, I need meatballs. Ginger snapped at my feet.

Amy grabbed a plate from the microwave and handed it to me. Three meatballs covered in sauce. She was amazing. I grabbed the plate and placed it on the floor for Ginger.

"Thank you," I said to Amy.

She looked up, wordlessly, offering only a small wave of her spatula. I raised my eyebrows at Caden, questioning why she wasn't speaking. He explained that she was telepathic and could hear people's thoughts.

"It's exceedingly rare and when everyone else her age was coming into their affinities, she thought she was going crazy. She stabbed pencils into her ears to stop the voices. It wasn't until she'd seen a doctor that she learned it was her affinity."

I put my hand to my heart. Fuck. I couldn't imagine.

Amy reached over the counter, and lifted my chin. She waved a finger at me and I squished my face in confusion. Amy grabbed a notepad from her apron, jotted something down, and slid it to me. *Do not feel sad for me.* When she turned away, I caught a glimpse of the scars that laced her ears.

Caden's hand grazed mine. I pushed up from the stool and walked away. He tried to follow, but I told him

I'd be right back. I needed a moment to collect my thoughts. Amy didn't need to hear me contemplating the weight of her scars.

Chapter 26

WITCHES WALKED AROUND the boat and chatted with each other. No one paid me any attention. They were all going home. At least I assumed they were. I was going to Arlynn, but not home. I didn't have one of those. Unless I counted wherever Caden was. This was all new to me and I was scared.

Yet part of me was selfish for being afraid. Amy had known magic her whole life and paid for it. Had that happened to me I would have done the same thing. I had animals talking to me and thought I was going crazy. To live in a world where magic was normal and still be different. Ugh, it had to be so hard for her.

The scars in her ears were puffy and discolored. Fat lines where the pencils had pierced the skin. She must have stabbed her ears numerous times. A chill ran up my spine. My stomach yelled at me; I had to get myself together so I could eat and not think of her scars.

"Well, you see, I took a sabbatical for a year, but when I return the lab will be waiting for me. I'm a big deal," Spencer said to a man in a trench coat.

I sunk deeper into the shadows from the captain's quarters of the boat. From the window, I could see Lucy steering the ship with a wheel. Spencer talked to a man about his job in Arlynn. I didn't want to eavesdrop, but Tool hadn't told me anything. I wanted information on him because he clearly knew me before.

"Isn't the lab you work at run by Doctor Apples?" Trench Coat Man asked.

"That old man is crazy. He left. Claimed we couldn't fix Duds. But I know we can. There is a very powerful woman. With her magic I can treat them."

Spencer didn't appear to be the type of person to want to fix anyone. Ever. Yet he was trying to help Duds. I didn't understand this man. He won't even tell me about my sister. Anger rose in me.

I pushed it down and went back to the table. Caden and Penny were eating their steak. As Penny sliced into hers, blood and juice flowed out. Of course she ate hers barely cooked. Caden's wasn't cooked much more.

Amy placed a plate in front of me. Steak, vegetables and fries filled every inch. I dove into the french fries, salty and cooked to perfection. Yummy, fresh sliced potatoes, not fries out of a bag. I sliced into the steak, well done. She cooked it the way I like without even asking.

It was soft and fell apart in my mouth as I chewed. It tasted like no steak I had ever had before. "Wow, this is amazing."

"Our cows are magical. Twice the size of cows from Earth." Penny chewed at her piece, blood dribbling down her lip.

"Cows?" My stomach turned.

I knew where steak came from, I wasn't stupid, but for some reason I had never thought about it. Cows. Fuck. Without ever having done it, I knew I could talk to them. And here I was eating one. Fuck.

My stomach tossed. Bile rose. I jumped from the stool and ran to the edge of the boat. Vomit erupted from me into the water below. Everything I had eaten in the last few days came up. I didn't even think I ate corn and yet it was there. Caden rubbed my back.

"Could you be any more disgusting?" Spencer asked from behind.

"Why are you even here? To find Savvy? Did it occur to you that she ran away from you? Yet here you are with a bunch of people that don't like you trying to find her. Maybe if you were actually nice we would like you. You know who I am and who my sister is yet you refuse to help me!" I spat. As harsh as I was, I couldn't stop the words. "Well? Why are you here?"

"You know nothing about me! I helped your sister get you into The Witches Protection Program. And I promised..." Spencer continued to talk but I couldn't hear what he was saying.

"You, um... you helped?" My head spun. He helped do this to me. Why?

My veins tingled. I wanted to hurt him. All of this was his fault. My entire life was a lie and he helped. Caden and Penny started yelling at him, demanding answers. Spencer knew so much about me yet told me so little. Like that I could mimic animals. Which animal could tear him to pieces? My vision blurred. Red.

"Relax," Spencer said.

"Did I relax when The Order stole my memories?" I

demanded.

I took another step forward and sniffed the air, smelling the fear of my prey. Spencer was scared of me—as well he should be. The power inside me was taking over, whispering to me.

Attack.

Caden and Penny took a step back. My pack did not need to fear me. The prey did. My mouth watered. I wanted to sink my teeth into him. Spencer whispered to my pack. Yes, he would know what was happening. He had explained that I could mimic animals. The scream at the motel was just the tip of what I was capable of.

A wolf growled inside me. I bared my teeth and my throat rumbled. I stalked Spencer with my eyes, looking for a weakness, waiting to attack.

"Harmony, I don't want to hurt you." Spencer took a step back and lifted his hands.

A weakness.

"Why didn't you tell me?" I asked. The wolf didn't care. I was toying with my prey.

His hand glowed orange. He would try and use magic on me. Foolish. My vision went black. This was him and his illusions. The wolf inside me didn't need sight. I could smell him. Sweat dripped down his temple. My prey took two steps back, his feet soft against the deck. Yet my hearing was stronger than ever.

I leapt into the air, launching myself with my hind legs. Arms forward, teeth bared, I was as graceful and terrifying as a wolf. Spencer leapt back, stumbled and caught his balance. My vision cleared as I landed on him.

A yell pierced the air behind me, but I couldn't make

sense of the words. The wolf was fully taking over. My claws dug into Spencer's chest as the railing slammed into his back. The momentum had nearly caused both of us to flop over the side. My feet landed on the bottom rung of the railing. Simultaneously, Spencer's hand grasped the top rung. I hadn't planned on tossing him overboard, but now the idea excited me.

Arms wrapped around my waist, pulling me away. I snarled and nipped at the intruding arms but failed to make contact. I was being lifted into the air, away from my prey. My arms flailed out toward Spencer, to claw his eyes out. Someone was pulling me further away. I struggled against the grip. Sniffing the air, electricity— my mate. Another growl erupted from my mouth. Why was he stopping me? Wolves kill and my prey deserved to die.

I tried to speak, but only the wolf came out of me in a low, keening howl. My mate had to understand. He was pulling me away from the hunt. I snapped my teeth and writhed against my alpha, but he continued to drag me. My vision blurred; I couldn't see where he was taking me. I sniffed the air again; my prey was further and further away. Lavender filled my nostrils. I crinkled my nose. The scent hurt. My alpha released one of his arms from my waist.

As cold water stung my face, I tried to run. I howled. Arms tightened around me as I attempted to jump away from the painful water. I blinked, fighting Caden's grip on me. Water splashed my face; the wolf was retreating. Caden held me in place as the water from the shower drenched us both. Fully dressed, I began to shiver uncontrollably.

Witch, are you okay? I'm going to nap on your pillow since you're busy, Ginger called from outside the shower.

"Why are we in the shower?" I asked.

"Cold water shocks the body, halts the magic," Caden replied.

"And I'm in the shower because?"

"The animal was taking over. I had to stop you from killing Spencer."

"Oh, well I'm still gonna kill him unless he gives me some answers."

Chapter 27

CADEN REMOVED HIS sopping wet shirt and tossed it out of the shower. *Thwap!* It slapped the tile floor. Water cascaded down his bare chest, like a waterfall against rocks. He removed his sneakers and socks, then unbuttoned the clasp of his jeans.

I stood, letting the water flow over me as I watched Caden undress, afraid that if I moved he would stop removing his clothes. I loved the view; my heart raced. The water was still freezing, so I reached down and turned the shower handle.

When he unzipped his pants, I could no longer control myself. I pulled him into me, mashing my lips against his. Sparks flew, the intensity undeniable—and in some ways the wolf was still there, hungering for my mate. I pressed my body against his, my nipples perked. I was soaked in more ways than one. Tasting the hot dewiness of the shower and the sweetness of his tongue almost undid me.

Caden ran his hand down my side to the bottom of my shirt. It clung to me as he pulled it up and over my head. My lips returned to his the second the shirt was removed. His hand went to my back, pulling me closer. His cock hardened against my stomach, our difference in height evident.

"I want you," I whispered against his pouty lips.

"I'm yours," Caden crooned as he ran his tongue against mine. I reached my hand behind my back and unclasped my bra. Caden laughed. "I could have done that."

"You take too long."

I placed my hand on his stomach and, with one finger, I traced his perfect V to the top of his jeans. They were already unzipped, allowing his cock to peek out of the top. I ran my finger across the slit at the tip, a bead of cum already on the head. I loved how hard he always got for me. In an attempt to release his cock, I yanked on his pants. The water acted like a suction cup; the jeans stuck. I huffed. My unclamped bra slid down my arms. Caden tore it off and bent down to take my puckered nipple in his mouth. I moaned; damn he was magic. His tongue twirled around my tiny pink nub as his hands slid down my sides to the top of my jeans.

I pulled my leg up to grab my sneaker. I slipped it off and tossed it outside of the shower, repeating the action for the second sneaker as Caden unbuttoned my jeans. I tried again to pull off his jeans, but the water and the angle didn't allow for it.

He unzipped my pants and slid his hand inside. Damn. The slickness was not from the water, I was ready for him. His finger rubbed against my pussy; I pushed against him. He released my nipple only to suck on the other.

Giving up on getting his jeans off, I pulled on my own. When I got them down to my knees, Caden slid his finger inside. Fuck. I gasped and cried out for more. He rubbed his thumb against my beaded clit as his lips returned to mine, pushing me against the cool shower wall. Caden rubbed his thumb with more intensity against my bead, and slowly slid his finger in and out of me. The new position allowed me to release the now throbbing member from his pants. I clasped my hands around it. He was large and ready. I stroked him with one hand and slid my panties down with the other.

"Take off your pants," I panted as I pulled away from his lips.

"You want me?" He gave me a devilish grin.

I nodded, biting my lower lip. He thrust his finger inside me, faster. I moaned at the ecstasy, on the verge of climaxing. I grabbed his forearm to prevent him from pulling away. I wanted his pants off—after. Closer. Caden's thumb pressed firmly against me, rubbing. His free hand pinched my nipple. With a cry, my climax reached its peak.

"Now. Pants," I breathed heavily, still trembling from the tingles of my climax.

With a smile, he obliged. While he took off his pants, I removed mine and my socks. I sucked in a breath as I inspected his body. There was a large scar on his right thigh that stretched from hip to knee. I would have asked about it but feared it would ruin the moment. Every time I saw it I wanted to ask, but never did.

Instead I knelt in front of him. His hands reached out, as if to stop me. I smiled at him and shook my head. He always pleased me and seldom allowed me to return the favor. Tonight he would not prevent this from happening. I took his shaft in my hand and began stroking. He released a moan when I ran my tongue along the vein bulging along the length of his erection and circled my tongue around the throbbing tip. I had never been able to take the whole thing in my mouth, but trying caused moans and grunts from him. Which I loved. Stroking the base of his penis, I wrapped my mouth around the tip. He let out a low growl as his hand grazed the top of my head. I took as much of him in my mouth as possible and sucked hard.

I alternated between stroking and sucking, sometimes gliding my tongue across the top. He tensed, I sucked forcefully, taking in his entire cock. He tried to pull away, but I dug my fingers into his rear-end to hold him in place, and he quivered.

He tangled his fingers in my hair and groaned, his cum exploding in my mouth. A lingering throb swept through my body as I looked up at the sexual ecstasy on his face. Standing, I smiled at him and he pulled me into him, hugging me.

Fuck that was hot.

Caden grabbed the lavender scented soap and lathered me up, taking extra time on my breasts. Once my body was washed, he grabbed the shampoo and washed my orange-blonde, tangled hair. I returned the favor, washing him. It was the single most sensual moment that I could remember.

When we got out of the shower, Caden grabbed us both a towel. They were white with a yellow duck embroidered at the bottom. He wrapped one around me and I snuggled into him as we walked into the rest of the room.

It must have been the quarters Lucy had prepared for us. It was bigger than our apartment back in Philly.

A king-size bed wrapped in blue linen was in the center of the room. Two leather sofas were on either side. A crystal chandelier hung from the ceiling and there was a picture of the boat above the bed.

Above the writing desk was a picture of a family. As I got closer I recognized everyone except a girl. It was Caden's family. Underneath was a gold plaque with the words 'The Royal Family.' Caden looked about the same age as the vision he showed me, sixteen.

"The girl is my sister Liz. This is the royal quarters on the ship. I hate the special treatment." Caden wrapped his arms around me.

I had never been treated special, except by Caden. To be royalty must be amazing. Having people always around serving you and tending to your needs. Yet Caden claimed to have hated it. Had I been treated special before? Didn't matter, none of that mattered. Whoever I was before was gone. And Spencer helped.

"Let's get dressed. Spencer still has some explaining to do." I went over to my bag on the bed.

Caden walked over to a gold dresser next to one of the sofas. I followed, wondering if there was anything I could wear in there since my clothes were all dirty. I hadn't planned on needing so many outfits. I didn't know how long I would be gone or where I was going. Running was as far as I had gotten in my thought process, and that was no longer an option.

One drawer contained multiple pairs of blue sweatpants, in a variety of sizes. Another was full of blue t-shirts. Not original, but it would work. There was no underwear, but I was thankful for the clothes. Caden explained Lucy kept the drawers fully stocked. Always the hostess.

Knock. Knock.

I quickly tossed on the clothes. Caden was pulling on his shirt as he opened the door. Penny walked through. Spencer stood in the hallway, chewing at his fingernails. He probably assumed I was going to attempt to kill him again. It was a solid plan. If he didn't talk.

Penny opened the closet and pulled out two pairs of flip flops. She tossed one to me and one to Caden. Her and Spencer were both wearing the same blue outfits as us. Penny had her swords strapped to her back.

"She threatened to slice you if you didn't come here?" Caden asked Spencer.

He nodded and finally walked into the room. Caden shut the door but Spencer remained by it. I wanted to growl at him to scare him.

"Well, I need you to explain what you know or Penny's swords won't be the only thing slicing into you," I said, sounding way more confident than I was.

"A little over two years ago, I was working in my lab," Spencer started. "A woman walked in asking for my help. She wanted me to remove her powers. I obviously refused, who would want that? Well turns out she may be the key to fixing Duds. Anyway, one day she asked me to help her because I had connections everywhere. And she wanted me to get her sister into The Witches Protection Program." He paced as he talked.

I wanted to ask him a million questions. It was obvious he was talking about my sister. Why would my sister help get my memories taken? Was she a monster or was I?

"So I agreed. But your sister made me promise not to tell you. And to protect you." Spencer took a step back toward the door.

"Why? I mean why agree to protect her?" Caden

asked, his jaw clenched.

"Because of Savvy. She was also going into the program. I love her and was going Earthside anyway. So I figured, why not? I told your sister I would protect you." Spencer shrugged.

"But why would my sister want my memories taken?" I didn't care about his love for Savvy.

"She never told me. That's all I know." Spencer turned and walked out the door.

Who was I before? What was my family like? Did my parents know? Did I have parents? My veins boiled. My sister had done this to me; Spencer was only a pawn. I had no clue how I was going to find her, but I would. And when I did, she was going to have a lot of explaining to do.

Could you guys keep it down? I'm trying to sleep. Ginger yawned.

Penny left, letting us know the border crossing was in thirty minutes. She promised to help me find my sister, and that she had to have had a good reason for what she did. The program was invented to help protect witches, not hurt them.

"I want to try something with you," Caden said the second the door shut. "It may not work, but I can show people my truth. I want to try and show you yours."

Chapter 28

"I HAVE NO TRUTH. My life has been a lie. The Order gave me a terrible life. What would seeing anything do?" I paced.

Caden meant well, I know he did, but I didn't have anything to show. I clenched my fists. My sister and The Order did this. I wasn't sure why and part of me didn't care. What if I really was friends with Vera and that's why they did it? It was the only conclusion that made sense. Vera claimed she needed help taking down the king, Caden's father.

The old me may have been okay with that, but this version wasn't. But maybe I hadn't been friends with Vera and she was lying. I ran my fingers through my hair. My head was spinning. It was too much to contemplate.

There were three things I knew for sure. My sister is out there, and I plan on finding her. My memories are also in Arlynn, I will locate them and hide them. And the last was my love for Caden. Whatever happened in my past life was that; my past life. Looking back would do me no good.

Once I found my sister and retrieved my memories, Caden and I could run and this whole mess would be someone else's problem. It was none of my business what happened in a land I didn't even remember. Um, and I would help Penny find Savvy.

"You don't know that. It's worth a shot." Caden raised both of his eyebrows at me.

He wouldn't give up, I knew that. He thought he was trying to help. I should at least humor him. I sat on the sofa beside him and he cupped my face in his hands, pulling me in for a kiss. His fingertips trailed up my cheekbone to my temple.

I was standing in an attic, the heat causing the wood to smell funny. A bucket sat in the corner for me to use when I had to tinkle. My blankie had been taken by Miss Lynn. She told me I would get it back when I learned to be a good girl.

A mattress was on the floor by the window. I sat on it to look outside. The bus went by with all the kids I used to play with, but last week I messed up badly and now I'm up here. I can't even go to school. My teacher said I was getting really good at reading, almost better than my class, like a second grader.

The attic door opened. Miss Lynn waddled in. She was a real big lady. I scooted back on the mattress, hoping she would let me go to school. Miss Lynn came over and leaned against the wall. She didn't breathe really well.

"Harmony, do you understand what you did wrong?" she asked.

I nodded. She told me kids aren't heard.

"Answer!"

"Yes, Miss Lynn. I ate past bedtime," I cried. I knew better. She told me the rules. But my stomach grumbled a ton.

Miss Lynn's breathing came out like a monster. I was scared of her. The wind in the attic slapped against the door. She'd left it open. I didn't think, I just got up and ran. She called after me, but I was faster. I ran out of the house and all the way to school. I didn't even have shoes on. I never saw Miss Lynn again.

The scene faded. I pulled away from Caden, but he yanked me back and placed his hands on my temple again. As a tear rolled down my cheek another vision played.

Mr. Benjamin slept on the worn brown lazy boy. He was always sleeping, which suited me fine. I didn't need a parent, I didn't need anyone. His mouth fell open and drool ran down onto his chin. Gross.

His three boys came into the living room, Ben, Berk, and Billy. I stood up and walked toward the kitchen. Being in the same room with them gave them permission to make me their punching bag. Ben, the oldest, who was only six months older than me, grabbed my arm and yanked me back into the room.

"Where you going, Cry Baby?"

Berk and Billy bounced on their feet, clenching their fists.

"To get, uh, outside," I whispered. No answer I ever gave stopped them.

"Uh, uh, gonna get outside? Stay and hang out with your brothers," Billy chimed in.

They weren't my brothers. They would never be. I hated them so much. When I first came to live here I told Mr. Benjamin and his wife Karen what was happening. I gave them great detail about how they would make me sandwiches with only the end pieces. And how they would wake me up in the middle of the night by dumping water on me. And the daily beatings.

Well, my lovely foster parents explained, 'boys will be boys. And sometimes boys that are coming into puberty do that when they like a girl. It's pulling pigtails.'

"You trying to think? I see your brain smoking." Billy got in my face and pushed his chest against mine.

I stumbled back. Next they would circle around me and start pushing me. It was always the same thing. Mr. Benjamin bolted upright in his chair. He mumbled for one of us to grab him a cold one from the fridge.

The boys couldn't be bothered with small chores while I was around so I walked into the kitchen. A calendar hung on the side that had big bold letters across the top. Seize the Day. I never seize any day. Mr. Benjamin called for me to hurry.

"Fuck you and your shit head children," I screamed.

I turned and ran out the back door. The boys shouted and chased me. If they caught me I knew I would be toast. They would beat me worse than ever before. I ran block after block.

Six blocks later and the shouting faded. I risked a look behind. They had their hands on their knees, panting. Yes. I outran them. Holy moly, I did it. To be safe, I didn't go back to the house till they were asleep.

Pissing them off then running from them became a daily routine. Not once did they catch me. I loved running.

Again the scene faded. I grinned. That was one of my favorite memories because I had won. Those shit head boys may have used me as a punching bag, but in the end... I won.

The halls buzzed with students chatting and laughing. Couples held hands and kissed in corners. I yanked on my shirt that I had outgrown two years ago. I couldn't afford clothes. Mr. Deter couldn't go shopping. He would buy one thing and spiral to an abyss of hoarding.

Amber sauntered toward me with her copy cats on both sides of her. They tried so hard to be like the popular girl. All were evil. I backed into the wall as she came directly at me. Her hair was in a tight high ponytail and swayed as she walked. The track pants she wore swished. I hated that sound, it meant she was getting closer.

"What do you own, like three shirts?" Amber stopped in front of me.

"You wear the same track suit every day," I shot back. Not the best response, but it was true. Miss star of the track team let everyone know it, every day.

"I am the best on the track team. I train every day. You would have no clue what that's like," Amber said and her copy cats agreed.

"I could beat you without training. Kids in this school are slow." I wanted to bang my head against a wall. I should not have said that.

"Let's put that to the test," Amber challenged. I didn't want to. The track team is the only winning team at the school.

A race against Amber would cause all the students to notice me. They already paid too much attention to me because of my old clothes and bruises that I come to school with. Being the foster kid had nothing good about it.

The copy cats linked their arms in mine. Shit. They

were dragging me down the hall. A few of the kids nudged others to find out why the copy cats were even touching me. Some followed behind us.

By the time we stepped outside, half the students were behind me. Amber led the way, taunting me every few seconds. She had challenged me to a race, and even if I wanted to I couldn't back down.

My sneakers were given to me by a neighbor; she would wear them when she cut her grass so they were covered in green stains. I had loose fitting jeans, and a shirt that showed my belly. Nothing I wore would give me the slightest advantage in this race.

I knew I could beat her. I had been running from people my whole life. She ran because she enjoyed it. I did it because my life depended on it. If I won, she would hate me more and the school would pay attention to me. If I pretended to lose, she would win.

Coach was on the race track doing sprints with the boys track team. Amber walked over to him and whispered in his ear. He dismissed the boys, who went over to the bleachers with half of the school.

Amber and I stood on the start line. Coach had his stop watch in his hand. My stomach turned. I still didn't know if I should win or not. No matter what, I was royally fucked. Amber mouthed 'foster bitch,' right as Coach blew his whistle.

I pushed off on my heels hard. Fuck that bitch, I was gonna win. She told me it would be one time around the track. That's all I needed.

The scene faded. That was the day I beat Amber and became a track star. The school still ignored me, except on the days of the races. That's when I was noticed.

In the next scene, an old man and the rat man from

The Order guided me onto a boat. My heart raced. I wanted to run. I wanted to hide. I shouldn't be here. The deck was cold and dark under my bare feet. Where were my shoes?

The sky was a bright orange. I shielded my eyes against the moon. It was as if the sun never set, I hated it here.

"Mister Donickey, Doctor Apples, welcome aboard. Your quarters are ready. Who do we have with you?" the captain asked.

Rat man whispered in her ear. I strained to listen. Nothing. I was a secret. What was my name? I tried to pull it to the surface and couldn't. A dark haze covered my mind every time I tried to think of anything.

Dr. Apples hobbled forward. Rat man placed his hand on my back and pushed me forward. I stumbled and was ripped upright immediately. Ouch. I didn't want to move.

I blinked.

The room was tiny. A chandelier hung above me on the bed. Dr. Apples and Rat Man were whispering. I strained to listen.

"You are a part of this. You don't get to back out now," Rat Man whispered.

"Branches are a part of trees. They were never asked what they want," Dr. Apples whispered back.

"All you need to do is erase the last couple days from her mind. The rest has been taken care of."

I sucked in a breath and Caden removed his hands. My legs tingled. Electricity trickled through my veins. What the fuck was that? It didn't make sense. Caden said he was going to show me my truth. Three visions were from fake memories. The third was the only one that may be true. I didn't understand.

"Most of those were memories The Order placed in my mind." I stood and paced.

"They were your truth. It's why you love to run. You may not be who you were before but that is who you are now." Caden pulled me onto his lap.

He was right. I am me because of those memories. I hated The Order for placing horrible memories in my mind, but it made me a pretty awesome runner.

One tear broke through leading the path for the rest to flow.

Border crossing in five minutes, the loud speaker boomed.

Chapter 29

A SONG MORE BEAUTIFUL than anything I had ever heard surrounded us in a chorus of enchantment. The melody was soft like a lullaby, but haunting. I leaned against the railing, staring into the dark night, the sea air pungent and salty. Roughly thirty people stood at the bow of the boat. Half were dressed in black pants and white button-up shirts with a duck emblem on the sleeve. I hadn't realized so many people worked on the boat. Penny had mentioned that this was a career favored by many of the witches in Arlynn.

The singing seemed to emanate from the other side of the ocean. I fell into a trance as I stared into the inky night, all other thoughts drifted away. Suddenly, as if a curtain were parting in the sky, a bright beam of light shone through, almost blinding me. I squinted, peeking through. The singing grew louder. On the other side of the curtain was a bright sky, swirling with brilliant pinks, blues, and purples. Sparkling black diamonds dotted the sky.

The ocean blood-orange, small waves tumbling over one another. The scene took my breath away. From Caden's visions I knew the colors of Arlynn were different. Even still, I was not prepared for the stunning beauty.

"Remarkable," I whispered.

I'm hungry. Ginger rubbed against my leg.

"I said the same thing last year when I crossed the barrier to the human world," Penny whispered back.

As they drew closer, a line of cloaked figures appeared along the Arlynn border. They floated inches above the water. The song was coming from them. The figures were human in shape, but unable to see their cloaked and hooded faces, I couldn't be sure.

"What are those?" I pointed.

"Sirens," Spencer stated matter-of-factly.

My hands flew up to my ears. I crouched down trying to block out the song. Everyone knew the tales of Sirens, luring lost-at-sea sailors to their deaths. They were evil creatures. Their song was so enchanting. Why is everyone just standing around?

Caden bent down next to me, laughing, and pulled my hands away from my ears. "What are you doing?"

"Sirens are evil. I've seen them in movies. I can't believe they're real."

"They are no more evil than you or I. They are misunderstood. Their job is to open the border between our worlds and guide the ships to Arlynn. Sometimes they accidentally guide humans to Arlynn. They don't mean to."

I stood staring as they crossed the border. Magic tremored through my veins. This was my home, yet it wasn't. I had no memories of it. My body trembled to run. This could be a mistake.

Water unexpectedly splashed my face, tugging me away from my thoughts. I smiled as what could only be described as mermaids played in the water. Beautifully opalescent, scaled tails merged into the torso of a goddess. Their gilled faces, though, were grotesque. Their hair was seaweed, eyes black as coal. I had always assumed they were exquisitely beautiful half-humans.

"Now those are evil." Penny pointed toward the mermaids playfully splashing water.

"Mermaids? How are mermaids evil?" I rolled my eyes.

"Nasty creatures—will chew you to pieces if given the chance. They are like sharks, but smarter," Spencer chimed in, stepping back from the railing.

My mind wandered. I imagined all the creatures that could live in Arlynn. The possibility that my affinity could be connected to magical beings delighted me. Would calling a sea serpent be a possibility for me?

The yacht crashed against a wave. All the mermaids slithered away. The sirens looked fearfully at the passengers of *The Ugly Duckling*, then turned and fled. Penny gripped the hilt of her sword. I grabbed the railings as another swell approached.

"What's going on?" Caden demanded.

Ginger ran off. The workers and passengers demanded answers. Lucy called for everyone to remain calm. My heart dropped. Shit. There was no way I did this. Fuck.

"Don't know. Arlynn waters are never this rocky." Penny grabbed the railing with her free hand.

Another crashing wave, this time leaving the deck

and everyone on it drenched. This was my fault. Um, um, I had to reverse this. Spencer took a few more steps back.

"I'm sorry. I didn't mean to," I pleaded with them.

"What are you talking about?" Caden asked.

Before I could reply, another wave rained down. From the depths of the ocean, the sea serpent emerged. A nasty, monstrous creature with slick, slimy skin. It peered at me with eyes the size of satellite dishes. Um, um, I took a step back covering my mouth with my hands. I didn't mean to call it.

A few of the crew and passengers ran, screaming of demons. The rest stayed, clinging to the railings and glowing their individual magical colors. Caden yanked at my wrist. I lost my grip on the railing, my feet sliding. He pulled me upright before I hit the deck.

"You need to get out of here," he said, pushing me away.

I swiped my blonde locks out of my face as more ocean water poured down on us. I did this, I had to fix it. But how?

Penny stood poised, both samurai swords firmly in her hands. Only a ninja princess could look so beautiful as a sea serpent encroached, ready to devour. Wind and water whipped around her as she whispered, "Wake."

The serpent stuck out its forked tongue, taunting us. Its tail sprang into the air and slapped down heavily against the water's surface. I tried to visualize the serpent going away, but Penny was directly in front of me. And it could eat her.

One of the crew started shooting electric-pink magic at the monster. It might have been Lucy, but this pink had an almost purplish hue. The monster didn't seem affected by the magic, so a few others joined in. It was a rainbow of colors against the murky, green skin and yet the serpent remained unaffected.

I tried to repress visions of the monster eating Penny in my mind, attempting to think of anything else. The yacht rocked from the waves, and I slipped again; knees crashed against the deck. I covered my eyes as if that could remove the image from my mind.

"No!" Caden screamed from a distance.

I removed my hands from my eyes; terror ripped through me. We were so fucked. The serpent was going for Penny, there was no denying that. It slithered closer, eyes focused only on her. Everyone on deck heaved magic at the monster. It remained unharmed.

Penny kicked off her flip-flops. In one swift motion, she leapt onto the railing. Her swords raised and ready to attack, she pushed off the railing toward the monster. For a moment she soared. I didn't know why Penny whispered to her swords, but hopefully it was enough.

The other mages ceased shooting magic the moment she jumped. The two samurai swords sliced through the sea serpent's eye as the ninja princess landed a forward flip onto the back of its neck. Hanging on by the katana, she pushed her feet against its cheek, and pulled a blade free. Blood poured into the swirling ocean waters as Penny jabbed the sword into its temple.

I had finally gotten control of my visions while Penny swished through the air. I imagined the serpent remaining perfectly still as she attacked. I could only assume, but it seemed to have worked, and Penny quickly sliced the monster a few more times. The crazy ninja princess turned to the crowd on the deck and waved.

I will kill all of you! the sea serpent screamed into my head.

It rocked back and forth, Penny grabbed the hilt of the katana still embedded in the serpent and managed to keep her balance.

"Please stop!" I screamed.

Heal me and I will.

Penny's body slapped against the serpent. His tail emerged from the waters and licked at her back. He was taunting me, teasing me, threatening me with knowledge that he could kill her with ease. I had to do something. Anything.

"Penny, I can fix this! Stop stabbing him!" I screamed. Penny fought against the beast. The waves crashed louder; there was no way she could hear me. If only I could talk to Penny the way I could with the animals. *Amy.*

I darted around the deck. Amy had been there a moment ago. Caden grabbed my arm shouting to me to get to safety. I shrugged him off and spotted Amy a few feet away. I ran over to her. *Please tell me you can speak into people's minds.* Before I could speak the words out loud Amy shook her head.

"But please try. If you can tell Penny to stop, I can fix this!" I shouted, although Amy already knew what I was thinking.

Amy shrugged and turned towards Penny. After an eternity, well probably mere seconds, Amy turned back to me. She gave a thumbs up. Penny removed her weapons one last time and performed a backflip into the ocean.

I kicked off my flip flops.

Arms wrapped around me. I turned to see Caden. His eyes were wide as he shook his head.

"No time to explain! Let go!" I didn't mean to sound so demanding, but I had to act fast.

He still held on tight. I tried wriggling out of his grip, but he wasn't budging. I looked him in the eyes, "Trust me, I can fix this."

Finally, he released me. I wasted no time and climbed the railing. My foot slipped and I fell toward the water. I attempted to regain my balance and do a fancy dive as Penny had. Instead, I belly-flopped and hit the water hard.

A wave crashed down and pulled me under. An arm wrapped around me bringing me to the surface. It was Caden, and he yelled something at me but the waves thrashing around us made it impossible to decipher.

I searched for Penny; she hadn't emerged from the water. Her head popped up not far from me. I almost missed her as she bobbed and went back under. I pointed at Caden and then in the direction I had spotted Penny. He nodded and swam away.

A slimy tail tapped me on the top of my head. The sea serpent was glaring at me with his one good eye.

"Promise to not kill anyone on the boat!"

I promise. Now heal me. That girl hurt me.

I sucked in a deep breath, bracing for the pain, and grabbed the beast's tail. Cold fire licked my hands. Fuck. The pain intensified, I wanted to let go. My arms shook as the pain climbed. The ice-fire was encapsulating my body. Too much, I tried to let go, but my body would no longer obey.

Water flooded my mouth.

I was being dragged down. My eyes stung as the salt water assaulted them. I couldn't release my hands. Nope, my body refused to acknowledge me.

You are useful. Come with me, the serpent

whispered.

He wrapped me in his slimy embrace. My lungs were inflamed as water filled them. My head spun. I was dying. Not even officially in Arlynn and a sea serpent was about to take me out.

Arlynn, a world filled with magic—a place I may finally belong—and a sister. Could a family be waiting for me, full of magic like me?

Magic! I had magic! I had to be able to spark tendrils like they did at the hotel.

The pain was so intense I couldn't tell if it was working. I concentrated on tendrils emanating from my hands, legs, eyes, anything that would work. The water and depth acted as a blanket; I couldn't see if I was doing anything at all.

Ah! Fine, don't hurt me anymore. The beast loosened his grip.

I kicked my feet to swim up to the surface. My body once again refused to listen. White twinkle lights covered my field of vision. No longer being held by the beast, I sank further down.

My lungs were on fire. I suppressed the urge to gasp for air. My skin tingled, the pain evaporating from me.

I wished I could tell Caden goodbye. Tell Penny it's okay to be nice. Feed Ginger more meatballs. Meet my sister. I closed my eyes.

A scaly sharp object rubbed against my arms. I peeled my eyes open with the last remnant of energy I had. It was a mermaid. It whispered, but I couldn't translate the words in my fading mind. Moments later a cold breeze licked my skin. My lungs were filled with water; I gasped for breath, but there was no room. My back slammed against the deck of the ship and I wiggled, struggling for oxygen.

The mermaid hovered over me. It hissed, then covered my mouth with his.

I cringed. His mouth cut at my lips. I felt a pressure inside of me as I regurgitated a spew of upchucked salt water. He pulled his mouth away and I grasped for air. Sweet air filled my lungs. The mermaid—or merman?—had removed the water from my lungs.

A certain dolphin begged me to save you. The merperson flopped to the edge of the deck, rolled, and was gone.

Pain throbbed through me; even my veins hurt. I crawled to the edge of the boat. Caden and Penny were still in the water. Caden had his arm around Penny, who had a death-grip on both of her swords, preventing her from swimming properly.

Floating through the air, the sirens had returned. They continued their song and encircled Penny and Caden. A pair drifted down and linked their arms in hers, then his. They gracefully floated them up, like angels, placing Penny and Caden on the deck.

I used the railing to pull myself upright. Penny returned the swords to their sheaths on her back before I threw my arms around her. Sea serpent guts squished between us. I squeezed her tighter, and Penny tensed. A slab of skin dropped from Penny's hair onto my shoulder.

"What are you doing?" Penny whispered in my ear.

"I'm so sorry. I didn't mean to call the serpent. And then I couldn't get rid of it. And you almost died. I would have felt responsible. Not that that's why I'm sorry. I mean I don't want anything to happen to you," I rambled.

"Shut up. And stop hugging me. It's weird." Penny pulled away from me.

"Are you okay, Harmony?" Caden grabbed me as I was slumping to the ground.

"Did you see that? I sliced that snake like bad meatloaf." Penny beamed talking to one of the others on deck.

"Okay. That's enough excitement for one border crossing. Everyone go shower. Penny, nice job, but you smell like monster guts," Lucy shouted to the crowd. "Get some rest. We still have a while before we hit Arlynn." The crowd dispersed.

I opened my mouth to speak; even my teeth hurt. Caden wrapped his arms around me and I closed my eyes.

Chapter 30

KNOCK. KNOCK.

I rolled over in the bed, a sharp pain stabbing my side. Ugh, it's too early. The sun shone through the curtains. A shiver ran through me. I was naked. A long dark bruise trailed down my left side. Fuck. The memories of last night slammed into my mind.

Knock.

If you don't get that I will claw your eyes out. Ginger yawned. Her fluffy black body stretched across the other pillow.

As I wrapped the sheet around me I crawled out of bed. The rotting smell of fish slapped me in the face. A pile of wet clothes were balled up in the corner by the sofa. Caden must have undressed me and tossed them there. Where was he?

The door flew open before I had the chance to open it. A tall skinny woman with flaming red hair busted into the room. She pushed a silver cart filled with plates and a large coffee cup. Fresh brewed beans and eggs mixed with the smell of sea serpent guts. My stomach growled.

Each plate was filled with a different breakfast food. Eggs, toast, pancakes, oatmeal, everything I could imagine, and no meat. Amy had heard my thoughts about eating cows. There was also a tiny plate of meatballs. Amy had thought of Ginger as well.

With a quick wave the woman rushed out of the room. I thanked her but she was gone before the words left my mouth. Pain sliced into my side. I yanked the cart toward the bed and sat.

Ginger stretched and came over to my side. She sniffed the air. That cat can smell meatballs anywhere.

"Ready to go home girl?" I scratched her back.

No. I don't like it there. It's not my home. Ginger grabbed a meatball and licked at the grease. For the first time her voice was low and strained.

"What if we bring you to the castle? Once I'm done with everything I have to do, I can come back and keep you forever and always."

Caden, Penny and I hadn't really come up with a plan for when we got to Arlynn. We had discussed certain things but nothing was solid. I wanted Ginger with me the whole time, but I was worried she could get hurt. If she stayed at the castle with Melon I knew she would be safe. And there was a chance she wouldn't be so upset about going home.

Instead of responding, she chewed on another meatball. I reached for the plate of eggs and my side throbbed again. There was so much I needed to do and being laid out from an injury didn't mesh well. I would have to ask Caden if he knew a people healer. That had to be a thing. I heal animals, so maybe witches could heal other witches.

The door flew open again. I yanked the sheet up to cover my breasts. Ahhh. That was painful. Penny bounced in. She seemed way too happy. What happened to the super serious ninja princess?

She came over, rolled up a pancake, dipped it in the syrup and took a bite. I put the coffee cup to my lips, ouch. They were sliced up from the mermaid's kiss of life. Worth the pain, but so gross.

"You stink," Penny said between chews. "We reach Arlynn today. Get dressed. We need to make plans. Caden is calling The Order. We had planned on not telling them we were back yet, but Lucy had to send them a manifest."

I nodded and chewed on some toast. Ugh. Knowing we need a plan, and actually figuring one out were two different things. Part of me thought when we reached Arlynn Caden would know exactly where to go and what to do.

In my mind Arlynn was some tiny little place on a map. It's in the Bermuda Triangle, it couldn't be that big. I was hoping we could wander around and stumble upon my memories, my sister, and Savvy. I rolled my eyes; that was beyond unrealistic.

Penny shoved another pancake in her mouth and left, shouting over her shoulder to meet at Amy's Place.

I jumped out of bed. Ouch. Bad idea. Hobbling over to the door, I locked it. No more intruders. Leaving the sheet on the floor with the wet clothes, I went to the bathroom.

Hot water cascaded down my body. The bruise on my side wasn't the only one. There were tiny ones over my legs and sides. New scratches blended with the ones that had begun to heal from the day Vera tried to kill me at the motel. My body couldn't handle any more attacks. I didn't get beat up this much in foster care.

After I dried off, I stepped into the bedroom. The smell of rotting fish slapped me in the face. Now that bits of sea serpent were out of my hair the smell was worse. Ugh. I tossed on fresh clothes and wrapped the wet one in the sheet. Whoever got stuck cleaning this room was so unlucky.

Ginger insisted on coming with me for the meeting. I scooped her into my arms and left the room. Bam. I walked directly into a person. Stepping back I realized it wasn't much of a person. Spencer glared at me, like I was the one in the way.

"I came to see you." He shoved his hands in his pocket.

What could he possibly want with me? I asked him numerous times for answers and it wasn't until I almost killed him that he finally told me anything. Not that his information was really helpful. I opened my eyes wide and sucked my teeth at him. It was my way of saying, what?

"When we reach Arlynn I will be going off on my own. You guys have a lot of stuff going on and I only have one priority." He rocked on his feet. Was he nervous?

"You know that's part of our plan too. We will get Savvy back." I should have told him to go. Good riddance. He was nothing but trouble.

"I know I said you should get your memories back. But when you do..." He paused and rocked harder. "Destroy them."

My jaw dropped. He was the one who had told me to get them back to find my sister. If it wasn't for him and his big mouth I wouldn't have even wanted them. I would have stayed Earthside and not come to Arlynn. It was his fault I was here and now he was telling me to destroy my memories.

Granted I had no intention of restoring the memories, but why had he changed his mind? I still didn't know what would happen when I had them. Would I remember me? Would I blend into one person? Would it work?

"The you before and you now are both broken. But you now can be fixed." Spencer took Ginger from my hands and snuggled his nose against hers. For a brief moment the nerdy kid from Caden's vision shone through.

Witch, he is right. Ginger purred, nuzzling his nose.

I pulled Ginger from Spencer's grasp. Their affection made my stomach turn. She is a mean cat and he is a tool. A match made in heaven. But she's my mean cat. I promised her forever and I would make sure she was okay.

"Who was I?" I hated asking him, but I had to know.

"Doesn't matter. You're better now." Spencer scratched his head and walked away.

Ugh, I wanted to hit him.

The boat buzzed with talk of Arlynn. It seemed that most people went on vacation Earthside for a few weeks. They found life without magic fascinating. I couldn't tell if anyone was in a similar situation to mine. No one else seemed to be in the Witches Protection Program. They were lucky. My life was turned inside out because of The Order. I didn't even know who I was before.

Penny and Caden sat on the barstools at Amy's place. Ginger ran up and jumped on the counter. There was a fresh plate of meatballs. Seriously, she ate five minutes ago. All that meat can't be good for her.

I sat down next to them and Amy set a cup of coffee in front of me. Being able to read minds must come in handy. She also set a dish of grapes on the counter. I popped one into my mouth, not wanting to interrupt Penny and Caden's argument.

They couldn't agree on where to go first. Penny wanted to find Savvy, then worry about my sister and my memories. Caden wanted to find my memories because Vera could try and get to them before we did. Then we could find Savvy and my sister.

"What did The Order say?" I asked.

"They would like you returned immediately and for Penny and I to find Savvy." Caden grabbed my hand between his and kissed my fingertips.

Well that wasn't going to happen. I didn't care what the rest of our plan entailed, but me going to The Order would not be part of it. Fuck that.

"We aren't going to do that. Yes, it breaks rule number one: always obey the leaders. But I think we need to discover why they took you first." Penny sipped her coffee. She was willing to break a rule for me. Wow.

"Penny, you don't have to be tied to this. I know how important The Order is to you. Spencer is going to go find Savvy, you can go with him." I didn't want her to go on her own. I wanted her by my side. She was one of my only friends.

"Penny and I will deal with The Order. If Spencer is taking off to find Savvy we can concentrate on your memories." Caden chewed on bacon. The poor piggie that had to die for that, ugh.

"Do we have any clue where The Order keeps the memories?" I asked.

Both shook their heads. Of course.

"Caden, will your parents help? They are king and queen. Maybe they will know something?" Wandering around Arlynn didn't seem like the best plan.

"No, but my gramps will help. He might know something. Big John was part of The Order," Caden replied.

We talked for the next hour about our plans for when we got to Arlynn. Penny refused to go with Spencer to find Savvy. She said she would find her, but first my memories. And at least Spencer was looking for her. If anyone could find her, he would. As a lab tech in Arlynn he had many connections.

Caden told me all about his gramps and how much I would love him. Penny had nicknamed him Big John and it stuck. The entire royal family called him that. My heart swelled at how his face lit up by the mention of his gramps' name. It was obvious he was closer to him than his parents.

We reach Arlynn in twenty minutes, the loud speaker boomed.

I turned to Amy. There were so many things I wanted to say to her. Thank you for last night. Thank you for the food. Sorry about what happened to you as a child. As the thoughts ran through my head, her hand grazed mine. She squeezed. There were no words, yet she was saying goodbye. I hoped it wasn't the last time I saw her.

The boat slowed. I went to the room to grab my belongings and Caden was right behind me. On the bed was my bookbag, purse, and Caden's bag. Someone had washed our belongings and folded them nicely in our bags. The crew on this boat thought of everything.

We returned to the deck and Caden propped himself

against the railing. Penny had her hands around the handlebars of her Kawasaki.

Arlynn was in full view. A stone castle towered above the other buildings and boats lined the harbor. To the far right, near the castle, there was a cliff. On the left was a beautiful beach. I had seen a movie about a fishing town in Massachusetts, and this reminded me of that place.

Lucy stood close to Caden, glowing a gentle pink. She must be calling the bridge to Arlynn. As we got closer I realized it was desolate. I had expected it to be bustling with life. People fishing and preparing boats. Others eating at the restaurants. Some tanning on the beach. But nothing. The dock sat in an empty harbor.

"Where is everyone?" Caden asked Lucy.

"It's been a long time since you've been here. Things are different. But don't forget it's also early. Some people still hang here, but not many," she replied.

When the bridge was fully raised, Penny pushed her bike onto it. Caden wrapped his arm around me and guided me off the boat. Other passengers followed behind us. Spencer nodded at us as he walked by. I waved. He may be a jerk, but he was growing on me. Well, not really, but hopefully he finds Savvy.

As soon as we arrived on the other side, Lucy dropped the bridge. A shower of water sprayed my back. I was so tired of the ocean.

I nervously grabbed Caden's hand. He was tense. This ugly place scared me. It was dark, lacking the signs of life I'd seen in Caden's vision. This was not the same place. It couldn't be. Lucy had said it was early, but don't fishermen prepare early?

"What is going on?" Penny asked as we marched forward.

"I don't know. It feels empty," Caden replied.

We walked through the harbor to a main road. A few cars drove by but not as many as I had expected and there wasn't a single flying broom. I peered through the windows. An old woman's face was pressed to the glass of one home. When she saw me looking, she snapped the curtains shut.

"I just... I have never seen it so... dead," Caden said as he gave my hand a squeeze.

As we turned down an alley, a woman stepped out of a brick wall.

"Not the welcome you expected, Prince Caden?" She giggled.

Chapter 31

TURRETS REACHED UP to the inky, iridescent sky. Clouds danced by, taking different shapes. Gray stone engulfed the entire castle. My veins tingled. I was about to walk into a castle. I had never done that before.

The girl that had walked out of the wall bounced in front of me. She was all bubbles and rainbows, wearing a bright pink shirt and shorts. She had the same hazel-green eyes as Caden and long dark brown hair that fell in curls down her back. His sister, Liz, encompassed everything happy and wonderful about the world. She appeared about sixteen but was actually twenty-one.

When we ran into her in the alley she had been down to the harbor to paint one of the buildings that had been graffitied. She had figured that early in the morning there wouldn't be anyone there. Our footsteps had scared her. So having a super cool power, she walks into walls. The girl can walk through walls and blend right into them. Caden called her a blender, which is such a funny name for it.

Liz skipped right through the door. Penny grinned as she pulled it open. She had leaned her bike against the castle wall. Caden sighed as he walked inside.

A small, fat dragon bunny-hopped down the hall. Melon's wings were so much smaller than his body and didn't appear strong enough to hold him in flight.

Get that thing away from me. It will singe my fur! Ginger hissed.

Melon let out a puff of smoke. It hadn't developed flames yet. Someday it will, but today wasn't the day. Caden knelt down and allowed the chubby dragon to climb into his arms.

"Caden, my man! How the heck are ya?" a man's voice boomed down the hall.

An older version of Liam from Caden's vision sauntered down the hall. He was slightly taller than Caden and twice the width. Caden had an athletic build, but this man appeared to be on steroids. His muscles were bulging out of his way-too-tight shirt. Not my type but from the drool in the corner of Penny's mouth, he was hers.

He reached us and pulled Caden into a bear hug. He released him and ruffled Penny's hair. His cheeks reddened. Oh. Wow. They were crushing on each other hard.

Liz jumped on her big brother. He picked her up with one arm, twirled her around and set her back down. She rambled on about the meeting in the alley before I had a chance to open my mouth. The girl was a fast talker.

"Hey, Liam, is Gramps home?" Caden asked.

"Yeah, in his room. Glad you're back, dude. Who is this beautiful creature? You been single forever, go Earthside, and bring home this hottie. Nice." Liam nodded as he spoke.

"Harmony. Nice to meet you." I put out my hand, a little scared he would crush it.

Caden grabbed my hand and pulled me down the hallway. Well, that was awkward.

The castle was a maze. We walked around for no less than twenty minutes. If I had to leave, I would be lost forever. Energy sizzled down the walls. So much magic was in this place.

I was about to ask for a water break when Caden finally stopped. Penny and Liz had kept pace with us.

During the trek around the castle, Liz rambled off facts about every hallway we were in. If I was tested later on what she said, I would fail. She talked so fast it was hard to keep up. I really liked her, but she must be a lot to handle full time.

This had to be Caden's room. He loved fishing, hunting, and would watch way too many baseball games. Along the walls there were trophies from his hunts, gross. He had a television with a baseball game on. It was kind of weird, considering it wasn't Arlynn baseball but Earthside ball.

The king-size bed on the far right of the room called to me. It wasn't that late in the day, but with everything going on a nap would be great. And since it's Caden's room, it was reasonable to lay on his bed.

"Caden, you're home. I was worried sick. Sit, sit. Tell me everything." A man walked out of the bathroom door. It had to be Gramps, which made this his room, not Caden's.

The older gentleman was not what I had expected. I

thought he would be elderly and fragile. This man stood tall, had minimal gray hair, and was pretty attractive for someone called Gramps. Naming him Big John made sense. Although Caden had many of his features, this man was extremely muscular like Liam. His hands were huge. I had no doubt he could crush boulders with them.

"Hey, Gramps. Looking good." Caden pulled him into a hug.

"Hey, Big John. Missed you," Penny said as Gramps pulled away from Caden. Then she jumped into his arms. Was that a tear trying to fall from her eye?

As he pulled away from Penny, Liz went into a full breakdown on what she knew. We had filled her in on everything, hoping she may have had any clue about the memories, or Savvy or The Order. She didn't know anything, but she reiterated it all to Gramps.

"You kids have put yourselves in a pickle." Big John sat and rubbed his chin.

I like him. Ginger leapt from my arms into Big John's lap. He rubbed her fur and nuzzled into her. Two more cats came from under the bed, one a bright orange and the other gray. Both looked like they had never skipped a meal. Ginger would fit right in.

"Do you know anything about where they keep the memories? Caden said you were in The Order." I rocked on my heels. Sitting down, this man was the same height as me standing. He was a few inches taller than Caden which made him more intimidating.

Big John's eyes widened. It was as if he just realized I was in the room. He shook his head then cocked it to the side. "You are?"

"Harmony Laverack. Do you know me?"

He kept his eyes on me. "Oh. No. Um, where do they

keep what?" Big John rubbed his chin.

"Gramps, the memories. The Order takes them from the witches in the program. Do you know where they store them?" Caden repeated my question.

"Yes, but that memory business is new. In my time, we crushed our enemies with our bare hands. Well, I did. Strength is my affinity." Big John held up his massive paw. The cats purred and rubbed against him for attention. "Anyway, I do know people, and they say the glass the memories are held in is actually steel."

Caden and Penny gasped. What had he said? Did it matter that it was made of steel? I cared about what was inside, not the bottle.

"In Arlynn, if you want anything made from steel there's one man you go to. He's the best. His affinity has grown to where he can weld anything with the tiniest amount of steel. The bottle being made from that makes it unbreakable," Liz rambled.

"So?" I still wasn't getting it.

"Koki Wren has the best steel affinity in Arlynn," Penny said, smirking. "And he's my father. We actually have a lead."

Wow. So cool. It made sense her father would be the best. She toted katanas and throwing knives. Her affinity was steel, so of course her dad had it too. I would have to look into genetics when it came to affinities. Not now, but in the future. Like if Caden and I ever had a baby, would they be truth detectors, animalist, or something different?

"Precisely. You guys must stay the night and catch me up on your past year. And in the morning you can leave," Big John said.

Knock.

"Liz, hide the girl," Big John whispered.

She grabbed my hand and ran us into the wall. Had I had time to complain I would have, and loudly, but the girl was so fast. One second we were in the room, the next we were part of the decor.

When we hit the drywall, tingles ran up my body. Vomit pooled in my throat and I was dragged deeper into the wall. Once inside, she turned me around, her hand always touching mine. We could see inside the room. This girl really had the coolest affinity.

"Come in," Big John called out.

Chapter 32

IN WALKED THE three men responsible for what happened to me. The Order leaders. Seeing them in person made me hate them even more. This was all their fault. They sauntered in as though they owned the castle. Smug assholes.

"Prince Caden Perry and Penny Wren, you are to come with us for questioning," Rat Man demanded.

Caden and Penny nodded. Their faces were distorted from looking through a wall to see them, but they looked scared.

Wittama, or whatever their leader's name was, looked around. "Let me guess, you also lost your charge, Prince Caden?"

"Sir, she ran away. She got scared when she saw how deserted Arlynn is. Why is that?" Caden asked. Was he trying to change the subject?

"The Unkindness are running amok all over Arlynn,"

Big John said. "They said their leader, Ember Raven, disappeared and we, the good people, will pay for it. Savages. As for my grandson, he isn't going with you." Big John stood and walked toward them. His size alone would be enough to intimidate, but the scowl on his face petrified me.

"Mister Perry, as you are retired, it would be best if you relaxed and didn't concern yourself with our ways. You remember how we handle things, don't you?" Rat Man stared him down.

My heart pounded. Could they hear it? Why was Big John so angry with The Order? He was one of them, wouldn't he be on their side? Why did it matter if Caden and Penny went with them? Would they kill them?

Big John sat back on the edge of his bed. The cats snuggled into him. He waved the men off as if to dismiss them. He backed down so quickly. Why? He seemed like the type of person to stick up for himself.

The men turned and walked out of the room with Penny and Caden following. Caden stopped, turned in the direction of where I was hiding and winked. Once they were gone, Liz pulled me out of the wall. I knelt and coughed. Shit, I hope they didn't hear that. I covered my mouth trying to suppress the noise.

"Nice job, Gramps. Your whole crazy talk works every time with them. They totally forgot about Harmony. And once Penny and Caden pass their lie detector test, they'll be back here and we can go to Penny's parents," Liz rambled. How did she breathe?

"Lie detector test? I'm confused by all of what just happened." I stood tall and stretched my arms above my head to open the airway.

"They were gonna take them no matter what I said. But by me challenging them they forgot about you. At least for now. As far as the test, they use people like Caden to make sure he told the truth about you running away." Big John pulled a kitty treat from his pocket. Ginger snatched it up. She would eat cat food for him, but not me.

"But I didn't run away."

"Right, well you're gonna have to. Then I can call him, say you did. And that way he won't be lying. Unless you want him to be punished, which is up to and including death."

If he said anything else I didn't hear it. I had decided to stop running and now I was being asked to run. The irony was not lost on me. Would they kill a prince? They fuck with people's lives for fun, so it wouldn't surprise me.

I rubbed my hands against my face. I had to leave. I would do anything for Caden, even take off in a brand new land. Fuck where would I go? I didn't even know how to get out of the castle. Big John could just lie and say I did. No, Caden would be able to tell. Shit.

Liz bounced on her heels. She wasn't much younger than me, maybe a year or two, but she seemed years younger. Maybe it was the bubbly, happy demeanor she wore so well. That only comes from never having struggled. Never having been through anything traumatic. She was a princess in a castle filled with magic. And I was jealous.

"If we go right now, Mom and Dad won't even notice me gone. What have you seen of Arlynn? I can show you the beaches. They were so great before The Unkindness made people fear leaving their homes. Oh, or we could go down into the village and help make blankets for people at the Center." Liz ticked off all her ideas on her fingers.

"No," Big John and I said simultaneously.

"You have never been here. I'm going with you. I can show you where to go and from there you can run away." Liz's voice went from cheerful to demanding.

I didn't want to put her in danger. She seemed like nothing bad had ever happened to her and I attracted bad shit, from summoning animals to having Vera try and kill me. I was a walking disaster. This sweet angel should not be going with me anywhere. If anything happens to her Caden would never forgive me.

Yet, I didn't have much of a choice. She was right, I didn't know where anything was. Fuck. This better go smoothly. I would have her get me out of the castle and far enough away, then demand she go back. My stomach turned; this wasn't a good idea.

I nodded, giving in. Liz jumped up and down, hugging me. She was a few inches taller, so she shoved her chest into my face. Awkward. I pulled away from her and looked over at Ginger. She had fallen asleep on Big John's lap. She had been scared to come to Arlynn, but she found someone she felt safe around. At least that's what it looked like. I asked Big John to take care of her until I returned. He stroked her back and told me to take care of his granddaughter.

Liz guided me out of the castle. Every time she heard footsteps she would pull me into a wall. The sickening feeling of becoming translucent never went away. Somehow she stayed upbeat as we snuck out.

On the way, she whispered to me about everything that had been going on in the last year. The Unkindness leader disappeared about a year ago. Which must have been when Vera came looking for me. When they both vanished, the followers became ballsy. They started attacking witches in the middle of towns.

It had been a real mess for The Order. They tried rounding up as many Unkindness as they could but they didn't have the manpower to keep up. Liz commented that sending their newest recruits Earthside for The Witches Protection Program may not have been their smartest plan. I agreed with her on that.

Since The Unkindness attacks, many witches stayed home. That's why Arlynn was no longer the loving, bustling place it once was. Liz has tried to bring it back to life; she plants flowers, paints over the graffiti, and tries to set up gatherings. But she's one person and it hasn't worked out yet.

I was impressed with her determination to try. She could stay in the castle, hidden and safe. Instead she keeps sneaking out to try and help. Her parents aren't thrilled with her plan and believed The Order would fix it. So far they hadn't.

We reached outside the castle and Liz started rambling, "We could check out the high school. They're on summer vacation. Oh, or the ponds. No, you should see The Fairy Museum."

"No. You need to go back inside," I demanded.

"Not happening. Oh, what about the beach?"

My mind went to the vision I had while Nurse Dara tried to recover my memories. The Order held them in the bottle and sand had scratched my skin. I could have been on a beach when they captured me. And then they transferred me to wherever I was in the memory.

"No beach," I replied. Going into town didn't seem like a great idea. The Order was looking for me. Being in plain view wasn't smart. We had to find somewhere we could hide and I could hopefully convince Liz to go back to the castle.

"We could go for a hike. The hills are gorgeous. And no one goes there." Liz turned her direction away from town and toward the hills in front of us.

Chapter 33

LIZ WAS FILLED with so much energy. She skipped and bounced up the hills. I trudged. My side hurt, a fairy buzzed around my head, and the plastic in the flip flops was digging into my toes. This was a terrible idea.

I wished I'd had more time to prepare. The headache began in the right temple and worked its way across my brain. I didn't want to blame Liz, but she didn't stop talking. The entire walk. Most of what she said flew past my mind and didn't stick.

The hiking trail curved in and out of a forest. The trees' bright yellow leaves hung low to provide a decent amount of shade. When the trail led out of the forest, the sun beat on my unprotected skin. Liz didn't seem bothered at all.

I should have ditched her as soon as we got out of the castle. I wasn't even sure how long I would have to be gone. Technically, Big John only had to believe I was running away so Caden could tell the truth. Did that mean I could return immediately? Was it even safe to return at all?

"Is it not gorgeous? I love hiking. Doesn't it make your body feel great? Want to race? So I was thinking, if you and my brother get married we would be sisters. I don't have a sister. I would love to be related to you. Oh, up ahead there's a bench and you can see the ocean. It's beautiful." Liz jogged backwards as she talked to me.

I did have a sister and I had no clue what she was like. This girl wore way too much pink and didn't know when to stop, but she would be nice to have as family. Because yes she was slightly annoying, but she left the castle with me so I wasn't alone. She was nice to have around, even if my head pounded from the pain.

By the time we reached the bench I was hunched over. My entire body was pissed at me. My toes were rubbed raw from the flip flops. The bruises on my side made it hard to breathe; I really hoped I didn't have broken ribs. I was sure I didn't, but the sharp pains made me second guess myself.

I sat down and Liz pulled a small hot pink change purse from her pocket. She reached her hand inside and yanked out two bottles of water. The purse had the same magic as Penny's fanny pack.

"Miss Wren, Penny's mom, made it for me. It's amazing how much you could fit in one of these. She has an affinity for fabric and makes these cool purses. Oh, I should see if she can make you one. Then you wouldn't have to lug that bag around." Liz pulled out a couple of granola bars and tossed me one. As she talked and talked, I pulled my journal out. I wrote a few sentences about Arlynn. I tried to write more but I couldn't stop thinking about the pain. A bubble bath and sleep for five days would do wonders for my body. Even an ice soak and aspirin would work.

"When do you think Caden and Penny will be back? Do you think we could go back after they returned?" I had debated taking off so they all stayed safe, but running away has gotten me nowhere.

"I'm not sure. We should probably stay the night here. Sometimes those question things last long. I could set up camp. Or we could go to my bestie's house, Audra, or we could sneak back into the castle," Liz replied.

"Do you have any sleeping bags in that change purse?" Penny would have them if she was here.

"No. But I have a couple of pillows and a blanket. We could share. An outdoor sleepover, so cool. I should call Audra and see if she wants to join. She could bring more stuff for us. Oh I have some bandages and aspirin. I noticed your feet. You poor thing." Liz pulled out a bright pink blanket from her purse.

We were still on the trail and camping out in the open wasn't a smart idea. I went back into the forest to see if there was a clearing. Sneaking back into the castle was the smartest idea, but The Order would be back. I couldn't risk it.

My feet stung with every step. There had to be some magical fix. This shit sucked. A few steps into the woods was a beautiful clearing. Purple moss covered the ground, and a few mushrooms popped up near bright orange and yellow flowers. It was beautiful and looked like something out of Wonderland.

Liz came up behind me, nodding. For a brief moment I expected her to warn me about poisonous plants and bugs. But nope, she agreed it was perfect. Then she pulled out her phone to call her bestie. I reminded her we were on the run, even if only for a day.

The moss was soft and squished between my toes; my flip flops had been kicked off and tossed in my purse. Liz and I stretched out the blanket and set up the pillows. She rambled the whole time about how much her bestie would love this adventure. I tried to be involved in the conversation, but luckily I don't think she noticed how little I talked.

Then she did the sweetest thing. She bandaged up my feet for me. I hadn't expected that and it made me regret getting annoyed by her. She explained that part of her princess classes was first aid, because no princess should be left without knowledge. I thanked her and lay down. She didn't have an extra blanket so hopefully the night would stay warm. If not, she and I would be doing some cuddling. Or we were gonna be sleeping on the moss and using the blanket to cover up.

I lay on my back and watched the yellow leaves swaying in the breeze. Clouds danced in the shape of witches. They literally danced. One puffy cloud was a man that twirled a tiny cloud of a smaller man. It was like a dream.

A group of what looked like birds with lion tails flew by. They crashed into the clouds, breaking them apart. Once they passed, the clouds reformed and danced again. It was beautiful.

Liz rambled about the different types of clouds. She had only seen snowy ones twice in her lifetime. The fact that they get any snow fascinated me since they're on the equator. But magic has different rules, I guess.

"So, this woman who is after me thinks your parents kill everyone that doesn't agree with them. Why is that?" I might as well get as much info from her as I can.

"Oh no. My parents would never hurt anyone. That Vera woman, I hate her. You said she's The Unkindness leader, right? It was Ember Raven originally, and my family hated her. Vera is worse, she's the murderer. Have my parents put a few witches in jail? Yes. But they deserve it. And the jail is great. It's an island off the far end of Arlynn. They basically do what they want, they just can't leave or have magic. Totally nice way of doing things. They would never hurt anyone."

She continued to explain how amazing her parents were. Stripping people of their magic and tossing them onto a different island they can't leave didn't seem nice. At least not if they did it for disagreeing with them. That was harsh. Regular crimes, sure. But according to Liz they only have one sentence. Forever. No matter the crime.

A dark shadow blocked my view. I squinted and Liz squeaked. Someone stood above us blocking out the sun.

Fuck.

"Hello. Have you changed your mind about helping me?" Vera's voice pierced my heart.

Two arms yanked me to my feet. Liz was pulled to hers as well. She didn't have time to hide. Shit. This was not good. Caden was going to kill me. If Vera didn't beat him to it. I struggled against the arms holding me.

"Seriously, how did you find me?"

"Your face is well known among our people. You were spotted. I told you we are friends." Vera cupped my face in her bony hand.

"We are not friends and never will be." I pulled my

face out of her grip.

"Oh, we are. Men, bring the girls and their belongings. That blanket is so charming. I'm sure her parents would love to know we have the princess.

Chapter 34

THE MEN DRAGGED LIZ and myself out of the woods. It was the first time she hadn't said a word. My headache should have gone away, but instead it got worse. I wanted to rip Vera's eyes out for scaring Liz. I ground my teeth.

A man stood by the bench and we were pulled over to him. Vera placed her hand on his shoulder. The men holding us pushed us close together so everyone was touching. Vera nodded at the man.

Whoosh.

It was worse than being pulled into a wall. My body was being ripped apart molecule by molecule. Then every ounce of me was placed back together. The pain in my side intensified as I reformed. One second I was standing by the bench, the next I was in an office.

There was a desk by the side with bookshelves lining

the walls. Thick black curtains covered the windows. A black and red carpet covered the floor. On the desk was a skull of what might have been a small animal, or maybe a child. A wine glass sat on a coaster with a thick red liquid inside.

Vera walked around and sat in the leather chair. Of course this was her office, it screamed Evil Bitch. She took a sip from the wine glass and smiled. Ugh, was that blood?

The man that had whooshed us here sat in a blue chair in the corner. He patted his forehead with a napkin. He may have an awesome power but it seemed to take a toll on him.

Liz whimpered next to me. Fuck. I clenched my fists. I had to get her out of here. A man grabbed my hands and placed them behind me, tying them with rope. I looked over and he repeated the process with Liz.

There had to be something I could do. I thought of all the animals I could possibly summon. We were in a house of some sort; I didn't think I could get one in here. Maybe I could have one charge through the wall. Were dinosaurs a thing here? I shook my head. What is wrong with me?

"Her father has been taking my men and killing them. For some reason you refuse to help me. Now I am taking away your choice. You will help." Vera dabbed at her mouth with a napkin.

"He doesn't kill them, you evil bitch. He puts them in jail where they belong. And so do you. You are their leader, tell them to stop hunting witches. Look at what Arlynn has become." Liz's voice quivered. Damn, good for her.

"Oh, sweet child, I'm not their leader. Not really. I am stepping in until their true leader returns. If she would get her head out of her ass and help me. Your people stole her memories and now she's a scared child who keeps running away!" Vera stepped around the desk and sat on it.

No. No. There was no way. She made it sound like me. And that wasn't possible. I wasn't their leader. Spencer had said my sister helped take my memories to protect me. Could she have been protecting me from myself? Vera has been claiming we were friends. The only way I would be friends with her was if I was evil.

Arlynn has been in turmoil since The Unkindness leader left. The members have been running rampant, destroying everything and people. I was taken a year ago. No. I'm good. I'm not evil. I'm not. I can't be.

Vera pointed at a woman that had been in the room when we arrived. She walked over and yanked my shirt down to expose my collar bone. Her hand covered the space between my breast and my collar.

When she removed her hand, a black raven tattoo appeared. The same one they all wore. It had to be a trick. I wasn't evil.

"Ember Raven, leader of The Unkindness and the most powerful witch I have ever met." Vera bowed to me.

No. Caden told me how evil she was. That wasn't me. It wasn't possible. Could that be what my memories contained? An evil witch?

"She's too good to be Ember Raven!" Liz shouted. At least she didn't believe it was me.

"Your people fucked with her mind. Made her a little blonde girl with a whole bunch of insecurities. The Order did a number on you." Vera sat at the desk again. "Take them away. Let Ember—oh, Harmony—think on this. Not that she has a choice anymore. I only need her magic and I finally have a way to get it."

We were dragged out of the room. I refused to lift my feet. It took two men to pull me down the hall. When we reached the stairs they had to carry me. We were brought to a room with two chairs in the center and they tied us there and left.

My name is Harmony Laverack. I am twenty-two years old. My parents died before I could remember their faces. I was placed in foster home after foster home. My name is Harmony Laverack. I am not this Ember Raven person.

Liz chatted in the distance. I am not Ember Raven.

She continued to talk. I didn't listen. I'm not that girl. I'm not.

Hours passed. Over and over I repeated, I am Harmony Laverack.

Of course I knew I had to be somebody before they fucked with my memories. I had assumed I was a big fat nobody. It would match who I was now. Not to mention I'm young. Like too young to be leading a group of crazy rebels hellbent on taking out the king. Which also happens to be my boyfriend's dad.

Ugh, Caden. How was I going to tell him? He was going to hate me.

"Just because some woman tells you that you're someone else, doesn't mean you are. Even if you are Ember Raven, that's not you now. Plus who is to say you're that bad? So let's say you are her. Which I doubt. But if you are. So what? You couldn't have been that bad. The Unkindness didn't go crazy until you left. For years they weren't even a threat. They would do a few rallies in the streets and demand democracy. That's about it," Liz whispered to me.

She could be right. I might not be Ember, but I might

be. And if I was, then maybe I wasn't that bad. Arlynn was being destroyed because I was gone. If I was her. Either way, I was given one option on what to do next. I had to get my memories back and take them. Wow, I was actually buying this story.

I didn't know if I would remember who I am now, but this land needed me. Caden, Penny, Big John, Ginger, and Liz needed me. They deserved to live in a safe place. Whoever I was before had the key to fixing this. Vera seemed to think I was gonna help her destroy the king. Nope. I was gonna take down The Unkindness.

Would my memories of Harmony remain when I got the old ones back? Even if I forgot Harmony, she would still be there. I would have to pull her to the surface somehow. Unless I remembered myself, then it wouldn't matter. Ugh this was all so confusing.

"Can you blend out of these ropes?" I asked Liz. I wasn't sure how her magic worked but it seemed to make sense that she could.

"No. I can get us through the wall if I could get out of these ropes." Liz grunted and tried to pull her hands free.

Shit. We had to get out of here. I just didn't know how.

The door opened. One of Vera's goons from the beach came strolling in, the one with the raven tattoos on his hands. I wanted to kick him in the teeth. He walked over to me and placed his beefy hands on my arms.

My body tingled. My skin was being pulled at. I screamed. My veins pulsed and I kicked at him. Fuck, I convulsed. Thousands of volts ran through me.

Liz yelled at him.

"If you would sit still this wouldn't hurt so bad," the

man pleaded with me. "I don't want to do this. Vera is forcing me."

"Fuck you." I spat at him.

A big fat boogery loogie landed on his eye. He wiped his face and left the room.

Whatever he was trying to do to me hurt. I couldn't handle much more pain. Liz yanked at her rope again, whispering that we had to leave before he came back.

A brown mouse scuttled into the corner of the room. Perfect.

Chapter 35

"HEY, LITTLE MOUSEY, can you help me out?" I whispered.

No. The mouse went back to licking the brick wall. Weird.

"I'll feed you meatballs." It worked on Ginger. Not sure if it would for this creature, but it was worth a shot. I didn't know what that man was trying to do, but it was as if he was pulling my magic from me. When he returned I would be in trouble.

Liz chimed in, "You could live in the castle with us. Food would be brought to you daily. My Gramps would carry you in his pocket. You could sleep in my room. Please help us. I'll sew you little pants."

"See, you can have pants if you help us," I added trying not to laugh as I spoke.

The brown mouse scuttled over to me and climbed

up my leg. He sat on my lap and spoke in my mind, *I could use some pants. What do you want me to do*?

"Chew at the ropes around my hands," I begged.

Mice are used for other things besides chewing, he huffed.

"Please," Liz and I begged.

He went around to my backside and chewed at the ropes. Thankfully. He pulled and gnawed.

"Faster," I demanded. I didn't know when Vera's henchmen would be back.

Shush or I will stop. Pants aren't that important to me. He nibbled at my finger, but then he managed to loosen my left hand.

I yanked it free and stood. The rope slithered off the other hand as I went over to Liz and yanked at her ropes.

Footsteps.

Fuck.

I pulled harder.

"Please hurry," Liz begged.

The mouse jumped up and chewed. We got her loose.

A key slid into the door.

Liz grabbed my hand. The mouse crawled up my sweatpants and into my pocket.

The hinges creaked.

Someone screamed.

We ran at the wall. The grossness of going through the wall hit me. Fresh air. We were free.

And falling. Shit.

The air whipped past me fast. Liz held onto my hand as we fell. Arlynn was an island but I was shocked when the waves crashed against the shore below us. Vera's house was on the edge of a cliff. Liz and I were falling toward the ocean below. Why am I constantly getting wet? I belly flopped into the water and Liz's hand slipped from mine.

A very angry mouse screamed at me, trying to get out of my pocket. I went under. Kicking hard, I pushed toward the surface. Air filled my lungs. Yes. I swam, looking for the shore. Something bit my side. Ouch.

I dug my hand in my pocket and pulled the mouse free. He crawled up my arm to the top of my head.

You idiot. Who jumps from a house on a cliff? Did you not know about the ocean? Had I known this was your plan I wouldn't have come. Idiot, the mouse yelled at me. Like I needed his crap.

The shore was a small patch of sand. Even if any of Vera's goons looked down, there was no way they could see us. We were so far below and hidden from view. I swam.

Liz was nowhere. Fuck. A wave crashed down, pulling me under again. The mouse grabbed my hair, almost yanking it out. I swam to the surface again. Still no Liz. What if she couldn't swim?

The mouse screamed at me for still being in the water. I swam to the shore and when I reached the beach, which wasn't much wider than me, Mousey scuttled down my body to the ground.

I searched the waters for any sign of Liz. I didn't want to scream in case the men after us could hear me. But how long could Liz survive? I jumped into the water again.

The waves calmed. There was no extra movement in the waters. Shit. I dove under and opened my eyes. Nothing. We had fallen together. When did our hands unlatch? I scanned everywhere.

There was a part of the cliff that stuck out further than

the rest where it touched the water. I couldn't see the other side of it. I swam towards it. She had to be over there.

On the other side, straddling a tree branch that stuck out, was a girl wrapped in pink. Liz. She was alive. My heart warmed.

"I can't swim!" she screamed.

"You live on an island." I swam over and put my back to her. "Climb on, I'll swim you to shore."

"I live on the island, not in the water. Too many creatures in the ocean. Caden's the only one of us that can swim. Gramps taught him. Guess it's one of The Order's requirements. Why are you swimming this way? The coast is closer that way." The silence while she was scared for her life was gone.

"The mouse is this way. We made a deal with him," I shouted over the crashing waves.

We reached the part with the mouse and Liz climbed off my back. She was already rambling. I hadn't even caught my breath.

You promised me a castle and pants. Let's go. No more water. The mouse climbed up my arm into my sweatpants. *You have a rock in your pocket. Why?*

The crystal from Nurse Dara. I had been carrying it with me. I placed my hand in my sweatpants and pulled it out. I put it in my other pocket so the mouse didn't scratch it up. I wouldn't be able to get another one from Nurse Dara. She swore I would see her again, I wasn't so sure.

"Fuck, my purse is back at the hiking trail. I didn't grab it." My journal was in there.

"Oh, I grabbed it. I knew it was too much trouble to lug that thing around. It's in my coin purse. And the best part, the inside is waterproof. So even though I almost drowned, nothing got wet. I can carry it till we go back home. I know we're supposed to be on the run, but I'm over running away."

I nodded. It had caused more problems than it solved. Ha. I must have swallowed too much ocean water to think that.

There appeared to be no way up off the small beach. We were on a tiny stretch of sand that traveled its way down the entire coast. My feet squished in the sand. The flip flops were tearing into my feet, but at least when I had them on I had some protection.

We trudged. The sun beat down on our skin. Every time I had thought it was the worst pain I felt, something else had happened to me. Whatever that man tried to do to me was the worst. At least for now. Rocks would probably come crashing down the hill and crush me. Ugh.

"It was a transporter that flashed us to that nasty lady's house, so we could be anywhere in Arlynn right now. I don't know how we're gonna get home. Do you think this ends? Oh right, it's your first time here. I wish I had extra shoes for you, but mine are wet. I think I'm gonna take them off and match you," Liz rambled.

Does she ever stop talking? Mousey chirped. His face poked out, probably because my clothes were still soaked.

Crabs in all colors popped in and out of the sand. They looked the same as the ones back home on the television except for the cool colors. I wanted to take a bright purple one and keep it, but the pinchers scared me.

We walked for hours. Liz somehow ran out of things to say. Or her mouth was so dry words wouldn't come out. If we didn't find a way up soon we were gonna be sleeping in the sand with the crabs.

The cliff pushed out into the water again and the sand stopped. I couldn't tell how much water we would have to swim through till we hopefully got to sand again. Not to mention I would have to carry Liz and Mousey.

"Nope. I'm not. There has to be some other way," Liz cried.

"I get that you're scared, but we don't have a choice. We can't sleep here." I pointed to a group of three crabs fighting with each other.

Liz opened her coin purse for Mousey to chill in. I warned him if he touches my purse our deal is off. No castle life for him. Liz climbed onto my back and I went into the water. Fuck, everything hurt.

The waters had calmed and swimming was easy, aside from the person on my back and the pain all over. For a brief second I thought of summoning an animal to help. Nope, that had gone poorly last time.

I swam close to the cliff side but far out enough so I could see if there was a shore. Liz clenched onto me. She stayed silent, thankfully. Up ahead was an alcove and the cliff separated to leave a small safe space.

We reached the alcove. It reminded me of a cave but didn't go deep into the land. There was a trail up the side. Yes. A way up.

Liz climbed off of me and I followed her up the trail. Tiny rocks sliced into the bottom of my feet. Of course. Why not have more pain? I was reaching my limit. So much of my body ached that I wasn't sure which part was the worst.

Halfway up the trail Liz reached into her little purse and pulled out a phone. Really!

"You have a phone!" I yelled. We could have called

for help hours ago.

"Yeah, but service is spotty. It doesn't work that far down. I'm gonna call Gramps. See if he can send help. The transporters will all snitch. And now that I know who you are... Well, that won't work." Liz held her phone toward the sky. She still didn't have service.

We walked further up the trail. Every few minutes she checked for service. Luckily she kept Mousey in her coin purse. She talked enough, I couldn't handle him as well.

My eyes stung. The wet clothes rubbed against my skin. My feet were numb. The sharp pain in my side intensified. Tingles ran up my arms. I had no idea how I kept moving.

Liz did a little jump and quickly dialed a number. What should have been a quick conversation took her way longer to explain. I sat down. This could take forever.

Little shards of rock, sand, and maybe glass, stuck into my feet and mixed with bits of blood. I shouldn't have sat down. I didn't know if I was going to be able to get back up.

Liz stomped her foot as she talked on the phone. "I don't know where we are. I'm all wet... A beach? Fine."

She clicked off her phone and walked up the trail again.

I pushed myself up. My body screamed to stop. "You gonna explain?"

"We have to reach the top so I can find a place to tell them where we are. Caden and Penny were screaming in the background. They're pissed. I was trying to help," she cried.

"This is my fault, not yours. You did amazing. You even yelled at Vera. That takes a really strong person."

I grabbed her hand and walked up the trail with her. We reached the top before I even realized it. In the far distance, the castle rose above all the buildings. A small town with all blue buildings was to the left of us. To the right were mountains.

Liz clicked on her phone. "We're by the ski resort."

"I thought it rarely snows?" I asked.

"We have magic. It's not real snow."

A few feet away, three people appeared from thin air. Penny, Caden and a gentleman in a black suit with a red undershirt. I guessed he was the royal transporter Liz didn't want Gramps to call.

Caden ran to me. He scooped me into his arms and I didn't argue. I nestled my head in the crook of his shoulder.

Chapter 36

THE HAIR ON MY head hurt. My elbows and side were on fire. A loud humming noise pounded against my skull. My stomach rumbled. Ugh, I had to poop. I ran my hand along my body. It was still all there. Barely.

The humming grew louder, people were talking. I was in a bed somewhere. Flashes of the water, Liz, Mousey, Vera, rocks on my feet. Man, I had taken a beating. Gurgle, I had to get up and go to the bathroom.

I peeled my eyes open. Bright lights stung. I shut them again. Penny, Caden, and Liz talked to me. A million questions flew at once. None of that mattered. If I didn't get up and go to the bathroom... well, hopefully I didn't get to that point.

Pushing up with my hands, I tried to sit.

"No, don't move. The healer will be here soon." Caden pushed on my shoulder.

"I gotta go tinkle." I swatted his hand. Swinging my legs off the bed, I placed my feet on the ground. I pushed up and swayed into Caden. My body was not obeying me. Gurgle.

"We will take her," Penny said. She pointed at Liz to grab one side of me. They locked their arms in mine and half dragged, half let me stumble, to the bathroom.

Luckily it wasn't far. I wouldn't have made it if it was any further. They helped me sit and turned away as I did my business.

Someone had dressed me in a baggy t-shirt that smelled of electricity and earth; Caden. It was his shirt. That same someone, which I was really hoping was Caden, had put me in fresh underwear. Since I didn't smell like seaweed, I assumed he had also bathed me.

Once I was finished, they helped me off the toilet, guided me to the sink and held me while I washed my hands. I glanced in the mirror. "What the fuck!"

Caden barged in. "What's wrong?"

"I have bangs? Why do I have bangs?" Before today, I had long pieces in the front that constantly fell out of my ponytail. But now, there were short straight-across bangs. Shit. I had multiple cuts along my face as well, but that was expected.

"Sorry. I didn't want to. But you had seaweed tangled in the front. And some in the back. I was able to blend the back a little better. And the bangs look better on your face. It covers your forehead. Not that it's huge, but it is a little on the bigger side. I did the best I could," Liz rambled.

She kept talking as I pulled away from her. My new haircut was the least of my issues. And she was right, it did cover up my forehead. Caden took over for Penny and Liz, scooping me up. I was in too much pain to protest.

Traveling to Arlynn had kicked my ass. Then reaching here, I got beat up some more. This may have been my worst idea yet. I should have stayed in Philly. As much as I wished I had, I knew being here was where I was meant to be. I had to get my memories.

Witch, you look like something I hacked up. Ginger leapt onto the bed as Caden lay me down.

At least she didn't ask for food.

Knock, knock. My headache increased. I wanted to go back to sleep and not wake up until my body was healed. Which could be a year or so.

A balding man with a hairy mole on his cheek shuffled into the room. He wore shorts with palm trees and a white tank top. The outfit seemed better suited to a teenage surfer dude.

He grabbed a chair from a table in the corner of the room. It screeched as it was dragged across the room. Penny and Liz stayed a few feet away. Caden sat on the bed and held my hand.

"I'm Doug. Sorry I was late. I was needed somewhere else." Doug sat in the chair.

Memories of when I healed the dog flashed in my mind. The pain in my hands. The burning. I couldn't put this man through that.

"No. I don't want you to heal me." I know it came out so rude, but I didn't want him to feel pain for my benefit.

Doug placed his hands on me, one on my side and the other on my hip. Shivers ran through my veins. Currents trickled up and down my arms. Warm waves cascaded across my skin. Heat rolled from him into every atom of my body.

For a moment, I was on a beach. The sun beat down on my skin. Children laughed in the distance. Boats floated on the surface. Palm trees rose in the distance. It was happiness. It was joy.

The pain was gone.

He removed his hands and clenched. My pain was now his. It wasn't fair. He shouldn't be hurting for me, yet he gave me no choice. I was grateful, but the cost was too much.

"Thank you. But you shouldn't have," I whispered.

"My gift is to help people. I will help as many as possible. The burn in my hands is worth it." Doug stood and walked out the room.

Caden chased after him and tried to give the man money, but he pushed the purple bills away. Arlynn has purple money, that's weird. The man shook his head, mumbling something about going surfing, and left.

My body was better than before. I sat and twisted my hips. Lifting my shirt, I looked for the bruise. I should have been embarrassed, but these people just helped me poop. Boundaries didn't exist anymore. The bruise on my side was gone.

I pulled the neckline of the shirt down. The pain, scratches and bruises had all disappeared. But not everything on my body had.

The fucking tattoo was still there.

"Yeah, I was gonna ask you about that." Caden sat in the chair Doug had dragged over.

I looked at Liz and she shrugged. She hadn't said anything. I had expected her to, the girl does talk a lot. But had she mentioned the tattoo he would have known who I was and why the tattoo was there. Now I had to tell him. Shit.

"Um, it's a long story. And I will explain, but we have to get to Penny's parents and find out what they know about the bottle." I was stalling. How was I going to explain to him I'm Ember Raven?

Penny reached into her fanny pack and pulled out black leggings, a black tank top, and a killer bad-chick, black leather jacket. Then she topped it off with matching leather boots. This girl even dressed like danger and I loved it. I had no style. Jeans and t-shirts were my go to, unless I was in sweatpants. I could never pull off something so cool.

"Put these on." Penny handed me the outfit. Whoa, I got to dress like her.

I grabbed the clothes and went to change. Liz and Penny had seen enough of me. And I didn't want anyone to see the raven tattoo again. I was embarrassed by it. There was still a tiny part of me wishing it wasn't real. That it was an illusion. Well, more like all of me was wishing that, but I knew it was the truth.

The boots were a tad big on me, but they wouldn't go flopping off. Everything else was skin tight. Penny was taller and skinnier than me. Luckily she had leggings or I wouldn't be able to wear her pants. I ran my hands against my legs; I didn't need a mirror to know I looked like a badass chick. Hopefully I wouldn't end up in the ocean again.

Caden was in the bedroom asking Liz what had happened. She remained silent. I was impressed. She could have told him everything. After all they were family, I was some girl she met a few days ago.

"I'm Ember Raven," I said as I reentered the room.

Penny and Caden's mouths dropped.

"I know. Impossible. All I know about her is that she's the leader of The Unkindness. From the looks on your faces, you guys know a lot more. Well, that's me. So I still hope you guys help me find my memories. And don't hate me." I grabbed my purse from a nearby table. I couldn't believe how straightforward and ballsy I sounded. Who was I becoming?

"No fucking way, you can't be her," Caden replied.

Chapter 37

THE PURPLE-COLORED brick house stood out against the vibrant red houses. Had Penny not stopped here, I would have kept on walking; she couldn't live here. As a prince's best friend, I had assumed her life and house was beyond extravagant. But from the look of the house, I was wrong.

The inside was charming and warm. Colorful throws were on every piece of furniture in the living room. Blues, greens, yellows, pinks, and browns all clashed and yet fit. Penny's mom had an affinity for fabric and obviously used it to make plenty of blankets.

Before we left the castle, Liz filled in Penny and Caden on everything that happened at Vera's, including the discovery of my identity. Once I admitted who I was, she rambled a mile a minute. The girl didn't miss a detail. She even showed them Mousey, who had made a home in her change purse.

Caden and Penny didn't believe it. They figured Vera was lying to me and somehow put a tattoo on me. They believed she would do anything to get my magic. I admitted that it sounded crazy, but I believed it.

We all agreed to put the discussion on hold until we could find my memories. Because that's what mattered. Vera wanted what was inside that bottle, so we had to get to it first. During the conversation, I left out the part about me taking the memories and trying to save Arlynn from destruction.

A short, dark-haired woman wrapped in multiple skirts and blouses bustled into the room. She pulled Penny into a hug and yelled at her for not eating. Penny's face rose to a bright red. The woman then turned to Caden and squeezed his cheeks.

She saw me and half smiled. I had to be wrong, but she didn't want me there. Her face changed when she guided Penny to sit, and she grinned at her and Caden. Yeah, there was no way she wanted me in her home.

"Momma Cakes, this is Harmony." Penny waved in my direction. "And, Harmony, this is my mom, Mrs. Wren."

"No, that is not Harmony. I know her. Why is she in my home?" Mrs. Wren snapped.

"You know me? How? What was I like?" Aside from Vera, she was the first person I had met that knew me before. I wanted to know what she knew. She might know if I was a good person or not. Granted her reaction to me made it pretty clear she didn't like me.

"Get her out of my home!" Mrs. Wren shouted.

A short stocky man with patches of missing hair scuttled into the room. He smiled when he saw Penny. He must have been her father. Penny was taller than both of her parents, and didn't resemble them much except for skin complexion and hair color. It was none of my business, but I believed she could have been adopted.

"Steel Man, I missed you. Mom is trying to kick out my friend," Penny whined. She even nicknamed her own dad.

"Well, your friend is the leader of The Unkindness and is attempting to overthrow Caden's parents. Do you blame Mom?" Mr. Wren wrapped his arms around Penny and squeezed.

"Sir, we are here to ask about the bottles you made. Harmony doesn't remember who she was and doesn't want to. Even if she is Ember, which she can't be, we need to find her memory bottle before Vera does." Caden stepped forward and shook his hand.

"Oh, she is Ember Raven." Mrs. Wren wiggled her finger at me.

Mr. Wren asked Mrs. Wren to go make some coffee for all of us. He then directed us to sit down. I sat on the sofa closest to the exit, in case Penny's mom freaked out again and forced me to leave. The blue blanket I was closest to was cool to the touch. Penny explained her mom infused heat levels into the blanket. Some were like magical heating blankets, others were magical air conditioners.

When Mrs. Wren returned with the coffee, she had forgotten my cup. I wouldn't have drank it anyway. She didn't seem to like me, and I was afraid of what she would have put in the coffee. She gave me second thoughts on who this Ember Raven was. Or who I was.

Mr. Wren began talking as soon as Penny and Caden settled with their cups of coffee. He started at the beginning, when The Unkindness started taking witches. A few years ago, eight to be exact, the king and queen had heard of a coven of witches out to take them down.

"Their leader was a man who went by the name Blue Raven. The king ordered the execution of him and his family. They managed to kill him, but his family survived the fire and that's when his daughter, Ember, took over. The Unkindness grew stronger. Witches disappeared, presumed dead. For a while, The Order was able to hunt down the coven and toss them in their prison. But no matter their efforts, more and more joined The Unkindness. They were losing control of their people.

"The Order devised a plan, The Witches Protection Program. It was to protect innocent witches and to hide witches they believed to be a part of The Unkindness. If the people knew they were taking memories, well they wouldn't have allowed it. So they lied about the program. Only members of The Order knew the truth. Them and the few people who helped them.

"I was one of those people. Memories are a tricky thing. Once removed, most materials couldn't hold them. They would go right back into the witches they were taken from. So the king asked me for help. I used steel and enchanted it to prevent that from happening. It worked. At first, I didn't know you were one of those people, Ember. But it made sense. It was the best way to keep control of you." Mr. Wren scratched his head.

"But the program is only for a year. What happened when the witches came back? Weren't they upset that their memories were messed with?" I asked.

"I haven't heard of anyone getting their memories back. Not yet. Not until The Order defeats The Unkindness. You guys are the first to return from Earthside." He rubbed his scalp and looked at Penny.

"That's why I didn't want you to go. They told you a year, but I knew it would be longer. Especially when I found out who Caden was guarding."

I wanted to ask so many more questions. I didn't understand why The Order was kidnapping witches and claiming to protect them. They knew who I was when they messed with my memory. If I was so bad why wouldn't they have killed me? Or sent me to their prison?

Mr. Wren continued with his story. "The Order came to me again for another bottle, stronger than all the others he had. It was for Ember Raven's memories. Her sister had come to them asking for help, begging to keep her safe. She had heard rumors of the program and said it was a better fate than prison or death."

The Order must have loved my sister's betrayal.

"But, after Ember Raven left, The Unkindness became reckless. Arlynn is being destroyed. People are afraid to leave their homes. Maybe she wasn't the problem," Penny said.

"I believe The Order came to the same conclusion. Which is why they didn't extend your stay Earthside. Penny, your charge is missing, so they needed you back to find her. But, Caden, you had Ember. They want her to control The Unkindness. This version of her without her memories. They believe they can control you, Ember, and, in turn, The Unkindness." Mr. Wren stood and paced.

They were trying to use me as a pawn in their war. Vera was trying the same thing. But I would be no one's toy. Neither would control me. I had other plans. Fuck, I didn't want to believe I was Ember Raven, but if I was, I could help the people of Arlynn on my own terms.

"Do you know where the memories are?" I asked,

trying not to sound desperate.

"No. But a man named Doctor Apples will. He lives in the dark forest. He helped them until they took you, Ember."

"Looks like we're off to see him. Thank you." I stood.

"Guys, I'm not going," Penny said. "I got you this far, but I have to find Savvy. Spencer has been unsuccessful. If she's part of The Unkindness like you, The Order will send her to prison or kill her. She's a good person, she doesn't deserve this."

I wanted to beg her to come with us. She had been by my side this entire journey. Not just that, Penny had become a good friend to me. I opened my mouth to argue with her, then closed it. Savvy needed her and I needed to get my memories. Afraid I would say the wrong thing, I nodded.

Penny smiled and waved goodbye to us.

Chapter 38

THAT WAS A MASSIVE info dump. My brain spun with everything Mr. Wren had told me. I was enraged with The Order and the king and queen. They were stealing witches' memories. No matter the reason, it was wrong. Then they had the nerve to justify it by saying they were protecting people.

All those witches Earthside had no clue who they really were. To top it off, my sister had placed me in the program. Was Ember Raven really that bad? No. Because even The Order had come to the conclusion that they needed her. Me. The memories. I wasn't sure how to look at Ember Raven. She was me, but wasn't me. It was so much to unpack. There were a few things I did know: Vera had to be dealt with and so did The Order. Before I got my memories back. I had a plan, but I didn't think Caden would go along with it. First I needed to locate my memories, because if anyone else got them, they would use them to control me.

Figures now was the time I stop running. It would have been so much easier. I guess I still could. But now I had a family and I had to protect them.

"You can't be Ember Raven. You can't be," Caden mumbled.

We were walking down an empty street. It would have been the perfect time for a run, but I wasn't dressed for it. Nor did I need it to clear my head anymore. I was confused, but my brain was working overtime fitting all the pieces together.

"Isn't there an easier way to get there? Like a broomstick or flying cars?" I asked. We had been walking for a while. He had repeated the same sentiment over and over. I didn't know how to respond, so we mostly remained silent. Penny's house wasn't close to the black forest.

"This is the easiest way without getting caught. In the air with flying bicycles people would see us. I don't have a car. Never needed one." At least Caden had said something different this time.

A sweet, earthy smell filled the air. I looked up as the clouds cracked open. Raindrops the size of golf balls erupted from the clouds and danced a waltz to the ground. *Boop boop dap*, they had a rhythm to their descent.

The first rain drop hit my forehead and rolled down my face. It left a sugary sweet taste on my lips.

"This is rain? It's the most beautiful thing I've ever seen."

"It is beautiful, but will get you drenched fast. Let's find cover," Caden said.

A few drops later and my new bangs were plastered to my face and my outfit from Penny clung to me. The crystal was warm against my skin compared to the cold damp drops of rain.

I followed Caden toward an alleyway sheltered by the adjacent building. There was someone else in the alley, a boy with a trench coat and hood, his face mostly covered in pimples. He couldn't have been more than fifteen. The boy approached us as we entered; I was still laughing from the dancing rain.

"Do you need anything? I got float gummies, flash bombs, mind erasers, love potions. I just sold my last fairy dust, but if you're in a pinch I can get some more. That stuff is addictive." He sniffled and rubbed his hand across his nose.

"Are you, like, a dealer? That's so cute. Do you have any crystals?" It would be a good idea to stock up on them.

"I am not cute, ma'am. But no, do I look like a seer? Those witches are weird."

"Scram kid," Caden demanded.

"Kid? I'm forty. Fairy dust keeps you young." But the kid walked away leaving us alone.

Nurse Dara had to be some sort of seer. It made sense. She always knew what was happening before it did. There had to be a reason she left Arlynn. If she was a seer, did she know who I was? She helped me on this path, it couldn't be a coincidence. Once this was done, I would go Earthside again to see her. Another thing she was right about.

Caden was as drenched as I was, his brown hair pasted to his forehead, green eyes glowing. Eyes that could always tell when someone was lying. I would have to tell him my plan for Vera and The Order. And somehow find a way to not tell him the whole thing. But not yet. Right now we were two people in an alleyway.

That's it.

Caden opened his mouth to speak, but seeing his mouth slightly parted like that gave me another idea. I grabbed his shirt, twisted and pulled him into me. His lips tasted sweet like the rain as I ran my tongue across them.

"Look, we need to talk. If you really are her," Caden began but I kissed him again. I didn't want to talk about this right now.

He groaned in response and grabbed me by the waist. I sucked on his lower lip and he picked me up. I wrapped my legs around his waist and he ground into me. A moan left me as I deepened the kiss. My back fell against the wall of the building.

"I love you," I whispered against his lips.

"Always and forever, but if you are her..." Caden began.

I kissed him deeper. This wasn't the time to discuss who I was. When that came up, I would have to tell him my plan. Right now, I had other things on my mind. Him bulging against me was one of them.

The alleyway had enough cover to stop the rain from soaking us. But not enough to stop passersby from seeing us. As much as I wanted him right here, I couldn't. He must have had the same thought because he pulled away from me. I dropped my legs and stumbled a bit. His kisses always put me off balance.

Big fat dancing rain drops continued to fall.

"We can't stay in the alley. We have to find Doctor Apples. Vera could have a lead on the memories." I grabbed his hand and walked into the rain.

"So what if she finds them first? You aren't taking them anyway, so who cares? I mean what if you are Ember Raven? You can't take them. We could go to

The Order. Maybe they can destroy the memories of her."

This was the conversation I was trying to avoid. He was part of The Order so of course he thought they were good people. That their intentions were just. He didn't have them fuck with his memories, so he couldn't possibly understand.

"Destroy them? But what if I am her? That would destroy part of me." Deep down I knew I was Ember Raven, the power inside me stirred every time her name was said. I had been ignoring it, but I had to admit who I had been.

"No. You can't be her." He grabbed my shoulders and shook me.

"Why? Because you were told she was such a bad person? Because your precious Order made Ember the bad guy?" Anger stirred. He refused to even take this into consideration.

"No, because Ember Raven is evil. And I can't love someone like that. We are finding your memories and having The Order destroy them. If, and that's a small if, you were her you will not become her again." He dropped his arms to his side. Green magic dripped between his fingers.

Caden was being ridiculous. He was flipping out over who I had been, like I had any control of it. As for me taking my memories, that was my decision. Not his, not Vera's, not The Order's. This is my life.

"Harmony, are you listening to me?" Caden asked.

"Wait, so if I take my memories then you won't love me anymore? So your love comes with conditions? A few days ago you wanted to run away with me. But If I'm really Ember Raven you will leave me?" I didn't wait for his answer. I stormed away.

Chapter 39

"WOULD YOU SLOW down and talk to me?" Caden yanked my arm and turned me toward him.

Rain slapped my hair, face, every inch of me. It tasted like sugar, but it was getting on my nerves. We had been walking for twenty minutes and it was still coming down. My purse was inside my jacket and I was positive it was as drenched as I was. Hopefully my journal wasn't destroyed.

Caden had been trying to talk to me the whole walk. I wasn't ready. I wanted to hit him, or call on some crazy creature to devour him. Since I actually have that power, I figured it wasn't a good idea to think about that too much.

Did he even love me or was this all a game? If I really was some evil witch he would leave me. He may have fallen for Harmony, but whoever I really was, he wasn't capable of loving.

At the end of the street, majestic black palm trees touched the sky. Even the leaves were black. We stepped into the forest and all the light disappeared. I couldn't see. Ugh. I hadn't brought a flashlight and I refused to ask Caden if he had one.

Luckily, he cast his hand out and his green tendrils slithered in front of him. The dim light cast enough of a glow for me to see a foot ahead. Even though it was dark, the trees did stop the rain from pelting me.

We stopped in front of a bright orange wooden shed. Bold black words were scribbled across it: GO AWAY.

This seemed promising.

A man with frosty white hair stepped out of the shed. His face was both ancient and youthful, but he was not handsome. The man's protruding jaw was not to be outdone by his bulging stomach. If this was the doctor, he was not taking his own advice.

"I'm so glad you're here," Caden said, offering his hand.

"Where else would I be? Cambodia, 1968?" The doctor stared at Caden's hand, not offering his own, but not looking away.

This is Dr. Apples. Wow.

Inside, the small room contained a bed and two chairs. To the right was a curtain, I hoped led to a bathroom. Sitting on one of the chairs was a young woman with fiery red curls. The hair on the back of my neck rose. I knew her from somewhere.

Ignoring Dr. Apples' rant about unwanted guests, I walked over to the woman. She turned her face away.

"Hi, I'm Harmony." I extended my hand. She stared at me. "And you?"

"I'm Savannah," she whispered.

Shit. It slapped me in the face. I had seen those locks

before, the day in Tech-fix when I met Caden. The name. Wow. She was sitting here in the middle of the forest like people weren't out looking for her.

Caden's jaw dropped.

The door slammed open and hit the wall. A tall man with black hair and grass-green eyes sauntered in. Asshole! Spencer being here solidified my theory. I jumped at him and pushed him against the wall.

"You had her here? How long? Penny is out searching for her!" I screamed in Spencer's face.

"Chill. I'm keeping Savvy safe." He shrugged me off him.

Caden's fists dripped with green energy. Once he calmed down, I would have him call Penny. She needed to know Savvy was alive and safe.

"How did she get here?" I paced. Penny had been searching everywhere for her and I stumbled upon her. Again, I didn't believe in coincidences.

Dr. Apples wobbled over and placed an envelope in my hand. "In my day, letters were safer. Phones track your information and mess with your brainwaves."

I pulled out the letter. It smelled as though it had been rubbed in herbs. I wrinkled my nose and unfolded the papers.

My Dearest Harry,

By the time you read this you will only have three hours to act. You have the chance to save a life. A girl with flaming red hair is being moved to a different location by Sapris beach. If you hide behind the high school, by the gym, you will be able to intercept her. The men who have her will stop for a smoke break. The girl is gonna try and run. She is shy and may fear you. Tell her Dara sent you. If you don't do this, they will kill her for her magic.

Love, your sister,
Dara

My jaw dropped. Dara was Dr. Apple's sister, and his first name was Harry. His parents must not like him much. Harry Apples. Weird. I read the letter again; Dara definitely wasn't a Dud, yet she lives like she is. I didn't understand why. I tucked the letter behind the next page and kept reading.

My Dear Harmony,

The future is never solid; it flows in different directions. Even the tide isn't predictable. People make choices that push the liquid one way or another. I'm getting off track. Point is, you decide your future. I only see it. I see two paths for you. Since you are reading this, you are on the path that keeps you in Arlynn. Neither path is wrong. But I must tell you of the other future I see for you. A normal life. You and Caden, here Earthside with two beautiful babies. You will be happy. But never content. You will always know you were supposed to be Ember Raven and that will leave an empty place in your life. The other path is not so easy. You will find your memories. You will become Ember Raven, but at a great cost. The river you are on will lead to your magic being stripped from you. Tragic, I know. But you will save a woman by the name of Penny Wren. She holds many secrets. And if they discover who she really is, they will kill her. I hope you still have the crystals I gave you.

Love,
Dara

P.S. You looked skinny in the vision, have you been eating?

I read it over and over. Caden hovered; he had read it as I did. I was still pissed and didn't want some normal life with him. His love was conditional. I had decided to take the memory potion and he would leave me because of it.

My brain bounced around from thought to thought. I sat on the bed and Dr. Apples grumbled. What was I supposed to do, let Penny die? No. I couldn't do that. But then lose my magic—I just got it. I still haven't learned to use it properly. And I'm supposed to give it up? But a life with Caden, if I wasn't so mad at him, maybe it would be an easy choice.

"Has Dara ever been wrong?" I asked Dr. Apples.

"Has a tree ever been struck by lightning when it wasn't supposed to?" Dr. Apples scratched his head.

Huh? I wanted to shake this man so his apples fell out of his brain. He made no sense.

"We can go," Caden said. "We can leave right now. I'll put a protection unit on Penny to keep her safe. I messed up. Even Dara is saying you're Ember Raven. I don't want to believe it, but I have to. It doesn't matter who you were. I love you."

He grabbed my hand, but I pulled away. "Prove it. Bring me to The Order. I need to make a deal with them. You will not turn me over to them. I will be no one's pawn."

"They will kill you. They must know who you really are," Spencer chimed in.

"How did you even get here?" I asked him.

"I used to work for Apples. I stopped by to see if he knew anything. Savvy was here. I got lucky." Spencer kissed Savvy's hand.

"Spencer is right. The Order will kill you," Caden whispered.

"If they wanted me dead, they would have killed me last year. Instead they sent me away with you. Take me to them, please," I begged.

I wasn't sure what side Caden was on. Him discovering I was the enemy either made him hate The Order as much as I did, or hate me. It would take time to trust him again. Not that I was sure I could ever trust him. The man of truth told so many lies.

Spencer was holding Savvy in his hands. The tool-like mask he wore disappeared around her. I couldn't stand him, but he did love her, that was easy to spot. If only I could see that love with Caden. I usually could, but not now.

"Doctor Apples, where are the memories kept?" I asked.

"At another one of my sisters' houses. The old hag. Spencer, write that old hag Ash's address on the back. Mushrooms never bloom around there." Dr. Apples walked over and pointed for us to leave.

There was no choice. I wouldn't let something happen to Penny if I could prevent it. I may not be strong enough, but Ember Raven was. I had to become her.

Chapter 40

THE WATER PULLED me down. A sea serpent wrapped his body around me and squeezed. I pushed my tendrils out at him. Inky black vines left my fingertips and wrapped around the monster. I struggled to breath. My vision blurred.

Witch, I need meatballs. Big John only feeds me cat food. Ginger pounced on my stomach.

I sat. My heart pounded. I grabbed the sheets as the sun shone through the curtains. I was in a spare room in the castle. Caden had wanted to sleep in the same room, but I refused.

The remnants of the dreams drifted away. I turned my hands over, no tendrils. I couldn't get them to come out. Black would be fitting.

Knock. Knock.

Something along the lines of 'come in' or 'leave me alone' rolled out of my mouth.

Penny flew into the room, ran over and hugged me. I sat frozen. She must be a shapeshifter or on fairy dust. Something. She doesn't hug people.

"Savvy is safe. And Caden told me about the letter. You don't have to stay for me, I'll be fine. Go live a normal life with him." Penny pulled away from me and adjusted her leather jacket.

There was a sister out there somewhere. A girl that's blood related to me. That was it. There was no real connection to that person. Penny was the sister I chose. She was crazy if she thought I was going to abandon her when I could help.

"Do people have black tendrils?" I asked.

"No. There are legends of a cursed witch with black tendrils and another with white. But that's a myth. Seriously, you should go Earthside with Caden." Penny placed her hand on my shoulder.

"I'm not going anywhere. I need a favor. Can I have a knife?" I had a plan. The Order would be here soon and I needed to embrace the side of me I never met.

I slipped out of bed and tossed on the outfit Penny had given me. I grabbed the crystal from Dara and stuck it in the waistband of my leggings. Then I took the knife Penny gave me and shoved it in the side of my boot.

"Liz said you needed one of these." Penny handed me a magical coin pouch.

My belongings easily fit inside of it. Liz had given me my journal back last night. I thought it was still in my bag. Luckily, it had fallen into her change purse. I also put the journal inside the gift from Penny. Then I put the pouch inside my jacket pocket.

Liz was right. It was so much easier to carry this around than my bulky bag.

Caden stepped into the room. I took a step forward. No. I stepped back. Still mad at him. He didn't get my forgiveness. He didn't deserve it. I needed him to accept all of me.

"The Order is in the throne room. Can I talk to you?" Caden ruffled his hair.

I walked out of the room. Then waited for them when I realized I had no clue where I was going.

When I discussed wanting a meeting with them, Caden finally agreed and explained it was perfect timing. His parents were away on another island. They visit the other islands to keep peace with them. Arlynn is one of many places in the Bermuda Triangle. I was fascinated to hear more about the different races. Elves, Fae, Lycan, and Sirens being among them. But I was too mad at Caden to give him the satisfaction of interest.

Penny walked out of the room and led the way. After way too many twists and turns we ended up at Big John's door. Before I could ask why we were here, he came out of the room.

"Caden told me what you wanted to do. Are you sure about this?" Big John asked me.

I'll stay with him. Ginger rubbed her body against his leg.

"Yes, I'm sure. Can you look out for Ginger? I don't know when I'll be back. After I make this deal, I'll have to act fast." I squatted and pet Ginger along her fur.

"I'm going with you to the meeting. The Order is not going to be happy with letting you go. Especially given who you are. And yes, I will look after her." Big John pulled me into a hug and whispered into my ear.

I nodded, then asked Penny if she could lead the way. Moths erupted in my stomach. This was a bad idea. The Order wanted me in captivity, they could toss me in their prison and I was willingly meeting with them. I was either dumb or brave. Probably both.

The throne room was... wow, I had never seen anything so... so... gold. The windows were lined with it and the two thrones were made of it. Even the floor had it infused in the marble. I almost missed the three men standing in the middle of the room.

These men had destroyed my life. Wittmeyer, Donickey, and Braxton glared at me as I entered.

I am Ember Raven. I am Ember Raven. I am Ember Raven.

My stomach turned. Fuck. I still had time to run.

"Miss Harmony Laverack, you are to come with us," Wittmeyer demanded.

"I am Ember Raven. I will go nowhere with you. I am here to make a deal." I stood tall.

Big John had whispered in my ear to not back down. They smell fear. And do not let them get close.

"So your memories are back. How?" Donickey asked, stepping forward.

"Why do you send innocent witches Earthside for a year?" I asked.

"Innocent? Ha. Every single witch we send is a member of The Unkindness." Rat Man laughed. "We are trying to fix them."

"How is taking their memories fixing them?" I stepped back. This whole time everyone thought they were protecting witches by sending them Earthside.

"By giving them new memories. It takes a year for the mind to adjust. When they come back we planned on giving them back their old memories. The mixture should make them better people. We give them happy, loving pasts, then we reintroduce their real lives. They should be healed of wanting to be part of The Unkindness. Well, everyone except you. We had different plans for you," Rat Man rambled.

"Shut up. She doesn't need to know this!" Wittmeyer yelled. "Now come with us!"

They were experimenting on witches. Holy shit. They tried Frankensteining their minds to control them better. The Order were truly screwed up people. All three took a step toward me.

I grabbed Penny from behind, the knife in my boot now against her throat. It was an awkward hold with the height difference. "Stay back or I'll slice her throat."

Caden and Big John gasped.

"You thought you could steal my memories. That you could hide me. Ha. Now look, Arlynn is tearing itself apart!" My heart hammered in my chest. I hoped they didn't hear my voice quiver.

"What do you want, Ember?" Wittmeyer asked.

"A deal. I give you Vera. You can do whatever you want with her. And then you leave me the fuck alone. Before you fucked with my memories, Arlynn thrived. Vera is to blame. Once she is out of the way, I can take back The Unkindness and fix this." My hand shook. The blade vibrated against Penny's throat. Her hand reached out and grabbed my leg. I pulled the knife away slightly.

"Let Penny Wren go and we will discuss this." Braxton stepped back.

"Just agree to her demands. You need her." Caden stepped beside me.

"Fine. But Caden and Penny stay. Do it yourself, Ember." Wittmeyer smirked. Somehow he knew I needed them. Fuck. I released Penny. He knew I wasn't going to hurt her.

"And risk her not succeeding? No. Arlynn needs this, Joseph." Big John walked over to Wittmeyer.

They whispered back and forth for a while. Penny and Caden tried talking to me, but I needed to stay focused. I needed to embrace Ember Raven. She would let nothing distract her. After a few minutes, Big John stepped to the side.

"Fine. If Caden and Penny go with you they are out of The Order. It's their choice. As for you, Ember Raven, for now you are free. But, The Unkindness need to be dismantled or I will kill you," Wittmeyer said.

Penny turned to me, tears in her eyes. I knew how much The Order meant to her. This wasn't a choice she should have to make. I nodded and hugged her goodbye. She walked over to Big John and he wrapped his arm around her.

Caden had always wanted to be in The Order. As mad as I was at him, I still couldn't ask him to go with me and give up his dreams. I touched his arm and turned. The Order had made it so I would have to do this on my own.

I am Ember Raven. I am Ember Raven. I am Ember Raven.

Footsteps slammed behind me after I was out of the room and I turned to see Caden. "Hey, I choose to go with you. You are more important than The Order. But wow, that part with the knife against Penny's neck. I got scared."

"She knew it was my plan. You didn't have to come. But thank you," I whispered.

I was still mad at him. But he picked me over The Order. That earned him a conversation about our relationship.

Chapter 41

RED GRASS COVERED the entire field. A few purple flowers popped up in random spots. Green mountains blocked us from anyone passing by. It was perfect for what I needed to do.

Caden had his transporter bring us here. My stomach was in knots. I hated traveling that way. It was almost as bad as walking through walls. If I had one of those affinities, I would have had an even harder time coming to grips with being a witch.

"What now?" Caden asked after he sent the man away.

I walked into the middle of the field. This was a terrible idea. I seemed to be making a ton of those lately. But it was the only way to keep everyone safe. I shook out my arms. This was crazy.

While holding my breath, I closed my eyes, picturing Melon. He was an adorable dragon, but still a baby.

According to Caden they grew to be monstrous creatures, which is exactly what I needed. If I could control it.

The sea serpent showed up on accident and then I had trouble bargaining with it. I was able to send the ravens away and the dolphin didn't give me any issues. It was possible, but I had to practice.

Long gray wings danced in my mind. I imagined a scaly body with a pointy tail. Fire rolled out of its forked tongue. Every detail was a larger scale of Melon.

"Are you sure this is a good idea?" Caden asked. I had filled him in on all of my plan, except the part about taking my memories.

"Yes. It's gonna work out perfectly." I kept my eyes closed, imagining the dragon.

"You know I'm a truth detector. I know you're lying." Caden huffed.

I shrugged. He shouldn't have asked if he didn't want a lie. This was a terrible idea. I was risking our lives. I could have left it up to anyone else to deal with Vera and The Unkindness. None of that was going to change my mind. I was going to make sure this was done. And when I got my memories back, I would be safe.

Wings flapped in the distance. Against the bright orange sky, a red dragon soared. As he got closer he would flap, flap, flap, soar. He repeated the process until he landed a few feet away.

The dragon stood on its hind legs and sashayed over to me. When he was dangerously close he sat upright and crossed his legs.

Hey, girl, hey. Love the jacket. How can I help you? he asked with a lisp.

"I need you to scare some people without killing

them. Can you do that?" Of course I summoned a sassy dragon.

Girl, I got you. But I might nibble a little bit. This figure is hard to maintain. He rubbed his claw against his stomach.

"No. You can't nibble." I wagged my finger at him.

My friend might be better at this. No one finds me scary. He pursed his lips.

"I need you. I don't have time to deal with another dragon," I begged.

Fine. Get on. Tell me where we're going? Is this your man? He's sexy. The dragon pointed at Caden. *Oh, my name is Sal.*

After introducing myself and Caden I walked over to the back side of Sal. My body vibrated. This was beyond insane. I bet Ember Raven had no issues flying on dragons. People who are feared by others do insane things and enjoy it. I couldn't back down. I had to do this.

Caden was walking toward me with his eyebrows raised. Not that long ago we were cuddled up on a sofa watching movies. Now we were about to fly on a dragon to fight an evil witch.

I had definitely lost my mind.

Climbing onto Sal was not easy. His body was slimy and I slipped a few times. Caden came up behind me and pushed me onto the dragon. I mumbled a thank you.

He straddled behind me and placed his hands on both sides of me. Caden dug his fingers under two thick scales and held on tight. Once we were secure, I explained to Sal where we were going.

Hang on tight, girl. I don't want that sexy piece of ham you got to fall off. Sal pushed off with his legs.

I intertwined my arms into Caden's and closed my eyes. None of my memories had me on a roller coaster. My guess is this would have been worse anyway. I would have to ask Caden if Arlynn had an amusement park.

Peeling my eyes open, clouds danced by. Nope. I slammed them shut again.

After hours, well maybe a few minutes, we landed. Sal had put us close to the ski resort that Liz and I had been at. Caden had seen the house on the cliff on the way here. Had I looked as well, maybe I would have seen it.

Stay on. We're gonna look so scary walking up. Sal walked toward the house.

A motorcycle rumbled above us and I looked up. A white Kawasaki flew toward us. Astride it was Penny. She had magicked her bike to fly. Wow. But she shouldn't be here. She landed a few feet from us and approached.

"Go home. I don't want you to get kicked out of The Order," I snapped as I climbed down from Sal.

"So we don't tell them I'm here. I had to track Caden's phone to find you guys." Penny smiled. "What's the plan?"

"I walk in and try to reason with her. That's not going to work so Caden is to pretend to get caught by them. Then Sal breaks down the wall, distracts them for long enough for Caden and I to get these cuffs on Vera." I held up a pair of magical cuffs Big John had from when he was in The Order. They will bind Vera's powers and that's exactly what we needed.

"Why wouldn't we all just walk in?" Penny asked.

"Vera is cocky. We need her to think she's won," I explained.

"It's not the best plan. But it might work," Caden interjected.

"Everyone know their part?" I asked.

They all nodded. Sal blew out a puff of smoke in the shape of hearts from his nose. It went toward Caden and he coughed through it. This dragon was something else.

Once they were all out of view, I approached the door. *Knock. Knock.* My bladder swelled. Shit. This was not the time to pee. Hopefully it was nerves.

The man that tried to steal my magic answered. I swallowed hard. He stared at me and I glared back.

"What?" he asked.

"I... I'm here to see Vera," I stuttered.

He waved me into the home and led me to Vera's office. She was sitting behind her desk again, drinking from her wine glass.

I stood staring at her. She really was beautiful if it wasn't for the fact that she was trying to destroy me. She had to know I was there, yet she didn't look up.

"Vera, we need to talk." I stepped into the room and sat in the chair across from her. I tried to act calm but I was sweating everywhere.

"Harmony, I gave you a chance. You refused to help. Your black magic is the only magic capable of summoning a demon that will destroy the royal family and their dictatorship. This was your plan for years. But now I will take your magic since our mutual friend has finally agreed to do it." She pointed at the man with the raven tattoos on his hands.

"I am Ember Raven and The Unkindness are mine. Give them back and I won't turn you over to The Order." I leaned back in the chair. No way would I summon a demon, and black magic doesn't exist.

Vera laughed.

The man chuckled.

I shook.

Vera stood and walked around the desk. She leaned against it and looked down at me, then she took her bony finger and put it under my chin, looking into my soul.

I was small. Nothing. The dirt under her shoe. I sank further into the chair.

"Harmony, you are no Ember Raven. You know nothing about her. She is darkness and fire. She is powerful. She would summon demons for me!" Vera wiped my bangs away from my face. "And Ember would never be caught dead with such a terrible dye job."

Run. Run.

I had banked on her believing I was Ember Raven.

The door slammed open.

I turned. Perfect.

Four men stormed in with two captives. One was short with black hair and another was skinny with a raven tattoo across the right side of his face. The biggest was almost the size of Big John. The last man looked like he hadn't eaten in weeks.

"Boss, found these two trying to sneak in the back." The biggest of the men pushed Penny forward.

Caden pulled, trying to break free.

I jumped up.

"Where's Sal?" I asked Caden.

"Got scared and took off," he whispered.

No. No. No. He was supposed to break down the wall as soon as Caden was caught. How did I manage to summon a scared dragon? We had to get out of here.

My brain went blank. I had to think of something. Anything.

The man that tried to steal my magic pushed me to the ground. My face smashed against the hard surface. Something broke, I think it was my nose. Blood flowed.

He rolled me over. I coughed up blood and ran my tongue across my teeth. My front tooth was chipped.

Penny screamed. From the corner of my vision, the starving man placed his hand against her chest. Bright blue electricity crawled over her skin.

Caden's hands glowed green. He shot out magic toward the man attacking Penny. The big man slammed his fist into Caden's face. Bones cracked. His eye socket caved in.

Tears flowed from my eyes. This was all my fault.

"Ember Raven would also never enlist the help of The Order," Vera cackled. "Brown, take her magic."

The Stealer stood over me. My veins vibrated. Every atom in my body screamed. Inky black tendrils flowed from my fingertips. Fucking black tendrils. Who the hell was Ember Raven?

Dara's words played in my head. 'The river you are on will lead to your magic being stripped from you. Tragic, I know. But you will save a woman by the name of Penny Wren. She holds many secrets. And if they discover who she really is, they will kill her.'

Chapter 42

WHEN I WAS LITTLE, running from fights wasn't always possible. Foster siblings would wait at home till I got there to use me as a punching bag. So as the punches would fly down, I learned to travel to a different place in my head.

I would imagine I was famous, like an actress or inventor of something cool like super speed running shoes. Everyone would love me. There would be parades in my name. No one would even imagine hurting me, let alone kick me when I'm down.

This little scenario always helped. Until this moment. Having a man stand over me pulling my magic from my veins hurts. The pain was unbearable. I tried to imagine I was anywhere else, but I couldn't. My tendrils flowed from me to his hands. There was no way to stop him. Dara was right.

Caden groaned in the distance. I should have ran

away with him when he asked me. Instead I kept postponing it. Saying after this, after that. And now it's too late to run.

When was the first time he asked me? Was it after I healed the dog? No. It was the day he gave me Ginger.

None of this would have happened had I left with him. Dara's vision of us and two kids would have come true. Shit. Caden had been willing to give up everything for me. He kept asking me to leave with him. He had always wanted to be in The Order and yet he chose me instead. Why didn't I see it before? No, I wait till our lives are at risk. Too late. Once Vera had my magic there was no reason to keep me alive, or my friends.

Could Caden even love me as Ember? I didn't know. None of it mattered if I was dead.

The tendrils stopped flowing. The man had my black magic. And I did nothing to stop it.

"Boss, you want her affinity as well?" he asked Vera.

Vera walked over and kicked me in the side. I coughed and clenched my stomach. She knelt, her face inches from mine. Copper crept up my nose; she definitely drank blood from that wine glass.

"Her pathetic little affinity? Ha. What would I need to heal an animal for?" She stood and took her position by the desk again. Vera pointed at the starving man beating on Penny. "Sunny, kill them all. Make it painful."

Penny screamed.

Caden pulled against the arms holding him.

I closed my eyes.

Shocks of electricity ran through my body.

I should have ran.

Darkness filled my mind. Black, like my tendrils that were gone. Like the ravens I had once summoned. Like my heart before I met Caden.

Vera was right, my affinity was useless.

Another shock of electricity slammed into me. I jolted up. The crystal in my waistband burned against my skin. I should have taken Dara's advice.

The crystal. It could clear my mind. Strengthen my power. What animal could help right now?

My vision blurred as I imagined animals raining down on Vera. Fuck.

The pain from losing my tendrils weakened my sight. I had to envision the animals to make the power work. I couldn't.

I wrapped my fingers around the crystal. Nothing.

"I'm sorry I have to kill you. Before all this happened we were friends. I never wanted to hurt you," Stealer whispered in my ear as he stroked my hair.

I slammed my forehead into his face. Liz was right, it was big. He stumbled back. He was going to kill me. I had to do something.

"Ember! I'm sorry!" Caden shouted.

He called me Ember. Had he accepted I was Ember Raven? Well, a poor excuse for her. I couldn't even summon anything.

The stone was still warm in my hand. Think of something! Any creature or animal would do at this moment. Something to cause a distraction like Sal was supposed to. Where was he?

To summon him I would have to see him perfectly in my mind and all I could think of was how Caden called me Ember. I am Ember Raven. Like a beautiful black bird soaring through the air.

Breaking glass vibrated the air. Hope squawked in the distance. Hundreds of tiny little wings flapped. A croaking sound filled the room and grew louder. Vera and her men screamed.

Opening my eyes, I saw hundreds of ravens pecking at The Unkindness. The men flapped their hands and swatted them away. The birds were relentless. It worked. The crystal strengthened my power, I didn't have to push so hard to summon so many birds.

Penny and Caden crawled toward me and each grabbed one of my hands. Time to finish this. Dust fell down. Then slabs of ceiling and drywall. Penny and Caden covered me as bricks hit them.

They prevented me from getting up, but I had to capture Vera or this was all for nothing. I peeked past their arms. What happened to the ceiling?

The sky opened up. The roof was gone. Large red wings flapped above. Flap, flap, flap, soar. The ravens stopped pecking, their little heads turned toward the dragon and they took off.

Sal perched on the side of the wall and blew a smoke heart toward Caden. Next to him, a majestic blue dragon with scales in the shape of a mohawk put his hand on Sal's. Two dragons?

Hey, girl. You look awful. Sorry I took off, I don't like fighting. But I got my friend Butch. Sal blew another smoke heart. *I'm a lover.*

Just a friend? Butch's voice boomed in my head.

Snuggy-boo, not now. Not in front of my new friends, Sal whispered.

The men tossed their magic toward Sal and Butch. Blue, brown, gray, and lime green tendrils flew up toward them. Both dragons laughed. The magic couldn't penetrate their scales. Instead it turned to dust, and ash rained down on us.

Penny jumped up and unsheathed her swords. She sliced at the short man and the katana cut through his jeans. He stepped back and tossed his brown magic at her. He was fast but Penny used her magical blade to ricochet it back. Brown tendrils slammed into his chest. He stumbled backward and fell.

Sunny turned his magic toward Penny just as Caden tossed green tendrils of magic at the skinny man. Sunny stopped fighting Penny and threw shock waves of electricity out. Caden shook and fell backwards.

Liz walked through the wall holding Big John's hand. I wanted to yell at her to run, but we needed help. She raised her eyebrows and immediately stepped back into the wall. At least she would be safe. And now we had Big John; his affinity for strength would be helpful.

Big John charged Sunny and slammed his fist into the man's face. Bones shattered. That man is strong. Caden stopped shaking.

I stood. There had to be something I could do. But what? I didn't know much about the animals in Arlynn. They have cats, but I didn't want to risk their lives. Even if they have nine. Think.

Butch breathed fire into the air above him. He then swatted a claw at Vera.

"Retreat!" Vera yelled.

I charged at her. Wind blew, slamming me against the wall. I got back up and ran at her again, but it made no difference. One flick of her hand and my back was hitting the wall.

You leave her alone! Sal scooped up Vera with his claw.

The short man stood and ran out the room. Sunny tossed his electricity at Big John. He responded with a growl and grabbed the man's arm, squeezing and bending. Sunny's arm was now a soggy wet noodle and he followed the short man out.

The large man who broke Caden's face went after

Big John. Their fight was a dance as each dodged the other's fists. It was mesmerizing. Their abilities were the same, but I bet Big John had this.

"He's getting away!" Caden screamed.

Skinny man was fighting Penny while the large man was getting his ass kicked by Big John. Shit. The Stealer was running away.

I ran out of the room with Caden, right behind Stealer. Caden reached him first and jumped on him. They both crashed to the ground.

Caden's eye socket oozed blood. It was too much blood loss. We were running out of time. Caden rolled the man onto his back and straddled him, pushing green tendrils into the man's neck.

"Give her back her magic!" he demanded.

"She has black magic. You know how dangerous that is! I was protecting Arlynn. I wasn't gonna give it to Vera," Stealer cried.

"Truth. But it's not your choice to make." Caden pushed more tendrils around Stealer.

Stealer closed his eyes. Black tendrils left his hands and shot out to me. They wrapped around my body and sliced through my clothes. These tendrils had thorns. Fuck. I was lifted into the air.

To my left, Caden was also in the air. The man was using my magic against us, and it was more painful than when he took it from me.

"No one should have black magic. This is why. The tendrils tear through everything. I could rip you in half right now. There has never been a witch with your color magic. And now because of me there never will be. I will find a way to destroy this, even if I have to kill myself." Stealer flicked his hands forward.

Caden and I soared through the air backward. This

part of the roof was also missing, but two claws scooped us up. Sal saved us from hitting the wall.

From this height, I watched Stealer run out of the house. He jumped off the cliff into the water below. I knew he could survive, but he was gone, for now.

"Sal, where is Vera?" I shouted.

I had to drop her. I couldn't let anything happen to this piece of ham. Bad enough he's bleeding. Sal rubbed his nose against Caden.

"Set me down!" I yelled.

Sal set me back into the room. Penny and Big John were still fighting. Vera was standing on her desk laughing. Asshole thought she had the upper hand.

Vera flicked her hands at me the second my feet touched the ground. I was sliding backward, wind slamming into my face. My vision blurred, but I pushed forward.

I was on a treadmill that was kicking my ass. There had to be a way to get to her. The crystal burned in my waistband again. What was it trying to tell me? Was there an animal I could summon?

I couldn't think of any, at least none that would be of any help. How many mice would it take to be of any use? Fuck, Harmony, think of something!

Mimic. I could mimic one. Which one? I tripped over brick and drywall. My head hit the ground. I sat up.

Vera remained on the desk. The glass of red, probably blood, was knocked over. She still had red liquid in the corner of her mouth. That was it.

A bellow escaped my lips. I rolled onto all fours and kicked my back legs against the ground. Dust and ash swirled, but I kept my eyes on the red on her lip.

When I last became the wolf, I'd lost control. This time, because of the crystal, I was focused. I became the animal I wanted, a fierce, enraged bull, and I didn't fall into his mind.

I tossed my head from side to side and bellowed, blowing hot air out my nose. Vera rolled her eyes. To her I must have looked like I lost my mind. She would be wrong. I had this.

The bull inside me was hungry for blood. I charged forward. We slammed into the desk and Vera flew against the wall.

Switching tactics, I mimicked a jaguar. The change was as quick as breathing. I pounced, inches above Vera, and she flicked air at me. I hovered above her. Shit.

Zoos. I had to think of animals. Which one could save me? The heaviest of them. No, that wouldn't help. I only needed a second to get close to her. I thought of the one place in the zoo I hated.

The rattle of their tail vibrated in my throat. Rattlesnakes freaked me out, and hopefully distracted Vera enough so I could get to her. The rattle grew louder and Vera scrunched her face.

I flopped on top of her. She moved her arm, about to toss me in the air again, but I bit down on her side. My teeth sank in hard.

She screamed.

My hand clenched around her throat cutting off the scream. She wriggled underneath me, clawing at my arm.

I squeezed.

Vera's hand flopped to the side until she passed out. I had her life in my hands. How easily I could kill her.

"Harmony, stop!" Caden shouted.

I would be free of Vera. The Order would owe me for taking care of their problem. A little longer and I would never have to worry about her again.

"Harmony, you're killing her!" Caden grabbed my shoulder.

A few more seconds and I would be done with her.

"Harmony, this isn't you." Caden pulled at me.

He was right. I released my hand and stopped biting her. Blood poured from her side. She lay still, eyes open.

I pushed all the animals from my mind. My heart raced. I did it. But I may have killed her.

Penny and Big John ran over and Big John scooped me into his arms. I didn't fight. My body burned.

"I'll call the transporter, and healer. The Order wants Vera alive." Penny sheathed her swords. "Hopefully, she isn't dead."

"I killed her," I mumbled. Fuck, who was I? I'm not the type of person that kills someone, yet... Vera still wasn't breathing.

I wriggled out of Big John's grip. Caden sat beside Vera with his fingers on her throat, checking for a pulse. I placed my hands on her chest and pushed down. I didn't know CPR but I had to do something. I couldn't let her die.

Every push caused blood to seep from her wound. Caden pulled off his shirt and held it against Vera's side while I continued CPR.

Doug and the transporter stood above us.

"Move," Doug demanded.

Caden and I scuttled back as Doug placed his hands on Vera. She gasped and sat up.

Fuck. I grabbed the cuffs and placed them on her.

"I'll get you for this," Vera whimpered.

Sal wrapped his claws around me. Before I could protest, he was soaring away from the cliff side.

Chapter 43

CADEN STEPPED INTO the room, his hands in his pockets. Doug, the healer, had fixed his eye, and the other bruises he had sustained. After Doug helped him, he had healed the rest of us.

"I love you, Harmony Laverack. I get that you are also Ember Raven. But I fell for you, not her." Caden chewed his lip.

As much as I understood what he was saying, he would have to accept us both.

"When did you fall in love with me?" I stood from the bed and walked toward him.

"Like the exact moment?"

I nodded.

"You were wearing blue leggings, a sports bra, and a baggy tank top. I knew I was going to see you that day, but I hadn't expected my heart to touch yours. You came into Tech-fix with your broken phone." He took a step toward me.

"That was the day we met." He had always loved me. My heart fluttered. "But I'm also Ember. You have to love all of me. Not just half."

"I know. Look..." Caden grabbed my hands. "You almost killed Vera. That part is Ember Raven. But you didn't. I like to think that had something to do with me. You need me by your side and I need you. I will love you forever and always and I will make sure Ember Raven doesn't destroy the good parts of you."

I hadn't told him I was going to take the memory potion. If we continued to talk about Ember Raven, he would insist I don't take it. But he accepted I was also someone he despises, and that was good enough for now.

I collided into him, mashing my lips to his.

He parted his lips and I invaded his mouth with my tongue. His hand slid down my back, caressing me. Caden growled into my mouth and I pressed my body into his.

He found my ass and squeezed it, grinding me against him. I needed him. I wanted him. No matter what happens after, we have this. Our love is real, even if my life wasn't. He lifted me up and I straddled him. My pussy rubbed against his cock through his pants and he swelled against me. A soft moan escaped my lips. He kissed me harder.

The bed slammed into my back as he tossed me down. I rotated my hips to grind against his cock, teasing him.

Heat screamed from my insides. I craved him. Caden stopped kissing me and I whimpered when he released my lips. He slid his hand up my shirt and pulled it over my head. Then he kissed the hollow of my neck and licked a moist trail down my collarbone. He paused when he reached my bra.

Fabric ripping pierced the air as he tore it off. I had two bras and that was one of them. I would have to ask Liz where to shop around here—that wasn't filled with pink clothing.

He ran his tongue across my nipple, bringing me back to the moment. Fuck the bra. He pulled away and went toward the other nipple.

I grabbed fistfuls of his button-up white shirt and yanked it apart, the buttons popping away, exposing Caden's perfectly sculpted chest. I reached for his belt, but he grabbed my wrists and placed them above my head, restraining me.

Fuck, this was hot. I pursed my lips at him. He smiled and shook his head. He let go of my wrist and ran his hand down to my temple, pushing a scene into my mind.

We were at our apartment in Philly, Caden was between my legs. Licking and sucking my wet clit. The vision was real and soaked me to the core.

"My affinity has some cool perks." Caden grinned, pulling his hand from my temple.

Lifting my leg into the air he kissed my ankle. He grabbed my pants and panties, pulling them off. Then he licked a path up my leg to my center. He stopped inches from my clit. The vision he placed in my mind still played. I needed to have his tongue against me.

He blew on my pussy. The heat from his mouth sent tingles through my body. His tongue slipped along my crease, parting my lips. I intertwined my fingers in his hair. With his tongue he flicked at my clit and I bucked my hips against his mouth. He pulled my clit between his lips and sucked.

Sparks erupted through my body. I cried out. The explosion shook through my legs and I pushed his head away for a moment. The intensity so strong I needed to catch my breath.

"I promise to accept who you are," Caden whispered.

"That's a start." I pulled his face up to mine and kissed him.

"I mean it. I know I fucked up. I'm sorry."

"You talk too much. I forgive you." I rolled Caden onto his back and straddled him.

A groan rumbled in his throat as I pushed his shirt off of him. The fabric of his jeans rubbed against my bare center. I lifted myself with my knees, reached underneath me, and unbuckled his pants.

He unzipped them and pushed them down to his knees, letting his cock spring free. My pussy throbbed in response. I needed him inside me.

As I ground against his cock, my nipples rubbed his bare chest. I trembled, rocking my hips back and forth. He wasn't even inside me yet and I was close to exploding again.

Caden picked me up by my hips and rolled me onto my back. A rush of air escaped my lips. He placed his hands on either side of my head and hovered above me. I used my feet to slide his pants down the rest of the way and he kicked them to the floor.

His tip rested against my entrance. I gasped. He kept it there, unmoving. Teasing me. I squirmed, and rubbed my slick pussy against his hard cock. He looked into my eyes, the green sparkling. His lips brushed against mine as he slowly pushed inside. A growl escaped his lips and I inhaled a moan. Slowly, he rocked back and forth inside me, pushing a little deeper each time.

"More!" I begged.

He pulled in and out slowly, pushing his entire length inside me. Placing his hand on my temple, he pushed another vision inside my mind. It was the night he bent me over the bed in our apartment, when he rammed inside me hard and fast.

The contradiction of the vision and his slow thrusts was driving me wild. He kept his hand on my temple as he slowly pulled in and out of me. Damn, his magic was amazing.

He slid out of me and pushed himself fully back in, filling me, sending an electric jolt through me. I moved my hips against him, yet he continued with the slow pressure. He began to tremble as he rocked inside me.

A tingling wave rushed through my body. I was getting closer to the edge. He moaned and I knew I wasn't the only one close. He pulled himself out to the tip, and thrust back in, pushing all the way. I cried out, the pleasure sending waves through me. I grabbed his hips, and wrapped my legs around him, fiercely pushing my pussy against him.

He thrust again and I exploded as he released himself inside me in long spasms. I wrapped my arms around him. He kissed my nose and pulled his hand away from my temple.

After a while, he slid out of me and rolled onto his side. It didn't take long before his little snores filled the air.

I crawled out of bed and grabbed my journal. While he slept, I wrote. I filled it with everything that had happened. Then I turned the page to write a note to someone I had never met.

Dear Ember Raven,

I don't know how this is gonna work. I don't know if I will remember me or if it will only be you in there. I started to journal to try and figure out why my memory was all fucked up. Now I know it was The Order. And I'm not even real, well my memories aren't. But I want you to know, if I am still in your mind I'm going to fight like hell to be remembered. To have a say. For you and I to be one.

This letter wasn't about how we may end up with a split personality or two heads. Hopefully not but who knows. This is about the man I love and the family I now have.

Tomorrow I am taking the memories to protect them. Arlynn is falling apart and it appears that you are the one who can fix it. I'm sure someone else could, but The Unkindness listen to you. They are the ones tearing it apart.

All I ask is that you don't hurt Caden Perry, Penny Wren, Liz Perry, Big John Perry, Dara Garcia and your cat Ginger. They are my family.

They are good people. And they mean well. They got wrapped up in The Order's promises and were raised to believe The Order was good. Maybe at one point it was a good thing, but not with its leaders now.

Oh, and as for your black tendrils, a man who works for Vera and has a raven tattoo on his hand stole them. Says it was to help Arlynn. Sorry I couldn't get them back.

As for Ginger, feed her meatballs and she will leave you alone.

Love,
Harmony Laverack

Chapter 44

THE SUN PEEKED through the curtain, hitting me directly in my eyes. Had I been sleeping, I would have been annoyed. Today was the day I would get my memories back. Nerves had kept me up all night.

Not Caden. He was snoring before his head hit the pillow. I stayed up and watched him. It may be one of our last moments together. I wanted to memorize every detail of his face. Fuck, I really hoped I was wrong about this.

I rolled over to crawl out of bed. Caden wrapped his arms around me and kissed me. My stomach erupted into butterflies as I deepened the kiss. This man was my soulmate. No matter what happens, I will find a way back to him.

"I love you," he whispered.

"I love you, too. Do you think Liz will let me borrow something to run in?" For some reason Caden walks everywhere, or uses a transporter. To get to the seer's house, I wanted to run. I wanted to clear my head one last time.

"You would rather run there?" Caden sat and swung his legs off the bed.

As I got up I nodded and went to the shower. Lately all of my choices had been beyond crazy. Yet, for some reason I hadn't stuttered on words or forgotten full sentences. The years of my life were still missing, but being in Arlynn made my brain relax. So it was all worth it. And now I didn't have an evil lady hunting me down.

Vera had been successfully transferred to the prison. The Order healed her first, so she could live out the rest of her long life stuck on Jail Island. It wasn't a thought-out name, but it worked.

The water smelled of fresh spring air. Magic played a part in it. As the seasons change the smell changes, at least that's what Caden said. I would have to experience that for myself, if I was around. I pushed back tears; I was making myself depressed.

I jumped out of the shower, brushed my teeth, and walked back into the bedroom. Caden was already back and wore black shorts, a black t-shirt, and a wide grin.

The clothes on the bed explained the smile. I should have realized when I asked for an outfit from Liz what I was going to get. The girl wears one color. Against my orangish hair, pink didn't look good. Pale pink leggings, with a salmon tank top. And in case that wasn't enough there were neon pink sneakers. It all clashed. I wasn't into fashion but this was a little much. I would rather have the different shades of black Penny gave me.

Rolling my eyes, I got dressed. I resembled a chewed up piece of gum.

"Is Penny around? Maybe I could borrow something from her." I tied the laces.

"She went to visit Savvy. Her and Spencer were planning on explaining the memory thing to her and giving her a choice on if she wants to take them. " Caden grabbed his phone and wallet and tossed them in his shorts.

"I'm taking them." The words flew out of my mouth before I had the chance to stop them. I grabbed the change purse and put my journal inside.

"Let's go." Caden kissed me on the top of my head and left.

"That's it?" I followed after him.

"Truth detector. There's no changing your mind, I can tell. Don't worry, I won't let you forget me."

We stopped at Big John's room before we left. He pulled me into a bear hug and warned me to be safe and not summon any more sassy dragons.

Witch, tell him to feed me meatballs! Ginger begged.

I squatted and petted her fluffy black fur. Being able to talk to her was so worth all of this. Vera may have thought I had a weak affinity, but she was wrong, it was cool and powerful.

"You look so cute. Pink really is your color. You can borrow my stuff anytime. Want me to go with you guys? You know what, no. I changed my mind. I had enough adventure to last forever. Maybe I will listen to my parents and work on being a princess. When you guys get back we can do dinner." Liz rocked on her feet. It had to take so much energy to talk that much.

"Yeah, sure. We can do dinner." I swallowed hard. "Big John, Ginger loves meatballs."

With that, I left.

Penny wasn't here so I couldn't say goodbye to her.

We could probably swing by Dr. Apples' place to see her. No. I would only be stalling. And Penny wasn't the type to get all mushy.

Caden led the way to the seer's house. As we ran down the streets, I tried to memorize every detail of this magical island. It was empty and had more of a dystopian vibe than Caden's vision. One day Arlynn would be brought back to life. I hoped.

Was Arlynn worth this? Worth giving up myself? Maybe. I wasn't sure. I didn't know enough about this place to be certain. But my family was. They deserved to have the home back that they grew up in. Becoming Ember Raven seemed like the best way to do it.

Hey, girl, hey. Need a ride? That piece of ham can ride me any day! Sal flap, flap, flap, soared above.

"No thank you, Sal. You take care of yourself!" I shouted to the sassy dragon.

Caden waved up to him. If dragons could blush, he definitely did. I would miss him.

We turned down a deserted street. We were in the country part of Arlynn. Two houses were off in the distance. The road went from pavement, to pebbles, to green sand. Huge palm trees lined the road. Florida-type beaches crashed into farmland, and I loved it.

Caden turned up a worn sandy driveway. The house looked even worse than the other one across the street. Broken wood panels hung from rusty nails, and all that was left of the gate were a couple battered hinges. The porch sagged heavily to the left.

It was probably a stunning home on the inside. The outside could be an illusion. Standing on the porch, and almost falling through a loose plank, Caden knocked on the side of the house. A peeling piece of siding fell to the ground. A frail, elderly woman with sagging wrinkles and flabby, bat-wing arms appeared. She looked through a hole in her wall with glassy, white eyes. Even her irises were a milky white.

"What do you two want?" she croaked. "Stop gawking at me, girl. I'm blind, not stupid," the old crone snapped.

"Ma'am, we're looking for the seer. Doctor Apples sent us," Caden said.

"Ech... don't call me ma'am. The name's Ashley. What would you want with my sister? The old bat. Mean as hell." Ashley fisted the air.

"Ashley, we believe she has something that belongs to my girlfriend here."

"Fine. But don't mind the mess." She stepped aside, waving us in. "Careful what you wish for."

Stepping over a loose brick, I stumbled inside. The wallpaper was peeling in dirty, ragged sheets. The holes in the floor were big enough to fall through. It was even worse than the outside. It smelled of death and rotting fish. I had expected glamour, but I was mistaken. I breathed through my mouth, but that didn't help. I could taste it. There were some foster homes that I lived in that had a similar smell.

"Mari, you old bat. Our brother sent some people to see us!" Ashley called out. She whispered to Harmony. "My sister... God-awful ugly. Don't look at her face."

From the rear of the house, a short, wispy Audrey Hepburn lookalike walked in. She was adorable, a luminous gem against the coarse foulness of the house. She swayed as she sauntered in, a smile spreading across her face. Despite the warning, I couldn't help but stare. A pink, puffy scar ran from temple to chin. Even so, the woman was exquisite.

"Hi... Oh! Prince Caden!" Mari bowed deeply.

"Ma'am." He bowed back. "We need your help."

"I know. Our sister Dara sent a letter. Help Harmony, blah blah blah. Best seer in our family and she followed our other sister Earthside. Thought she would come back after our sister was murdered, but no. She stayed." Mari waved her hands in the air.

"Dara sent a note?" I asked. The woman knew what path I was on. So far she had been right about everything except Penny getting killed. And only part of my magic was taken. Maybe this was the right road for me. She knew I would show up here.

"Yes. She said to give you your memories. But to warn you there will be no turning back." As Mari spoke, a golden strand of magic trailed from her fingertips, dancing behind her.

I rubbed my palms against my leggings. The warning was confirmation. I wouldn't be me anymore. Clenching the change pouch in my waistband, I thought of the note I wrote to Ember Raven. I would never stop fighting. I would return, no matter what.

"Would you like some tea?" Mari asked.

The yellow tendril had returned, attached to a tray holding a kettle and two teacups. I shook my head. Caden took the tray and set it on a wobbly coffee table in the center of the living room. He poured a cup and offered it to Ashley. She shook her head, and he offered it to Mari. When she also refused, he set the cup back on the tray and stepped back.

"I never understood why The Order didn't keep the memories themselves. They think a seer would be a better defense if anyone came looking for them? Well, it's hogwash." Ashley stomped her foot.

"Careful, sister. The Order pays us very well for our services." She turned to Caden. "Are you certain about this?"

"Yes," I answered.

Mari walked from the room. Ashley sat on the sofa, exhaling a puff of smoke from a cigarette. She mumbled to herself about prophecies and stupid memories. I barely heard any of it. Mari had seemed apprehensive about the memories. Why had she asked Caden if he was certain? How badly could this actually go wrong? Do I really need them?

Mari returned donning a yellow oven mitt. Her hand was clasped around a miniature black bottle. She walked past me, handing the bottle to Caden. He raised his brow at her as he took it from her.

"Remember the day she was brought to you, Mari? They still haven't replaced the door," Ashley snapped.

"You give this to her outside. I don't need any more destruction to my house." She peered into his eyes, squinting. "You will never have the throne. A woman will rule Arlynn. Someone close to you. Today will always bring you much sorrow."

"I don't want the throne," he snapped.

"Sorry. Life of a seer. I don't always know what these things mean. Now go."

I wanted to say thank you, but the woman didn't even look in my direction. Caden gripped the bottle until we reached the street. His brows scrunched as he hesitantly handed it to me. His hand trembled. I took a step back and smiled. Blowing him a kiss, I inspected the bottle. Maybe I was supposed to drink it? I glanced back at the house; Mari stood on the porch.

"Wait!" Caden shouted. I looked at him, my thumb pressed to the cork.

"What?"

"What if it doesn't work? What if your memories are

gone? What if you aren't Harmony anymore?" Caden grasped the hand that wasn't around the bottle.

"Then you will have to remind me. I love you, forever and always." I pushed my thumb against the cork on the tiny bottle.

Pop.

The cork tumbled down and bounced to the ground. I looked back to the bottle and my jaw dropped. Wisps of black smoke curled menacingly from the tip. They were coming for me. Tingles of fear rippled through every cell in my body.

A car pulled up beside us. Someone actually drives around here? Spencer, Penny, and Savvy jumped out of the car. They were all shouting. The words barely reached my ears before they dissipated.

"It's Savvy!" Penny screamed.

I shook my head. I didn't understand.

"She's your sister. Spencer told me why she put you in the program. Cork the bottle!" Penny shouted through the mist.

Too late.

I dropped the bottle. It hit the ground softly. I stepped back, my heart hammering in my chest. What did I do?

Black, oily vapor tumbled and rolled over itself, creeping toward me—a serpent of smoke slithering across the ground. I hastily took another step back.

The seer screamed, but the sound was so far away. I looked around for her, for Caden, for Penny. Where did they go?

My feet were numb and tingly as the black cloud poured over them. I could no longer move. I watched as the smoke traveled up my legs, slowly, almost cautiously. The vapor caressed my fingertips. It grew and engulfed me. I couldn't see, blanketed as I was.

Then the familiar ice-burn returned.

I wanted to run. I couldn't.

Ember Raven was taking over.

The memories filled me—consumed me—and I laughed.

To Be Continued...

Find out if Harmony Keeps her
Memories in...

UNTAMED
WITCH

Coming Spring of 2022

ABOUT THE AUTHOR

Melody Caraballo binge watches shows so send her your recommendations. She loves video games and lazy days by the pool. She lives in Western New York with her boyfriend, John and her three children. Unhinged Witch is her debut novel. The first in The Unkindness Saga. Keep up to date by signing up for her newsletter on her website melodycaraballo.com

Twitter: @authormelodycar
Facebook: AuthorMelodyCaraballo
Goodreads: MelodyCaraballo

Acknowledgements

I have been writing for so long and so many people help me along the way. I am beyond grateful to have such wonderful friends by my side.

First my family. This would be impossible without you guys. John Schubert, my love, you read every chapter as I wrote it and pushed me when I needed a strong loving shove. Thank you. I love you forever and always. Eli, Ian, and Zoe my wonderful children. So many nights you gave me breathing space so I could write, and even got so excited with every step of the process. I am lucky to be your mother.

Dad, I got my creativity from you. Being your daughter has always been such a joy. Mikey Caraballo, you are my favorite brother and a huge pain. Mom and George Elliott, thanks for being awesome parents. John and Maureen Schubert, thank you for having the most amazing son, he is my rock and you guys raised him to be amazing. Ashley, heaven is too far away. You come to life for me when I write about you. Time will never heal the hole you left behind.

Jenn Howell, you are my person. I can't express how much you have helped me over the years. No matter how bad my grammar was you always read everything I wrote and helped edit so many of my stories. You made me a better author.

Jolene Bryman, how can I thank you enough. Your witchiness made this a better story. You taught me about crystals, well a little bit, and natural magic. Not to mention all the love and encouragement.

My Writer Family, you guys changed my life for the better and made me a better writer. Abby Glenn, Beck Erixson, Christy Dirks, Geetha Krishnan, Jen Davenport, Laura Donald, K.J. Harrowick, Lauren Hazan, Maha Khalid, Megan Van Dyke, Sanyukta Thakare, and Talynn Lynn. Let's not forget all the people from Revpit, Positivity Pass, Rewrite it Club, Ocean's Eleven, and all the many writers of Twitter.

Owen Timm, thanks for falling at work.

Ashely Machie-Richeal you would run up the stairs to grab the next chapter that I wrote on scraps of paper. I'm so thankful for you.

Jessica Manning, Zhu Ren, Tom Caple, and Jay Cross, You guys read my story when it was such a rough draft. Thank you for believing in me from the beginning.

Stacey Timberlake-Sowinski (Athans), Rena Chombardo, Janet Medeiros, and Mary Russell, my hype girls. Having a strong team always cheering me on has helped beyond words. For that I am forever grateful for you ladies.

Jeanne Gates, if I had a cheer squad you would beat them up so you could be first to be there for me. Thanks for calling me daily to make sure I did my edits. Missy Labuz thanks for helping me with words for weapons.

Larry Milton, thank you for all the words of encouragement.

Andy Walker, thank you for leaving me alone so I could write this.

The Portal World Publishing Team: Guild Command General K. J. from the House of Harrowick, Drinker of Beer, Creator of Worlds, Mother of Dragons, Queen Instagator of Gators, and Wielder of Villains. Taco Fiend be thy name. Jen thy Town Crier of House Davenport. Writer of explosions. Not the quiet ones. Megan Storyweaver of House Van Dyke, first of her name, writer of twisted tales, lover of magic and kissing, promiser of happily ever after. Lady Talynn of the House of Lynn, Lover of Exquisite Vineyards, Chocolate Connoisseur, Teacher of Pleasantries, and Writer of all things fantasy and science fiction in the world of young adult.

K.J. Harrowick for designing my cover, it's beautiful.

Last but not least my amazing editors Jess Lawrence and Carly Hayward. You two helped me take a story that was meh and turned it into something magical

CPSIA information can be obtained
at www.ICGtesting.com
Printed in the USA
LVHW020031011021
699178LV00006B/24/J